"I just like saying your name…Tanner."

"I like hearing you say it." He grinned.

Suddenly the dog was back from wherever he'd been exploring, pushing between them. Natalie laughed. "Hey. What's your deal?"

"He's just jealous." Tanner smiled. "He thinks all affection should be directed his way."

Natalie dropped to her knees in the snow and wrapped her arms around the furry dog. "You are a handsome thing, Vitus, and a good boy in spite of wanting to hog all the hugs." Vitus wagged and wiggled.

Tanner chuckled. "You go ahead and take him inside. I'll get the wood and be right in."

"Okay." Natalie returned to the cabin, switched on a battery lantern and glanced at the cozy common room. She set the board game back on the shelf and looked around for any other tasks she needed to complete, but they'd already left the cabin neat and tidy.

She was going to miss this place.

Not just this place. *But this man.*

Dear Reader,

What would you do for a friend? Natalie Weiss doesn't trust many people, but Brooke Jenkins has had her back ever since they roomed together their freshman year of college. So when Brooke discovers she's pregnant and can't locate the father, Natalie jumps into action. She's determined to find him and make sure he lives up to his responsibilities to Brooke, even if it does mean staking out his post office box the week before Christmas. In Fairbanks, Alaska. At thirty below zero.

Friends and family are what Christmas is all about. The tree, the food, the gifts—they're all just a way to show the people in our lives that we love them. Natalie's childhood was less than ideal, but thanks to an impulsive decision and a case of mistaken identity, she's about to experience an old-fashioned family Christmas the likes of which she has never imagined possible.

I hope you enjoy Natalie's story, and that your Christmas is just as magical. I'd love to hear about it. Drop by my website at bethcarpenterbooks.blogspot.com, where you can find my email and other contacts, sign up for my newsletter or enter the occasional giveaway.

Merry Christmas to you and yours!

Beth Carpenter

HEARTWARMING

An Alaskan Family Christmas

—

Beth Carpenter

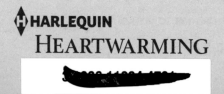
HARLEQUIN
HEARTWARMING

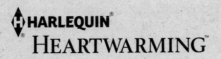

ISBN-13: 978-1-335-88995-9

An Alaskan Family Christmas

Copyright © 2020 by Lisa Deckert

This edition published by arrangement with Harlequin Books S.A.

For questions and comments about the quality of this book, please contact us at CustomerService@Harlequin.com.

Harlequin Enterprises ULC
22 Adelaide St. West, 40th Floor
Toronto, Ontario M5H 4E3, Canada
www.Harlequin.com

Printed in U.S.A.

Recycling programs for this product may not exist in your area.

Beth Carpenter is thankful for good books, a good dog, a good man and a dream job creating happily-ever-afters. She and her husband now split their time between Alaska and Arizona, where she occasionally encounters a moose in the yard or a scorpion in the basement. She prefers the moose.

Books by Beth Carpenter

Harlequin Heartwarming

A Northern Lights Novel

The Alaskan Catch
A Gift for Santa
Alaskan Hideaway
An Alaskan Proposal
Sweet Home Alaska
Alaskan Dreamsa

Visit the Author Profile page
at Harlequin.com for more titles.

In memory of my grandmother, with her listening ear, generous heart and bottomless cookie jar. So many stories. So much love. Thanks, Mom.

CHAPTER ONE

How could Natalie's favorite mystery writer have been so wrong? K. Krisman's stakeout scenes always included tasty snacks, witty observations and, most importantly, relevant information. The only useful detail Natalie had gained in the last three days was how long it took for the layer of frost on the windshield to grow so thick it obscured her view of the postal store. She estimated another twenty minutes before she needed to scrape the glass.

A muffled ringing disturbed the silence inside the car. Natalie pulled off her mitten, unbuttoned her down coat, unzipped her wool sweater and managed to extract the phone from her flannel shirt pocket before it rolled over to voice mail. Brooke.

Natalie smiled. "Hi. How are you feeling this morning?" The plus side to this stakeout was that it got Natalie out of Brooke's house early enough that she didn't have to listen to her friend toss her cookies every morning.

Not that Natalie wasn't sympathetic, but why should they both suffer?

"Pretty good. Your crackers in bed idea helped. I have crumbs on my sheets, but it's totally worth it."

"I'm glad. The dean's assistant mentioned it. Her second baby is due next month." She'd also mentioned far more than Natalie ever wanted to know about overcrowded bladders, labor and episiotomies, but at least her advice was helping Brooke. Natalie checked her watch. "You're up early."

"I know. I'm catching a ride with one of the maintenance guys. Somebody called in sick, so they asked me to cover the desk."

"Again?" Brooke had a degree in hotel management and was part of the supervisory team at a big resort in Fairbanks, and yet they were always getting her to fill in at registration or even clean rooms whenever they were short-staffed. Natalie bet Brooke's boss never pushed a vacuum cleaner.

"I don't mind. So, any sign of him yet?" Brooke's voice was hopeful. Always. Which was the only reason Natalie was sitting in a frozen parking lot in Fairbanks, Alaska, at six in the morning. Because Brooke deserved answers.

"Sorry, not yet. Oh, wait, there's somebody." Natalie glanced up as a car pulled into the parking lot, but she quickly recognized the red Jeep. "Never mind. It's just the barista to open the coffee cart. I'll stay as long as I can today, but remember, I have to catch my plane to Anchorage this afternoon."

"Yeah, I know you have the department Christmas party tomorrow. Are you taking a date?"

Natalie laughed. "You know I've had zero time for dating, especially in the last few months."

"Well, you always said once you get your doctorate and a teaching position, you'd find time. I'm holding you to that."

"Fine, once I move and start my new job, I'll look around."

"Good. Did you get the message from the dean in Anchorage yesterday asking you to call back so he could congratulate you on earning your PhD?"

Natalie scoffed. "He spent about two seconds on the congratulations and the next ten minutes trying to talk me into dumping my new job to cover for someone who's going out on maternity leave. There's always an ulterior motive."

"That's not true. Look at you. You're doing me a huge favor without asking for anything in return. Although I really don't think it's necessary. Dane said he'd be back. Maybe he'll pick up his mail this morning, and he'll get my letter."

"Maybe, but I'm starting to think he's abandoned his post office box, or possibly he's getting his mail forwarded somewhere else."

"I hadn't thought of that. That could be why he hasn't answered my letter." Brooke spoke as though Natalie had given her good news. Her mother really should have named her Pollyanna. "Maybe his mail hasn't caught up with him yet."

Natalie made a noncommittal noise. More likely he was married and kept a post office box his wife didn't know about, but it was no use sharing her suspicions. Her friend would find out soon enough. Really, though, a PO box as his only means of communication? No cell phone? Not even a landline number? That didn't ring any alarm bells for Brooke? "Are you sure you got the address right?"

"Yes, Dane wrote it down for me."

Natalie frowned. Dane Rockford. Was it just her, or did that name sound as made-up as the rest of the story? Whatever. "Okay. I'll keep watching until I have to catch my plane."

"I really appreciate it. Just leave the car in the airport lot. I've got the extra keys. I'll get someone to drive me over to pick it up after work. Oh, and don't forget to plug it in. The battery's not always reliable when it gets too cold."

"I will, and I'll call you if anything happens in the meantime. Have a good day at work."

Natalie returned the phone to her pocket. Maybe she should cancel her flight and stay a few more days. Trouble was, she'd promised her coworker Marianne that she'd be at the party in Anchorage tomorrow night to say goodbye to everyone before she left the university, and she never liked to break a promise. But she could fly back to Fairbanks after Christmas for a few days if necessary.

The teenager at the coffee cart opened the shutters and turned to wave at Natalie. Sheepishly, Natalie waved back. So much for being inconspicuous. She'd only been there for a couple of hours the first day before the barista had knocked on her window and asked if she was okay. She'd been forced to come clean about why she was loitering around their parking lot. Fortunately, once she'd explained, the barista had been in full sympathy with the cause. She'd even shared the key to the bathroom in the adjoining mini mall.

Hopefully, Rockford—if that was his real name—wasn't avoiding his mailbox because he'd spotted Brooke's car in the parking lot. It didn't help that it was a bright yellow car with a blue driver's-side door. The original door had been damaged beyond repair in a parking lot mishap and, of course, the perpetrator had given Brooke a fake phone number and insurance information. Things like that happened to Brooke. They never seemed to dampen her outlook, though. She'd just gushed about how lucky she was to find a replacement door in the junkyard and how nice the guy at the garage was to install it on the cheap.

Natalie shivered. Despite the ridiculous number of layers she was wearing, she found it impossible to stay warm at thirty below zero while sitting still. According to the weather report, this cold would break and the weather would warm into the single digits around Christmas, but that wasn't much help today. Growing up in Anchorage, Natalie thought she understood winter, but compared to Fairbanks, Anchorage was the tropics.

Speaking of tropical weather, Natalie checked the forecast for South Central New Mexico. Tomorrow's high was sixty-eight, equivalent to a summer day in Anchorage. Bliss. She would be starting her new position as an associate professor there in exactly twenty-seven days. Assuming she didn't die of hypothermia first.

She couldn't leave Alaska, though, until she was sure Brooke was going to be okay. If nobody showed up today, it might be time to hire a professional to find this guy and serve him papers. Brooke wouldn't like the idea, but then Brooke lived in her own reality.

Natalie considered starting the engine and running the heater, but she was down to a quarter tank of gas and she had another seven hours to get through. The Christmas lights draped over the coffee cart winked invitingly. Time to warm up from the inside out.

She wedged her puffy coat out from behind the steering wheel and made her way across the parking lot. Her barista friend, Tiff, a local college student, had a double cappuccino and a friendly smile waiting by the time she arrived. "Anything new in the manhunt?"

"Nope." Natalie tugged her mitten off with her teeth, dug around in her coat pocket until she found her wallet and handed over her bank card. "Hopefully something will break today, because I have to fly out this afternoon."

"I hope the jerk shows up soon, and you nail him to the wall."

"I can't," Natalie admitted as she dropped a dollar into the tip jar. "I have strict orders to find out where he lives, report back and let my friend be the one to tell him about the baby. She wants to break it to him gently."

"Really? I'd want to break something, and I wouldn't be gentle." Tiff slid her card through the reader and handed it back. "Say, could that be him?"

Natalie spun around, dropping her card and mitten as she turned. Sure enough, a man in a blue parka was getting out of the back seat of a small SUV and heading toward the door of the postal store, carrying a leather satchel. By the time she'd fished her bank card from the snow, spilling part of her cappuccino in the process, the man was already inside.

Natalie galloped across the parking lot but slowed to a casual saunter as she arrived at the door and went inside. An iron grate separated the store side from the post office boxes. She turned the corner and spotted the man in the second aisle. His hair looked freshly trimmed, but it was the same rich cocoa color as the shaggy mop on the man in the poorly focused selfie Brooke had shown her. It could be him.

Her quarry fished out a key and was inserting it into—yes!—box number 437. She stood farther down the row and pretended to be searching her pockets for a key. He removed a wad of mail, including a distinctive yellow envelope, and shoved it into his satchel. She only caught a brief glimpse of his face when he turned.

"Excuse me," he muttered before stepping around her and walking out the door. As soon as he was inside the car, the driver shifted into gear and pulled toward the parking lot exit. Natalie had to race across the lot to Brooke's car. She skidded on a slick spot and dropped her coffee cup. Stupid mittens. She almost turned back to pick it up—Natalie despised litterers—but realized the SUV was pulling out. She jumped into the driver's seat. Miraculously, the car started on the first try. She fishtailed across the lot and reached the exit in time to see the gray SUV turn left at the stop sign.

She zoomed to the sign, waited for a snowplow to pass and turned left, but the SUV was nowhere to be seen. She drove on ahead and was just about to give up when she spotted it at the next intersection turning right. She switched across two lanes, almost clipping the bumper of a black truck. He laid on the horn. "Sorry," she mouthed as he passed her. He shot her a rude gesture, not that she blamed him.

She made the turn and was able to follow the gray SUV without further incident until it pulled up in front of a barn-red building with a clock tower and a glass-fronted entryway. The train station. Two men got out and walked to the back of the SUV. When the liftgate opened, an enormous dog jumped out. This had to be the malamute Brooke had described.

They unloaded a large backpack, a crate, a satchel and an ice chest onto the sidewalk. The men exchanged a few words, and the SUV pulled away, leaving the guy Natalie was tailing standing there holding his dog's leash. A porter pushed a trolley in his direction.

Now what? Natalie's strategy had been to follow him to his house or job. Somewhere where Brooke and her lawyer—which Brooke would say she didn't need but Natalie would insist upon—would be able to find him. The train station put a crimp in the plan.

Well, Natalie hadn't sat in the cold for three days to give up now. She drove on to the parking lot, plugged Brooke's block heater into the rail provided for that purpose, grabbed her tote and her suitcase, and went inside. The man with the big dog was talking to a woman in uniform, gesturing toward the blue-and-yellow train outside. While keeping one eye on him, Natalie made her way to the ticket window. "Where is this train heading?"

"Anchorage, passing through Denali."

Perfect. She could follow Brooke's mystery man and make her way to Anchorage at the same time. "I'll take a ticket, please." She pulled off her mittens and hat, tucking them into her coat pockets.

"One-way or round-trip?" the man asked.

"One-way."

"I'll need to see your identification." He took her driver's license and credit card and did his thing on the computer. She kept an eye on Rockford to make sure he wasn't slipping out, but he was still engrossed in conversation. "Here you go." The clerk handed her a ticket. "Train boards in twenty minutes. Arrival time is seven fifteen."

She looked at her watch. "Tonight?"

"Yes. Enjoy." The man smiled as though taking an entire day to cover the ground she could fly over in an hour was a bonus. At least she'd probably be warmer in the train than she would have been on the stakeout.

She tugged her roller bag away from the window. Her quarry was buckling a muzzle onto his dog. The huge malamute didn't seem to be offended about this, judging by the sweep of his plumy tail. Must be a regulation of some kind. Rockford handed over the leash, and the train employee led the dog toward the train. Rockford wandered over to inspect the art on the wall of the waiting area. He carried only the satchel, so he must have checked his other luggage.

Natalie looked down at her suitcase. It was small, and since she was wearing most of the clothes she'd brought to Fairbanks, quite light. She could keep it with her instead of checking it, and that would give her a chance to find a taxi in Anchorage while Rockford was waiting to claim his luggage. Then all she had to do was follow him home, assuming taxi drivers really would "follow that car."

She had a plan. Now it was time to check in with Brooke. Natalie slipped into the bathroom and pulled out her phone. It rang seven times before Brooke picked up.

"Natalie?" Brooke whispered. "Did he come?"

"He did! I followed him to the train station." A woman came out of a stall and shot her a suspicious look. Natalie tried for an "I'm kidding" smile. The woman walked past her to the sink and turned on the faucet.

"That's great," Brooke was saying, but Natalie could hear someone in the background calling her over. "One minute," she told them before she returned to the phone and whispered, "I'll be there just as soon as I find someone to cover. We're short-staffed today."

"No time." Natalie moved farther from the

woman washing her hands and lowered her voice. "I have your car, remember, and the train boards in twenty minutes for Anchorage. I've got a ticket for the same train. Once we get to Anchorage, I'll follow him to wherever he lives and let you know. Then you and your lawyer can pay him a visit, okay?"

"Are you sure it's him?" As usual, Brooke was ignoring the words she didn't want to hear. Like lawyer.

With one last suspicious look in Natalie's direction, the other woman in the restroom pushed her way out the door. Natalie adjusted the strap of the tote that was sliding off her shoulder. "He has a malamute with him."

"Vitus is there?"

"Who?"

"Vitus. The dog. He's a sweetie pie."

"Oh." Too bad Natalie hadn't been close enough to hear him call the dog. There couldn't be too many malamutes named Vitus. "Besides the dog, he collected the mail, including your letter. I saw it."

"Did he look happy when he saw the envelope?" Brooke asked eagerly.

Natalie knew what Brooke wanted to hear, but she couldn't lie. "I'm not sure he noticed. Listen, I plugged in your car and left the keys under the mat. You're okay to find a ride to pick it up?"

"Of course. Thank you, Natalie. I can't believe you're doing all this."

"Thank you for letting me stay with you these last few weeks. Take care of yourself. I'll call as soon as I know something."

"Okay. And enjoy the train trip. I hear it's beautiful."

"I'll send you some pictures. Bye." Natalie shook her head and smiled. Leave it to Brooke to see the upside.

Natalie had lived her whole life in Alaska. Yes, winter was beautiful, in a monochromatic sort of way. But after thirty-two Alaskan winters, she was ready for something different. Ready to start the life she'd been working toward for so long. But Brooke was right. This train ride would be a last glimpse of what she was leaving behind. She might as well enjoy it.

After a quick call to cancel her flight, Natalie took a moment to remove a few layers of clothing before she passed out from the heat. She packed the sweater, hat, mittens and outer layer of socks in her suitcase, ran a brush through her hat-hair, and returned to the lobby, carrying her coat and dragging her suitcase. She looked around. No sign of Rockford.

Her heart rate jumped into overdrive. Had he

slipped away while she was talking to Brooke? She should never have let him out of her sight.

But then she spotted him across the room as he straightened. He seemed to have gathered a bottle of water and some other spilled items and was handing them back to a woman who walked with a cane. She tucked them into a quilted bag and thanked him. Okay, he *seemed* nice enough.

Brooke claimed he was. They'd met when her tire had gone flat, leaving her stranded on a lonely road halfway between the hotel where she'd filled in for the late shift and her home. Her spare was flat, as well. She'd been about to call for a tow when he'd stopped to ask if she needed help. Natalie would have locked the doors and called the police, but Brooke the Trusting just climbed into a car with a total stranger. It was pure luck that the guy driving by at two in the morning happened to be an amateur northern lights photographer rather than an intoxicated ax murderer.

He'd given her a ride home. The next morning, he'd gotten the tire repaired and installed on her car before he'd shown up at her house to give her a ride to pick it up. Brooke said it was her idea that he should check out of his hotel and stay with her for the two weeks he was in town. In fact, Brooke claimed almost everything about their time together was her idea, but Natalie had her doubts. Nobody did anything for free. He probably had an endgame in mind from the moment he saw Brooke's car on the side of the road, and it had all worked out just like he planned. A juicy little affair with no repercussions. Little did he know a bomb was about to drop.

An announcement came that it was time to board. Ignoring the seat assignment on her ticket, Natalie followed Rockford through the train. The seats all faced forward, except for the front seat of each car that faced backward with a table between it and the second seat, forming a sort of booth. In the third car, he chose the backward-facing seat. Good, that made him easy to watch. Natalie found an unoccupied seat about three rows back and across the aisle. The car was only about half full that morning, and the window seat beside her was vacant, as well. She lifted her small suitcase into the rack above her head, pulled out her latest K. Krisman mystery and settled in for a ride.

The train pulled forward. Rockford took out his phone and made a call. Natalie strained her ears, but she couldn't hear him over the click-clack of the wheels on the track. Too bad she'd never learned to lip-read. He tucked the phone into his pocket and opened his satchel, pulling out a laptop computer which he booted up on the table in front of him. His face took on an expression of rapt concentration. His lips moved as he read. Natalie giggled to herself.

He squeezed together the finger and thumb of each hand, but she couldn't see what he was holding. His left hand remained stationary, while his right moved in a circular, wrapping motion. Now that she was watching more closely, she didn't think he was holding anything at all. After a moment, he nodded and pulled the computer closer to type something into it. Then he pushed it back again and repeated the winding motion. Very odd.

Anyway, he wasn't going anywhere for a while. Natalie turned her attention toward the window. A pink glow painted the horizon, visible between the trunks of birch trees. Snow covered the ground like a plump down comforter, with a curving line of animal tracks forming the quilting. It really was quite lovely.

When she looked back, Rockford had stopped to admire the landscape, as well. He gazed out the window for several minutes, a small smile on his face, before he returned to his computer.

As the sky lightened, the details of the landscape began to become clear. Mountains, trees, rivers, all decorated with a blanket of pristine snow. An announcement came over the speaker. "Passengers, we have a moose sighting coming up ahead on the left."

Natalie scooted over to the window seat to watch. There he was, a young bull rubbing against a tree trunk. He glanced toward the train, but he didn't seem to be particularly alarmed. After a moment, he reached up to nibble at the twigs overhead.

Moose were common in and around Anchorage, but not so much that it didn't spark a little thrill whenever Natalie spotted one. They were such bizarre creatures, their spindly legs all out of proportion with their chunky bodies. They thrived in the bogs and snow of Alaska, spending the winter extracting enough nourishment from twigs and bark to keep themselves alive until spring arrived.

Sometimes Natalie had felt like a moose in winter, surviving on part-time jobs, teaching freshman online courses, holding it together until she could earn her doctorate. But now she had her PhD, and that associate professorship in New Mexico was hers. She'd been lucky enough to have applied just as noted mathematician Dr. Benarjee had been recruited to a think tank in D.C. She'd taken over his classes and the lease on his apartment. All her worldly possessions, other than what she carried right now, were waiting in storage at her destination. Spring had finally arrived. She just needed to make sure Brooke was taken care of before she left Alaska.

The train rounded a bend, and the moose was lost from view. Natalie picked up her book and opened it to the bookmark, ready to settle in until Rockford made his move.

TANNER PAGED DOWN on his manuscript to the instructions for tying another variation of the classic Woolly Bugger. This would be his fifth book on fly tying, and he'd built a reputation for precision and clarity, which he intended to maintain.

He read through the steps he'd listed, acting them out with his hands as he read to make sure he hadn't skipped any. Mentally, he tied off the thread and snipped it with scissors. Yes, that was correct.

Before moving to the next fly, he glanced up to see that woman looking at him again. Immediately she turned toward the window. All morning, even back in the train station, he'd had this eerie feeling someone was watching him. Was she the reason?

He studied her for a few seconds while her gaze remained on the window. Thick brown hair pushed back behind her shoulders, revealing silver drop-shaped earrings. A nice profile, with prominent cheekbones. She looked familiar. In fact, wasn't that the same woman he'd almost bumped into in the post office that morning when he had been picking up Dane's mail?

He supposed it was possible. Fairbanks wasn't that big, and just like him, she might have made a quick mail run before she caught the train. She turned, and their eyes met for half a second before she picked up a book and opened it. He recognized the cover because he'd read the mystery last month when it first came out. Whoever she was, she had good taste in literature.

He turned back to his manuscript. He needed to get this final edit finished and the sample flies ready for the photographer by the middle of January, and he wasn't likely to get much work time once he arrived at the family cabin, especially with Gen and the girls there. He loved his two nieces, but their presence was not conducive to accomplishing anything that required cohesive thought. The cabin was a great place for them to run off some of that pre-Christmas energy, though, and his cousin's dog, Vitus, would be happy to run along with them.

Good thing Gen's girls had been around

to play with Vitus at Tanner's place in Anchorage while he was dog-sitting. You'd never have guessed that up until last month Tanner's nieces had spent their entire lives in Florida. At his house, they played outside in the snow for hours every day, gliding down the hill in his backyard on inflated rings and chasing Vitus in circles. Gen was going to have her hands full next fall when Evie started kindergarten and Maya didn't have anyone to play with.

Tanner was glad he could offer them a place to stay while they regrouped. Starting over was never easy, especially when there were kids involved. Poor Gen had been completely blindsided when her husband of eight years informed her that he was quitting his job to pursue a career in stand-up comedy. Oh, and by the way, moving out, because he needed to surround himself with people who were "supportive." Meaning a woman he'd apparently been seeing—or rather, cheating with—for some time. Tanner would have liked to fly to Florida to teach the jerk the definition of *supportive*, but for Gen's sake, he stayed out of it.

Gen had been a stay-at-home mom. They had no savings to speak of. Gen got the house in the divorce, but by the time she'd sold it, paid off the mortgage and the real estate agent, and driven herself and her two daughters home to Alaska, there wasn't much left over. She and the girls had moved in with Tanner. The last few weeks she'd been in supermom mode: baking cookies, wrapping presents, basically trying to make sure the girls had such a wonderful Christmas when they went to the cabin that they wouldn't even miss their father.

Tanner had done his part, obtaining every item on his nieces' extensive Santa list. On Christmas Eve at the cabin, he and the rest of the family would help the girls set out milk and cookies for Santa and read *The Night Before Christmas*, just like his dad used to read it to him and Gen when they were kids. Evie and Maya deserved a great Christmas.

He went back to the edits. When he got to the Russian River variations, he remembered that he hadn't called about the samples Rob had sent for his approval. The train was coming into Healy, and his phone showed three bars. He dialed quickly. "Hi, Peggy."

"Merry Christmas, Tanner. How was the signing?"

"It went very well. You did a great job with the publicity. Say, I may be about to go out of cell range. Is Rob handy?"

"Sure. I'll transfer you."

"Thanks. Merry Christmas." A few seconds later, he heard the click as Rob picked up. "Hi, it's Tanner. Listen, those bucktail samples you sent aren't going to work. Too brittle, and the dye is uneven. We need to go back to the old supplier."

"Are you sure we can't make them work?" Rob, his partner, asked. "The price is—"

"Not relevant if the quality's poor. Their peacock herl is fine and the marabou is excellent, but don't order the bucktail." That woman was watching Tanner again, but when their eyes met, she quickly looked away.

On the phone, Rob gave a long-suffering sigh. "Fine. I'll order more of the bucktail from the supplier you like. How was the book signing?"

"Good. I'm on the train, so I might lose you any minute, but I'll tell you more when I see you. I'm going to be at the cabin for the next few days, so no phone. I'll get back to you after the new year."

"No problem. I'm closing up the office and giving Peggy time off until January second."

"Sounds good. Merry Christmas, Rob."

"To you, as well." The call ended.

Tanner shook his head. Rob was always tempted by bargains, but Tanner wasn't going to put his name on anything that didn't meet quality standards. Fortunately, Rob trusted his judgment. He opened his laptop again and went back to work. Several hours passed without Tanner realizing it until the porter came to announce the dining car was open for lunch. Right on cue, Tanner's stomach growled.

The woman three rows back was still reading, but he could see her eyes dart toward him before disappearing behind the book. He couldn't imagine what it was about him she found so fascinating. Tanner packed his laptop in his bag and looked toward her again. Curiosity won out. Instead of heading directly to the dining car, he moved to the aisle beside her. She pretended to be entirely engrossed in her reading.

"Excuse me." When she didn't look up, he touched her shoulder. "Ma'am?"

"Yes?" She held her place in the book with her finger and frowned at him.

"Would you care to join me in the dining car for lunch?"

CHAPTER TWO

NATALIE SWALLOWED. Now what was she supposed to do? Apparently, she hadn't been nearly as subtle as she thought. This surveillance thing wasn't easy.

"Lunch?" Somehow, she managed to speak in a normal tone.

"You know, the middle meal of the day," he was saying. "The porter says the dining car is open."

Natalie hesitated. Rockford stood there, swaying slightly to the motion of the train, waiting for her to make up her mind. Judging by the smirk on his face, he considered this a bit of a joke. He'd obviously noticed her watching him, and it wasn't going to do any good to pretend she hadn't been. She might as well go along and gather as much information as possible, just in case her plan to follow him home didn't work.

"I suppose so."

He moved back to make room for her to

step into the aisle. "I'm Tanner Rockford, by the way."

Tanner? So he had given Brooke a fake name! Or else he was lying to her now, although she couldn't see the point. And why hadn't he lied about his last name? If he didn't want to be found, hiding his surname would make more sense. In fact, she should follow that advice, just in case. "I'm Natalie."

"Hello, Natalie. Nice to meet you." He gestured that she should go first, so she grabbed her bag and stepped into the aisle. They made their way through another passenger car and into the dining car, where a server waved them to a booth for two and handed them menus.

Natalie quickly settled on the taco salad. He'd probably order the cheeseburger. He looked like a cheeseburger kind of guy. She peeked over the top of her menu at him while she considered how best to go about gathering information without making him suspicious. Nice face, regular features. Little laugh lines at the corners of brown, no, hazel eyes. Thick brown hair and wide shoulders, appropriately dressed in a fleece zip-neck and jeans. She could see why Brooke found him attractive. The question was whether he was honest. And/or responsible.

Once he'd set his menu aside, she adopted

a friendly smile. "So, are you a visitor to Alaska?"

"No, I live in Anchorage. You?" he asked.

"I'm from Anchorage, as well. What part of town?"

"Lower hillside."

"Around O'Malley?"

"Yes. Not far from the zoo."

Bingo. With a last name and a general location, she should be able to find his house even if she couldn't follow him. Assuming he was telling the truth about where he lived.

"What part of town do you live in?" he asked.

"Actually, I'm in the process of moving."

"Right." He flashed a sheepish grin. "Sorry. I guess I shouldn't ask a woman I just met where she lives. Or her last name. So, what sort of work do you do, Natalie? If that's something you feel comfortable talking about."

So he'd caught that. Observant. Natalie decided to stay as close to the truth as she could. "I teach math."

"Cool. I'm a big fan of teachers. My sister had an adversarial relationship with math until this one teacher in middle school took some extra time to help her catch up on a couple of basic concepts she'd missed along the way. She said it was like algebra suddenly came into focus, when before it had just been a bunch of random numbers and letters on a page. Do you teach at one of the high schools?"

"No. Actually next semester, I'll be starting a new job in the lower forty-eight."

"Ah, so you decided to take one last farewell sightseeing trip before you go?"

"Exactly." Good of him to make up her backstory for her.

The waiter came to take their orders for her salad and, no, not a cheeseburger, but a Cuban pulled-pork sandwich. Once he'd gone, she decided to dig a little deeper. "And what do you do for a living, Tanner?"

"I tie flies."

"Like, fishing flies?"

"Yes."

Hmm. Natalie couldn't imagine anyone could support themselves, much less a baby, tying flies. But he was riding the train, which wasn't terribly cheap, and his clothes weren't the sort you picked up on the clearance rack at a discount store. He hadn't paid for that laptop he'd been using earlier from couch cushion change either.

"How does that work? You sell them online, or…?"

"In a way. I have a line of fly-fishing supplies

that distribute through the major sporting goods chains as well as online. And I write books."

Better. "About flies?"

"How to tie them. In fact, that's why I'm here. I was signing my latest book in a sporting goods store in Fairbanks."

"How did it go?"

"It went well. Lots of people picking them up for Christmas gifts. I'm working on the next one now."

"Fascinating." Natalie had never had much interest in fishing, but it would be hard to cast a line in Anchorage without reeling in an avid fisherman. She had a faint memory of a book on her department supervisor's desk with a picture of a red-and-white fishing fly and the name Rockford. Of course, it was entirely possible "Tanner" had assumed the identity of the author to impress her. "How many different fishing flies are there?"

He laughed. "That's like asking how many flavors of ice cream exist. Fishing flies are designed to mimic bugs or larvae or whatever the fish are eating. People are always coming up with new ideas on how to do that. We sell kits with the basic supplies, but I also like to experiment with unusual materials. Last week, I invented a couple of flies using pearlized plastic gift wrap I found when I was Christmas shopping. I'm liking the way it looks, but I'll have to wait for summer to see if the fish agree before I put it in a book."

Before she could ask another question, the waiter brought their food. The salad was surprisingly good. She'd expected something along the lines of airplane food, but her salad had a nice blend of shredded chipotle chicken and salad greens, served in a stoneware bowl.

Rockford picked up his sandwich, but before he took a bite, he nodded at the window. "Another moose."

Natalie turned to see. They were high on a hillside, overlooking a deep valley. A river ran roughly parallel to the tracks, mostly frozen and covered with snow, but a twisting line of fast-moving water in the center had outrun the freezing temperatures. A cow moose was making her way beside the stream. A moment later, two smaller moose appeared from the woods behind her, probably her yearling calves. It was clear from their slow progress that the snow was deeper than it appeared from the surface.

Natalie looked back to Rockford, studying him while his attention was on the moose. He turned toward her, and this time she didn't look away. His eyes met hers, hazel eyes brimming with intelligence and curiosity. She was beginning to suspect he might be deeper than it appeared on the surface, as well. Maybe Brooke wasn't so far off.

THE CLOUDS IN the west were beginning to turn the blush color of a Peace rose. Natalie closed her book and watched out the window as the tint bled across the snow like watercolors. Truly beautiful. The train had run near the highway for most of the trip, but now their paths had diverged, and Natalie was observing a part of Alaska she'd never had the chance to see before. Despite her reason for taking the train, she'd enjoyed the journey. And, if she was being totally honest, she'd enjoyed her lunch with Rockford.

They'd continued to chat as they ate. He'd listened when she'd talked about some of her experiences in teaching and he'd asked intelligent questions. He'd tried to pay for her lunch but had surrendered gracefully when she'd insisted on buying her own. She'd hoped for a peek at the name on his credit card, but he'd paid in cash. Afterward, he'd excused himself to work on his book and she'd returned to her seat and noted his approximate address in the spiral notebook she always carried. Occasionally she would look up to check on him, but he remained engrossed in his computer.

She pulled out her phone to take a picture of

the sunset to send to Brooke later, and to check the time. They still had almost five hours to go before the train was due in Anchorage. The plane she'd been booked on would be taking off from Fairbanks right about now and landing in Anchorage in another hour. She should have called her hotel from the train station to make sure they would hold the room for late arrival, but it should be fine.

Natalie had given up the lease on her Anchorage apartment at the end of November, when she'd gone to stay with Brooke in Fairbanks while she'd finished up the loose ends and officially received her degree from UAF. Tomorrow night was the math department's annual Christmas party, and Natalie could enjoy it with a clear conscience once she'd tailed Rockford home and reported back to Brooke. Everything was falling into place.

Her phone showed two bars. Maybe she could get off an email to the hotel. *Arriving late, but please hold reservation for Natalie Weiss.* She returned the phone to her bag and glanced over at Rockford. He'd closed the lid to his laptop and was stashing it in his satchel. Probably planning to stretch his legs. She could use a stroll, too, but following him up and down the train would be a little too obvious.

He pulled his coat down from the over-head shelf and put it on. Hmm. Maybe he was changing cars for some reason. She supposed it didn't really matter. He'd have to claim his luggage in Anchorage, so he couldn't get away before she did.

He came to her seat and touched her shoulder. "Goodbye, Natalie. I hope you enjoy your new job." Without waiting for a reply, he walked down the aisle toward the rear of the train.

Wait. Why was he telling her goodbye? They still had several hours before they arrived in Anchorage. What was he up to?

They'd come to a sort of village now, or at least a cluster of cabins near the tracks. The voice on the PA system was saying something about dry cabins and flag stops. The train seemed to be slowing. She could see someone sprinting down a shoveled path toward the tracks. Apparently, they were going to take on another passenger.

In the book she was reading, the protagonist had lost a tail by jumping off a subway car just before the doors closed and taking another train to a different destination. Could Rockford be planning the same? But if so, why would he tell her goodbye?

To gloat! The same reason he'd asked her to

lunch. He knew she was following him, and he'd made up that whole story about writing books to throw her off the trail. Now he was going to leave the train early, no doubt catching a later one. Well, she hadn't lost him yet.

She pulled on her coat and grabbed her suitcase from overhead as the train came to a stop. A family with three small children in the next car blocked her way as they gathered their belongings. The oldest, a girl around six or seven, dragged her feet until her father mentioned that Santa might be watching. Immediately, she picked up her purple backpack.

Meanwhile her mother nestled a phone against her shoulder while zipping a toddler into a snowsuit. "Yes, we're just going to check on the cabin. Don't worry, Mom, we'll be on the next train."

So there was another train! Natalie trailed along behind the family, dragging her suitcase. By the time they got to the open door, the passenger was getting on and Rockford was gone. The porter nodded at the couple with their kids. "You know this is just a flag stop, right?"

"Sure, just stopping by our cabin." The father adjusted his huge backpack, took two kids by the hand and followed his wife and toddler off the train. Natalie buttoned her coat, clutched her tote and suitcase, and tagged along. The family made a beeline toward a small white cabin not far from the tracks while Natalie peeled away to look for Rockford.

She spotted him farther back on the train, collecting his motley assortment of luggage, including his dog, who wagged his tail wildly. A moment later, the train pulled forward, and Natalie started in his direction.

The noise from the train covered the sounds of her boots crunching in the snow, and Rockford was busy pulling on a warm hat and removing the dog's muzzle. He gave the dog a vigorous ear rub. When he stopped, the dog pricked his ears and then galloped in Natalie's direction.

Natalie stiffened. Having a hundred-pound wolf-like animal bounding at her was triggering an adrenaline spike, even though the wagging tail and friendly expression reassured her. She braced herself for a collision, but he slid to a stop and pushed his head under her mitten, demanding petting. She laughed. Brooke had said the dog was a sweetie pie. She stroked his head.

"Natalie! What are you doing here?" Rockford had followed the dog.

She shrugged, playing along. "This looks like an interesting place. I thought I'd poke around a little bit. Catch the next train to Anchorage."

"The next train." He was giving her an odd look.

"Yes. Are you taking it?"

"I…no, I'm staying through Christmas."

Hmm. "Do you happen to know the train schedule?"

"I do in fact. Ordinarily, they only run trains on weekends, but there's a special Christmas train going to Fairbanks on the twenty-third and returning to Anchorage on the twenty-fourth."

The twenty-third? Today was only the twentieth. Was he jerking her chain? "But—"

He tilted his head as he studied her. He didn't look like he was kidding. "Where did you plan to stay while you wait for the next train?"

What had she gotten herself into? "I— Is there a B&B or something? Maybe a rental cabin?"

He shrugged. "Not that I know of. I suppose you could ask Red."

"Who's Red?"

He waved toward the blue cabin nearest the tracks. "Red runs the closest thing we have to a store, and sort of keeps track of the people around here."

"Where are you staying?"

"In my cabin."

"I thought you lived in Anchorage."

"I do."

"But—" If he was staying at his cabin, how was she going to find out his residence? And more urgently, how was she going to survive for three days?

"Natalie, what is going on? You've been watching me since this morning. Why?"

She couldn't tell him. She'd promised Brooke. "I saw you get off the train and thought you were just taking a break, that there would be another one later today."

The line between his eyebrows deepened. "You don't seem like the type who would do something so impulsive."

She shrugged. "You don't really know me, do you?"

"Obviously not." He grabbed her suitcase. "Well, come on."

"Where are we going?"

"To talk to Red. Maybe he knows of a place you could stay." His voice held out little hope, but he led her toward the blue cabin. The inexpertly painted sign over the door read "Red's Stuff." Tanner held the door open so Natalie could enter first. Rough shelves held boxes, cans, winter hats, mosquito repellent and several other items Natalie couldn't immediately identify. A voice called out from the shadows in the rear of the room, "Who's there?"

"It's just me, Tanner Rockford."

"Oh, hey, Tanner. Your family already stopped by on their way to the cabin, and your uncle left the utility sled out back for you. Those girls are sure excited about Santy Claus."

Girls? Natalie's jaw began to ache under the strain of holding her tongue while pretending she didn't know anything about Rockford. Married, just as she had suspected. Worse, he had kids. Brooke would be devastated. But at least Natalie knew his real name.

"Yeah, the girls are excited all right. Say, Red, this lady got off the train by mistake, and she needs a place to stay. Do you know of any rentals?"

A gnome appeared, peeking around a stack of boxes. The top of his head shined even in the gloom, and if the remaining hair had ever been red, the color had long ago faded. Natalie didn't like the speculative gleam in his eye. "Well, now. This time of year, most part-time cabins are locked up tight. Time was, folks would leave them open in case someone needed a place to stay, but nowadays…" He shook his head sadly. "I suppose, if you're in a bind, I have a place out back—"

"Are you talking about your woodshed?" Tanner asked.

"Well, yeah, but there's room for a cot."

"There's no stove, is there?"

"I'd throw in a good sleeping bag—" the old man gave a sly smile "—for a fair price."

"Never mind," Tanner told him. "She'll be staying with us."

Us? Like Tanner and his wife and kids? That would be beyond awkward, especially if he figured out she was connected with Brooke. "Wait. I never said—"

"It's that or camp out in Red's woodshed. Our place has heat and beds. Your choice."

Well, when he put it like that, Natalie supposed she'd survive awkward.

TANNER FASTENED THE last buckle on Vitus's harness and turned, only to bump into Natalie. Again.

"Sorry," she said. Again.

"It's all right." He stepped around her. She'd been dogging his steps the whole time he was loading the utility sled. She was probably afraid he was going to leave her behind. Which he was sorely tempted to do.

What was the woman thinking, jumping off

the train at a flag stop with no forethought? It wasn't as though she was from outside, with no knowledge of Alaska and wilderness. Even if she'd never left the Anchorage city limits, she must know how unforgiving this climate could be. She had to realize she couldn't just call a taxi.

When he'd caught her staring that morning, he'd wondered about her, but their conversation at lunch had reassured him. She'd seemed smart and genuine, and she clearly enjoyed her profession. But now, he didn't know what to think. Had she developed some sort of bizarre fixation on him? He was well-known in some circles, but not exactly famous. Certainly not the level of famous to attract stalkers, and he could have sworn she had little if any interest in fly-fishing. Maybe he was wrong.

Anyway, it looked like they were stuck with her for a few days. He couldn't leave her to fend for herself, and he couldn't very well let her freeze in Red's woodshed. And now, rather than acting grateful, she was frowning in his direction as though he was the one acting sketchy.

Tanner lifted Natalie's suitcase onto the sled along with his gear. "If you have any calls to make, you should make them here. The cell phone coverage at the cabin is spotty at best."

She nodded and walked a few feet away. He could hear some murmuring while he connected the pull rope from the sled to Vitus's harness. The dog obeyed Tanner's command to stay, even though he was quivering from the effort not to take off at a full sprint. Tanner mentally calculated the weight of the plastic utility sled packed with a full ice chest, his crate and Natalie's suitcase, then cast an eye over her. She looked reasonably fit, but he'd better play it safe.

As soon as she finished her call, he gestured to the sled. "Get in."

"In the sled?" She seemed surprised.

"Yes. I know it's a tight fit, but…"

She looked at the sled and then at the dog. "Are you sure he can pull that much? I could walk."

Tanner's opinion of her softened a little. "He'll be fine. It's only a mile and a half to the cabin, and the trail should be broken for most of it."

She opened her mouth as though to argue, but she seemed to think better of it and climbed into the center between the ice chest and the crate, hugging her knees in front of her. "Like this?"

"That's good." He jogged to Vitus's side. "Hike!"

Vitus gave a yip of joy and leaned into his harness, his tail waving over his back like a flag. The sled jerked forward. Natalie gave a little gasp and clutched at the tie rope holding the crate in place. Once he'd established some momentum, Vitus broke into a trot, easily pulling the sled across the snow.

When Tanner looked back, Natalie seemed to have forgotten her earlier beef. A big smile spread across her face and her eyes sparkled. Tanner grinned to himself. He'd observed this phenomenon with his nieces, and it held true with adults, too. It was almost impossible to maintain a surly attitude while playing in the snow.

CHAPTER THREE

THIS WAS THE most fun she'd had since she was in elementary school, zooming down the sledding hill. Natalie realized she should feel ridiculous. After all, she was sitting on a piece of plastic, wedged between a crate and an ice chest with her own suitcase forming a backrest behind her. It wasn't as though she was fulfilling her childhood dream to be one of the celebrity IditaRiders in a dogsled through Anchorage during the ceremonial start of the Iditarod. But still, it was a blast.

It helped that the temperature here was considerably higher than it had been in Fairbanks; she'd guess in the teens. Not bad at all. The sun had set, but an almost full moon had risen to light the way. Judging by the number of parallel tracks, mostly snow machines used this trail, but she preferred their current method of transportation. The big dog ahead of her was clearly enjoying himself, trotting along as though the sled weighed nothing. Rockford didn't look like he was even breathing hard as he ran beside the dog. That rat.

Just as she'd come to think he might actually be a decent guy, she had to find out he was not only married but had kids. How did a guy who'd spent two weeks playing house with Brooke almost two months ago have the gall to sound so…trustworthy? He was obviously a practiced liar. His poor wife. And poor Brooke.

How often did he do this kind of thing, anyway? He lived in Anchorage but had a post office box in Fairbanks. Did he tell his wife he was going to "work on his book" while he played around on a regular basis?

But it was hard to focus on her loathing of him while dashing through the snow in a one-dog open sleigh. She'd make sure Rockford paid, but meanwhile she might as well enjoy this opportunity. Vitus was at least twice the size of the racing huskies she'd watched, and not nearly as fast, but the ride was still exhilarating, especially as the slope changed to a slight downhill and the dog broke into a gallop.

When they reached the bottom, momentum carried them partway up the next hill, but soon Vitus slowed to a walk and Rockford grabbed on to the towrope to help him pull. "Wait," Natalie said. "Let me get out and help."

"You're okay," he told her, but she scrambled

out anyway. She could pull her own weight. She always had.

They climbed to the top of the hill, Vitus tugging the sled with ease now that she was out of it. When they reached the summit, Rockford paused to unhook the dog from the sled. Natalie soon realized why—the slope on the other side of the hill was steeper and the sled would have run over the dog. Rockford suddenly stopped. "Wanna ride it down?"

"Me?"

"Sure. Why not?" His grin held a challenge.

Why not, indeed? She'd loved sledding as a child. "Okay, I will." Natalie climbed into the sled once more and before she could change her mind, he gave her a push.

The sled quickly picked up speed, whooshing over the snow. Vitus ran after her, galloping down the slope and yowling joyfully. She hit a bump and bounced, along with everything else in the sled. Natalie let out a surprised yelp, and Vitus yipped back as if he approved.

As she slowed at the bottom of the hill, the sled hit a deeper patch at the edge of the path, which sent it into a spin. After completing a full nine-hundred degrees of rotation, the sled came to a stop against a bank of snow, facing uphill. Behind her, Rockford was making his way down at a more cautious pace, laughing as he did.

Natalie laughed, too. "Gosh, that was fun. I haven't been sledding in ages."

Vitus ran to her, his tail lashing from side to side and his mouth open as though he was laughing, too. She ruffled his ears. Tanner grinned as he reached the bottom of the hill. "Nice ride. I'd pull it up and let you go again if it wasn't full of freight."

"That's okay. One ride was enough." She got up and dusted the snow off her coat.

The packed trail headed off toward the right, but Rockford dragged the sled over to the left where only two sets of snow machine tracks marred the snow. He opened the crate and pulled out a pair of snowshoes. "I'll break trail from here. You can ride. It's only a quarter mile now, and the trail's fairly flat."

"Are you sure? I can walk."

"You'd posthole, and I don't have an extra pair of snowshoes with me. Don't worry." He patted the dog's head and clipped the towrope to his harness. "Vitus could pull twice this weight for a quarter mile."

"All right." She repositioned herself into the sled while he strapped on his snowshoes.

He gave a command to stay and walked forward a few paces. The dog whined, but Rockford continued forward until he was about twenty feet ahead. He turned. "Okay, Vitus. Hike."

The dog leaped forward and, for a moment, Natalie wondered if he was going to bowl the man down, but once the sled hit the unpacked snow he was forced to slow and settled into a steady walk.

Clouds covered the moon, leaving only Rockford's headlamp to illuminate the path. After another twenty minutes or so, lights from the windows of a log cabin came into view. Vitus walked right up to the steps and stopped, waiting to be unhitched before he jumped onto the porch and stood beside the door expectantly.

Rockford offered Natalie a hand up. She ignored it and climbed out of the sled on her own, despite a stiff back. He gestured toward the front door. "Well, this is it."

Natalie swallowed. Suddenly, it wasn't fun anymore. People didn't help strangers without an expectation of something in return. She'd better be clear up front that this was a business arrangement. "I'll pay you the going rate, of course, for room and board until the next train."

He gave a short laugh. "I don't need your money." He grabbed the crate from the sled and carried it to the steps, and then went back for the rest of the baggage.

Natalie grabbed her own suitcase. "Nevertheless, I'll pay."

He shrugged and continued to unload the sled.

Natalie sucked in a fortifying breath. She was about to spend several days in a cabin with a man she didn't know. A man she didn't like. Worse, a man she could easily start to like, if she didn't know he was a cheater and a liar. What if he was dangerous, too? Before she'd gotten into the sled, she'd cancelled her hotel reservation and called Marianne to say she was delayed and wouldn't make the party. Her text to Brooke said she was going with Rockford to his cabin and that if Brooke didn't hear from her by the twenty-third to call the troopers, but that was days away.

And even if Rockford wasn't a threat, what about his family? Should Natalie tell his wife about Brooke? If Natalie was in that position, she'd want to know. On the other hand, she hated to ruin Christmas for the innocent wife and kids. She'd better play it by ear.

Vitus came to stand in front of Natalie and looked up at her. She ran a hand over his noble head. He wagged his tail and leaned closer. His owner might be a louse, but the dog wasn't.

"You're a fine dog, Vitus. Good job pulling that sled." His tail wagged faster.

Footsteps sounded inside the cabin and the door flew open. Vitus jumped onto the porch to greet the two little girls who burst outside. They threw their arms around the big dog's neck. "I said I heard something," the smaller girl declared.

"You thought you heard them ten times already. Merry Christmas, Uncle Tanner," the bigger one called. "We waited for you to get the tree."

Uncle Tanner? Did that mean—

"Who are you?" The younger girl left the dog and was standing close to Tanner, eyeing Natalie suspiciously.

"Maya, manners." Tanner put his hand on the girl's shoulder. "Natalie, these are my nieces, Maya and Evie. Girls, Natalie had a mishap and needs a place for a few days until the next train, so she's going to stay with us."

"Are you hurt?" Evie stepped closer. "Mommy has Band-Aids."

"I'm just fine, thank you," Natalie told the girl.

"We found a cat one time," the girl volunteered, "but we had to give it back because the people who lost it put up a poster and said they were looking for it. Is somebody looking for you?"

"No," Natalie laughed. "Nobody's looking for me. I'm on my own."

"I'm four years old," Maya announced suddenly, holding up four fingers and carefully folding in her thumb.

"Wow." Natalie tried to look suitably impressed.

It must have worked because the little girl smiled. "Evie's five. She's bossy."

"Am not—" her sister started to say, but she was interrupted by the appearance of a dark-haired woman at the door.

"Girls, I asked you to keep this door shut— oh, hello. I didn't realize you'd made it from the train." She flashed a questioning glance at Tanner.

"Natalie, my sister, Genevieve. Gen, Natalie. Where's Mom?"

"Out back with Uncle Russ. Hi, Natalie. Come on in. Tanner didn't mention he was bringing anyone with him."

"He didn't know," Natalie admitted as she stomped the excess snow off her boots and followed Gen into the cabin. A lantern cast a pool of light over a long wooden table surrounded by mismatched chairs. Glimpses of towering log walls and high rafters made Natalie realize the cabin was much bigger than she'd first thought. On the left, a kitchen area consisted of an antique-looking stove with a big stewpot on top, a worktable and lots of open shelving stacked with kitchenware and dry goods. On the other side of the room, a leather couch kept company with a recliner, rocking chairs, a padded bench and a corner fireplace made of river rock. Packed bookshelves lined one wall and several framed photos of the northern lights hung on another. Vitus had stretched out on the rug in front of the fireplace. The back of the room was lost in shadow.

"You can leave your boots here." Gen pointed to a tray where the girls were already setting their boots beside several other pairs. "What do you mean, Tanner didn't know?"

"She needs a place to stay," Maya told her mother, "'cause she had a mis-cap."

"Mishap." Tanner set Natalie's suitcase inside the door. "That just means an accident. Natalie accidently got off the train before she was supposed to."

"I didn't realize there wouldn't be another one today," Natalie hurried to explain.

"I see," Gen said, although she clearly didn't.

Natalie removed her boots and hung her coat on the peg near the door where Gen pointed, being careful not to bump into a table in front of the window, which held a flowerpot. "I'm really sorry to impose this way. I'd stay somewhere else, but there don't seem to be any rentals or B&Bs available."

"No, not in the winter," Gen confirmed. "Well, good thing Tanner got off the train, too. You can share Mom's room. There's a trundle bed. Tanner, you're with Uncle Russ in the loft."

"I figured." He set down the last of the luggage, pushed the door closed with his heel and nodded toward the flowerpot, which contained a long stalk leaning toward the window. "Where did that come from?"

"The amaryllis? Mom brought it with her." Gen turned the pot so that the stalk leaned away from the window. Four buds were just beginning to unfurl on the top. "She didn't want to miss it blooming."

"Oh, okay. I'll start the generator."

"Uncle Russ said he'd do it once they've collected more firewood."

Tanner nodded. "Any word from our long-lost cousin?"

"Russ says he's coming on the train on the twenty-third."

"Good. I can drop Natalie and collect him at the same time." He smiled. Natalie wasn't sure if it was his cousin's arrival or her departure that gave him the most pleasure, but she relaxed a little.

The situation was looking up. Rockford wasn't married, or at least there was no mention of a wife. His sister and nieces seemed nice. There was an exit plan in place. Now all she needed was to somehow find his official address in Anchorage, and she'd be golden. Perhaps if she stuck around, she'd get an opportunity to sneak a peek at his driver's license. Just out of curiosity, Natalie took out her phone and checked reception. No bars here at the cabin. He hadn't lied about that.

"Didn't you make your calls back at the train?" he asked Natalie. He'd carried an ice chest to the kitchen and was picking up her suitcase and a battery lantern.

"Yes." Natalie looked to see if Gen was listening, but she was adding another log to the fire in the fireplace. "I called several people and told them where I was and to call in the troopers if they didn't hear from me by the twenty-third." She caught his gaze and held it.

"I'll make sure you're on that train." His tone made it more threat than reassurance. "Come on. I'll show you your room."

"I can carry that." Natalie reached for the suitcase.

He ignored her and carried it to the rear of

the room. As they passed into a hallway, Natalie spotted a ladder that had been hidden in the shadow of a beam, as well as two curtained doorways. Tanner pushed one aside and she followed him into a largish room with a quilt-covered bed beside the window. A duffel bag rested on a blanket chest at the foot. He reached underneath and pulled out a low bed on wheels, rolling it across the floor to the other wall. He moved the duffel and opened the lid of the chest to pull out a neat stack of plaid sheets, releasing the clean scent of cedar.

"I can make the bed," Natalie told him.

"All right. I'll be in the other room if you need anything." He hung the lantern on a hook near the doorway and left.

Natalie picked up the light and held it high to better examine the room. The cedar chest looked hand-carved, with a whimsical design of a squirrel among branches. A long dressing table held a standing mirror and an old-fashioned enamelware bowl and pitcher, along with a scattering of toiletries. A tall cupboard filled the space near the door. The room was charming.

She returned the lantern to its hook and made up the bed with flannel sheets and two quilts she found in the cedar chest. Hopefully Rockford's mother wouldn't mind sharing her room too much. There were no pillows in the chest, but she found one on the top shelf of the cupboard.

She slid it into a pillowcase and was setting her pillow on her bed when the significance of the bowl and pitcher hit her. That's what they meant on the train when they talked about dry cabins. No plumbing. Predictably, she felt a sudden urgent need for facilities.

A faint hum from an engine carried through the window, and light from the hall washed through the doorway. She returned to the main room to find Tanner alone, peeling potatoes. She could hear the girls laughing and thumping around on the porch. "Could you direct me to the outhouse, please?"

"Um, sure." He smirked. "Just go out that door and around the cabin. It's about twenty feet back."

"Thank you." She pulled on her coat and stepped into her boots.

He cut the potato into quarters and dropped it into a big pot on the stove. "There's a snow shovel on the porch. You might need to shovel a path to reach the door of the outhouse."

"Right." The urge was getting stronger. She'd better shovel fast. She was buttoning her coat when Gen stepped inside.

"Where are you off to?"

"The outhouse."

Gen looked puzzled. "Why don't you use the composting toilet?"

"There's a composting toilet?"

"End of the hall," Tanner said as he expertly sliced a carrot into pieces. He pointed with his knife toward the rear of the room. "And to the right."

She stared at him. "Why didn't you say there was an indoor toilet?"

He shrugged. "You didn't ask."

Gen rolled her eyes. Natalie shed her coat and marched across the floor, through the curtain and down the hall to the room he'd indicated. If Gen hadn't been there, would he have let her shovel the path all the way to the outhouse before he mentioned this option?

Once she'd finished, Natalie returned to the kitchen area, with the intention of making it clear she didn't find his little joke funny, but Gen and the girls had returned, along with two more people all donning coats and boots. "There she is," Gen said to the older woman beside her. "Mom, this is Natalie."

"Debbie Rockford." The woman took an uneven step closer and offered her hand. Natalie noticed a brace on her leg, and then forgot it as she took in the sunny smile Debbie was offering. "I understand we're going to be roommates. You're in luck. According to my late husband, I don't snore."

"Me either, as far as I know. It's nice to meet you." Natalie shook her hand and smiled back. "I truly appreciate you taking me in like this."

"The more, the merrier. This is Russ, my brother-in-law," she said, gesturing at a middle-aged man in a flannel shirt who stepped up to shake hands, as well. "And I gather you've already met Evie and Maya. Now that Tanner has brought Vitus, the girls want to snowshoe over to a neighbor's house to drop off some cookies."

"Why don't you take the snow machine?" Tanner suggested.

"No need. The girls could use the exercise," Debbie told him. "And so could I."

"We're taking Christmas cookies we made to Miss Jackie," Maya said.

"She loves Vitus, so we waited," Evie explained. "Wanna come?" she asked Natalie.

Natalie glanced toward Tanner, who didn't seem to be making any moves out of the kitchen. Maybe she'd have a chance to find out more about him while everyone was gone. "It's been a long time since I tried snowshoeing," Natalie told Evie. "I think I'll stay here for now, but thanks for the invitation."

"Okay. We'll be back for supper. We're having s'mores for dessert." Evie snatched up a cookie tin and dashed toward the door.

"I wanna carry the cookies!" Maya raced after her, with her mother right behind. Debbie and Russ followed more slowly. Natalie moved so that she could see them out the window. Russ paused to help Debbie negotiate the porch steps and bent to fasten her snowshoes, but once she was geared up, Debbie seemed to be able to keep up a reasonable pace.

"Polio," Tanner said.

"What's that?" Natalie turned toward him.

"My mom. She had polio as a child, and that's why she wears the leg brace. I assume you were wondering."

She had been, but she didn't like to admit it. "She seems to do very well with it."

"Yeah. It costs her, though." Tanner sliced an onion in half in one stroke. "More than she'll admit."

Natalie stepped closer to the kitchen island. "What are you making?"

"Caribou stew."

"Can I help?"

"I don't know." That smirk of his could get irritating. "Since you're paying me the 'going rate' I'm not sure I'm allowed to let you lift a finger. Are there guidelines I should be following? I probably should have made your bed, huh?"

She didn't roll her eyes, but she was tempted. "Why don't I set the table?"

"If you think it's proper." He chuckled and tipped his head toward a shelf at the end of the kitchen. "You'll find what you need there."

She picked up a stack of heavy pottery bowls. They looked hand-thrown. On the shelf beside them, she found napkins and a tray of monogrammed silverware, with a swirling *R* embossed on the handles. Who kept monogrammed silver in a cabin? This place was the oddest mix of rustic luxury.

"Nice silver," she commented.

"It was my great-great-grandparents'," he said. "My grandfather brought it with him when he came to Alaska in 1937."

"Really? That long ago?"

"Yep. His oldest brother inherited the family farm in Wisconsin, his sister got the house and furniture, and somehow he ended up with the family silver and a horse. He sold the horse, traveled to Alaska and applied for a homestead."

"That doesn't seem fair."

He shrugged. "It was the Depression. His brother ended up losing the farm to bankruptcy. My grandfather probably made out better than either of the others, although I gather it was a hard life at first."

"So, this place is your grandfather's homestead?"

"Yes. Well, not the original cabin. It burned down in 1958 and they rebuilt."

"I don't suppose they're still living?"

"No. My grandfather died ten years ago. He was ninety." He sliced a mushroom and dropped it into the pot. "An amazing man. I still miss him sometimes."

Natalie set the bowls and spoons on the table, wondering what it would be like to be part of a family with roots. Her parents had divorced when she was eight, and she'd never known any of her grandparents. During Natalie's senior year of high school, she'd turned eighteen and her mother had announced she was moving to California with her latest boyfriend. Natalie could stay or go. Never mind that moving states would mean Natalie would lose the honors scholarship she was counting on for college. Or that she wasn't particularly fond of her mom's new boyfriend.

Her dad, to everyone's surprise, had volunteered to let her live with him while she finished high school. It wasn't until her spring semester of college that she discovered the credit cards he'd taken out in her name, ruining her credit rating in the process. Thanks to accepting her father's offer to help, it had ended up taking her fourteen years to pay off his loans and earn her doctorate.

What would it have been like to have a family that supported her instead of taking advantage of her? Did families like that really exist? Or did people like Tanner pretend they'd had a happy childhood to project a certain image, just as he'd pretended his name was Dane when he met Brooke?

Rockford sprinkled in some spices and put the lid on the pot. He plucked a jar off the shelf and opened the lid. "Olive?"

Natalie wrinkled her nose. "No thanks."

"Not a fan, huh?" Tanner fished one out with a fork and popped it into his mouth. "We have other snacks if you're hungry."

"I'm fine for now. Thanks."

Tanner ate another olive, and then replaced the jar and removed a dish towel from a bin beside the stove to reveal two loaf pans filled with white dough.

"What's that?" Natalie asked.

"Ah, this is my family's heirloom sourdough bread. My mom started it earlier." He picked up a knife to make three parallel slashes across the top of each loaf and set the loaves in the oven.

"Heirloom?"

"That's right. This particular sourdough starter belonged to my grandmother and has been in the family for at least sixty-five years."

"What? How?"

"Sourdough starter is a living thing." He pointed to a canning jar on the shelf behind him filled with a bubbly white solution. "Mom scoops out a couple of cups of starter and adds it to flour and other ingredients to make bread dough. Then she feeds the starter with flour and water. The yeast grows and produces the gases that make the bread rise. If you don't care for and feed your starter, it can die."

"Interesting. I've never made bread."

"Well, if you'd like to try, I'm sure we'll be making more in the next couple of days. The stew should be ready in about an hour." He grabbed his satchel from a hook by the door. "I'm sorry to be unsociable, but I do need to get some work in."

"Sure. I'll just read my book." She started toward the fireplace.

"It's a good one," he said as he unpacked his bag. "Have you gotten to the part with the two poodles?"

She laughed and turned toward him. "And how the groomer mixed them up and gave the detective's poodle to the mafia guy? Wasn't that hilarious? You read K. Krisman?"

"Every chance I get." He pulled out the wad of mail, with the bright yellow envelope on top, and laid it aside before setting his laptop on the table and opening it.

Natalie looked at the envelope and back to him. "Aren't you going to read your mail?"

"What?" He glanced over at the pile. "Oh. No." He sat down at the table and typed something into his computer.

"Why not?"

"Why not what?" he asked, his mind obviously on the document he'd opened.

"Why don't you check your mail? It might be important."

"I doubt it," he said without looking up.

She picked up the yellow envelope. "This one's handwritten. It looks personal."

He finally looked up to scowl at her. "Could you put that away, please?"

"Why?" She waved the envelope at him. "Do you know who it's from?"

"No. It's none of my business."

"None of your business who mails you letters?"

"That's not my mail. I picked it up for my cousin."

"Your cousin?" Maybe it was going to be all right after all. "Dane Rockford is your cousin?"

"You know Dane?"

"I…no."

"But you said his name."

"It was on the envelope."

He narrowed his eyes. "If you read the envelope and saw Dane's name, why were you so insistent that I open it?"

"I…" she hesitated.

"What? Can't think of a lie to answer that question? What is going on, Natalie? You've been watching me ever since I got on the train. In fact, that was you at the post office this morning, wasn't it?" He nodded to himself as though totaling up points. "It was no accident that you got off the train when I did. You purposely arranged it so I'd have to bring you here. Why?"

"That's ridiculous. You've been reading too many K. Krisman books."

"Or maybe you have. What sort of caper are you pulling?"

"Why would you think I—"

"Don't give me that. I want to know who you are and why you're here."

She swallowed. "Okay, I'll explain. But before I do, may I ask one question?"

"What's that?"

"Is your cousin married?"

He gave a short laugh. "That's your question? No. Dane is not married. Now talk."

"All right." She sucked in a long breath. Where did she start and how much did he need to know? "My best friend, Brooke, lives in Fairbanks. She met your cousin, Dane, about two months ago."

"Okay."

"A couple of weeks ago, she noticed symptoms. Nausea, fatigue."

"You think this has something to do with my cousin? Is it some communicable disease?"

"No." A nervous laugh escaped. "It's not a disease. She's pregnant."

"Pregnant? And she thinks Dane is the father?" A line formed between his eyebrows.

"She knows he is. She wrote him a letter, but she never heard back."

"You're sure she said Dane?"

"Yes. Dane Rockford." She waved the yellow envelope. "This is the letter she wrote. Why is that so hard to believe?"

"Dane is really not the type."

"What type?"

"The type to pick up a stranger and get her pregnant."

Natalie pushed her shoulders back. "Are you implying my friend is the type?"

"Well, since I've never met your friend, I wouldn't make that claim, but I do know Dane. Maybe she's mistaken?"

"There's no mistake. I'm sure a paternity test will confirm it when the time comes."

"I'll advise him to ask for one when I tell him about this."

"Oh, you can't tell him." Natalie had to make that clear.

"What? Why not?"

"I promised. Please. Brooke only agreed to let me help if she could break the news to him. The letter she wrote just says she has something important to talk with him about. She wants to tell him in person."

"So, let me get this straight. You thought I was Dane."

"Well, you did have a key to his mailbox."

"Fair enough. You were watching the mailbox and followed me on the train and allowed yourself to get stranded here just to find Dane for your friend?"

"Yes."

"Couldn't you have just waited for him to read the letter?"

"She wrote it two weeks ago, and he never answered. It seemed clear he didn't intend to answer."

"He's been away."

"Well, I didn't know that."

"Wait. I told you on the train that my name is Tanner."

"Yes, but—"

"But you figured I was lying about my name. Or that Dane was lying."

She nodded.

He shook his head. "Did anyone ever tell you, Natalie whatever-your-last-name-is, that you have a very cynical mind?"

"My name is Weiss." She allowed a half smile. "And I might have heard that once or twice, although I maintain I'm a realist, not a cynic. But come on. Only a PO box? No cell phone? Doesn't that seem suspicious? Like maybe Dane was married?"

"I suppose it would if you didn't know Dane," he acknowledged.

"So, where can I find your cousin?"

He shrugged. "I have no idea."

"Oh, come on. You might as well tell me. I'm going to find him sooner or later."

"Seriously. He dropped off his dog with me right after Thanksgiving and said he had some business to take care of. As you mentioned, Dane doesn't carry a cell phone, and he's not good about checking in."

"Then why did you pick up his mail?"

"He promised he'd be here for Christmas, so I thought I'd bring it to him."

"Great. You can give him the letter and

make sure he understands it's vital that he contact Brooke."

"I guess I could do that." Tanner tilted his head. "Are you absolutely sure it was Dane?"

"Are you saying my friend is lying?"

"No, it's just that it's so out of character. Dane is—well, there's a reason he lives out here in the middle of nowhere most of the year."

"He lives here? In this cabin?"

"Yes. Well, most of the time, anyway. I think his official residence is still his dad's house in Anchorage."

"Can you give me that address?"

"I suppose, but you're not going to find Dane there very often. He's usually out here, by himself."

"Are you saying he's a hermit?"

"No, not at all. Just that he's not always comfortable with new people. He's fine when he knows you, or in a familiar situation. He works as a fishing guide on the Kenai during the summer, and he's great with clients. But as far as I know, the only date he's ever been on was when my sister set him up to double with her and her college boyfriend. It didn't go well."

"What happened?"

"I don't know. Gen said he hardly spoke two words. Her sorority sister wasn't impressed.

That's why I find it hard to understand how he could have met your friend and—"

"Brooke got a flat tire at two in the morning. He stopped to help."

"Ah, that sounds more like him."

"She did mention that he was shy at first, but really opened up once you got to know him better."

"Yeah, that's Dane." He took the yellow envelope from her hand and looked at the looping handwriting. "Your friend sounds like a nice person."

"Oh, nice doesn't begin to describe Brooke," Natalie assured him. "She makes Mr. Rogers look like a tyrant."

He laughed. "Maybe things will work out, then, for the two of them."

"I hope so." Natalie wasn't convinced successful long-term romantic relationships existed outside of fairy tales, but if anyone deserved happily-ever-after, it was Brooke. She crossed her fingers on both hands. "I sincerely hope so."

CHAPTER FOUR

AFTER THIS REVELATION, editing was the last thing on Tanner's mind. One of his earliest memories was when he was six years old, when his mother asked him to keep an eye on his four-year-old cousin to make sure Dane didn't get into any trouble. Old habits were hard to break.

He closed the lid on his laptop. "Listen, I know this Brooke is your friend, but tell me honestly, what has Dane gotten himself into?"

Natalie frowned. "What do you mean?"

"What sort of life does she live? Does she party a lot?"

"Why would you ask that?"

"I was just wondering why she was out at two in the morning." At Natalie's glare, he held up his hands. "I'm not judging her, just wondering about their compatibility. Because Dane is not a party kind of guy."

"For your information, Brooke was on her way home from work. And the reason she was going home from work at two in the morning is because she stayed overtime to fill in for someone on the night desk who couldn't make the first half of their shift." Natalie huffed. "She's always doing that. She has a degree in hospitality management and she was hired as a manager, but whenever they're short-staffed, Brooke is the one who pitches in."

"Oh."

"She's very responsible, and she'll be a great mom. Believe me, Brooke is good enough for your cousin. My question is if he's good enough for her."

"Dane will live up to his responsibilities, if that's what you mean."

"How? If he lives here most of the year, how could he make enough money to support a child?"

So that's what she was concerned about. He stood up and grabbed his coat. "Come with me."

"Where?"

"I'll show you. Come on."

She shrugged and pulled on her boots and coat. "How far are we going?"

"Not far." He grabbed the lantern from the peg beside the door and led her along a shoveled path through a grove of trees to what looked like a large shed. The heavy door on the front was secured with a padlock. "Here, could you hold this?" He handed her the lantern.

She held the light while he worked the combination lock until it snapped free. He opened the door and flicked on the lights. She stepped inside. The scent of sawdust filled the room. On the far side, an ATV and snow machine were parked in front of a small garage-type door, but the entire rest of the building was Dane's workshop. Saws, axes, clamps and other tools hung neatly on a pegboard-lined wall. The center of the space was dominated by Dane's lathe and a large custom workbench he had created. And the far wall was lined with shelves, holding a row of wooden bowls.

Natalie stepped closer and picked up a bowl, one made from bird's-eye birch. Dane would be able to tell him exactly which variety of birch. The bowl had been roughly shaped and then polished to a sheen, letting the natural curves of the wood form undulating edges. Dane had filled a natural split and three knots in the wood with green jade. Natalie ran her finger over the wood. "This is amazing."

"Yes." Tanner had always been in awe of his cousin's talent. "He sells them through galleries in Anchorage and Fairbanks, and a major online art auction site has expressed interest in featuring some of them."

"Brooke had a wooden bowl similar to this one on her coffee table."

"Dane must have given it to her. Does she like it?"

"She loves it. I thought it was because it's beautiful. I didn't realize it was a special gift." She turned the bowl over and checked the signature on the bottom. "Just *'Dane'*?"

"That's how he signs them all." Tanner reached for another bowl, this one of dark and light woods, glued and stacked into an intricate pattern and then turned on the lathe into a tall urn-shaped vessel. "The galleries sell Dane's bowls for anywhere from two hundred to two thousand dollars apiece, depending on size and complexity. He does them all by hand, no power tools. Even his lathe is pedal-powered."

She paused in front of the shelves. "There must be almost two dozen here."

"There are usually a lot more. He probably delivered most of his inventory before he took off on whatever it is he's doing. He's not getting rich, but between guiding and wood crafting, he makes a decent living." He turned to catch her eye. "Feel better?"

She gave a little smile. "I do, actually. I don't mean to sound mercenary—"

"But kids are expensive. Yeah, I get that you're just looking out for your friend." On the other hand, who was looking out for Dane? Maybe he shouldn't have clued Natalie in on Dane's talents. Tanner should run a background check on this woman to make sure she hadn't pulled any scams in the past. "What did you say Brooke's last name was?"

Natalie stiffened. "I didn't."

"And you're not going to tell me?"

She returned the bowl she'd been studying to the shelf. "I don't see that it's any of your business. If your cousin wants you to know, he'll tell you himself."

"I could just read it off the return address on the envelope, you know."

She huffed out a breath. "Fine. Her name is Brooke Jenkins. She works for the Chinook River Resort. Feel free to investigate her. I doubt you'll find so much as a parking ticket."

"We'll see."

"You won't mind if I do the same for your cousin?"

"Of course not. In fact, I'm surprised you haven't already."

She shrugged. "Without an address, I couldn't find him on the internet."

"Ah. That's probably because Dane's first name is Norman. He's named for Norman Dane Vaughan, the Alaskan explorer who was one of the first to reach the South Pole."

"I know who Norman Vaughan is. What I wanted to find is who Dane Rockford is."

"Well, you can look, but you're not going to learn much from the internet. You'll find he owns one third of this cabin along with Gen and me, has resident fishing and hunting licenses, and has no social media presence whatsoever."

"What about his art? Doesn't he have a website?"

"No. I've offered to set one up for him, but he says he just wants to make bowls and let the galleries worry about marketing." He stepped toward the door. "Are you ready to go inside?"

"Yes."

Tanner locked up behind them and followed her back to the cabin. Vitus met them at the door, waving his plume of a tail. "Ah, they must be on their way home. Vitus is the advance guard."

Natalie stopped to stroke his head. "Vitus. I get it now. After Vitus Bering, another explorer."

"Right. Dane is a history buff, like his dad."

"Your Uncle Russ?"

"That's right." They stepped inside the cabin and shed their outerwear.

"What about Dane's mother?"

Tanner shrugged. "Long story. She's out of the picture."

"So does Dane make a habit of taking off like—" Clattering steps on the porch announced that the others had returned.

Tanner gathered up Dane's mail and returned it to his satchel. "Let's not tell the rest of the family about this until Dane has had a chance to read the letter and decide what he's going to do."

"What do you mean, decide? He's—"

"Not now," Tanner insisted as the door flew open and the girls rushed inside, followed by their mother. Vitus ran to meet them as if he hadn't seen them in hours, rather than minutes.

"Is it supper time?" Evie asked, as she hugged the dog. "I'm soooo hungry."

Tanner lifted the lid to the Dutch oven and gave the stew a stir. "It's ready. Wash up and we'll eat."

"Yay!" Evie and Maya stepped out of their boots, dropped their coats, hats and gloves, and ran toward the washbasin in the back of the house.

"Girls. Put away your things first," Gen called and followed them into the hallway.

"We'll talk more later," Tanner whispered to Natalie. And they would. Because he was sure by tomorrow, he'd have many more questions for Natalie Weiss.

THE GIRLS HAD returned to put their boots on the tray and coats on the rack, but ran off leaving hats, a scarf and gloves where they had fallen. Natalie went to help Gen gather the girls' things. "Here's a blue mitten, but I don't see a mate."

"Maya insisted on wearing one red and one blue today." Gen grinned. "Pick your battles, ya know?"

"Absolutely." Natalie was used to dealing with college students rather than preschoolers, some of whom weren't that different than Evie and Maya. "Where are your mom and uncle?"

"They'll be along soon. Mom was getting tired, so they stopped for a rest."

Tanner made a growling noise from the table area where he was slicing bread. "She shouldn't be snowshoeing that far."

"She knows her limits," Gen replied.

"Does she?" Without waiting for an answer, Tanner stepped into his boots and reached for his coat. "I'm taking a sled—"

The creak of the front step stopped him. A moment later Debbie and Russ entered the cabin, laughing together. "Something smells good," Debbie said, and then she noticed Tanner's coat in his hand. "Going somewhere?"

"No." He toed off his boots. "Dinner's ready."

"You were coming after me, weren't you?"

"Well, I was—"

"I'm fine. And Russ was with me. He wouldn't have deserted me."

"I just thought you might need a ride."

Debbie laughed and patted his cheek. "You're such a worrier. I'll go wash up and make sure there are no water fights going on back there." She followed the sound of giggling to the back of the cabin.

Russ gave Tanner a pat on the shoulder. "She's okay. She's tough, you know."

"I know. It's just that she pushes herself too hard."

The two girls dashed from the rear of the house to the dining table, both heading for a yellow chair. Evie arrived first. "Mine."

"You had it at lunch," Maya complained.

"Hey, who's going to sit by me?" Tanner asked, as he set the pot of stew on a trivet near the end of the table farthest from the yellow chair.

"I will!" Evie shouted.

"Nuh-uh. You already called the yellow chair. I get to sit by Uncle Tanner." Maya grinned and waited for Tanner to set a booster in place before climbing into the chair at his right. She patted the other chair beside her. "Miss Natalie, you can sit here by me."

"No fair," Evie whined, but a stern look

from her mother quieted her. "Grandma, will you sit by me?"

"Sure." Debbie smiled at her granddaughter, but Natalie noticed a faint grimace as she settled herself into the chair at the head of the table.

Tanner's frown indicated he'd noticed, as well, but he didn't comment as he set butter, salt and pepper on the table. Gen sat beside Natalie, and Russ chose a chair across from Tanner. Natalie started to reach for her napkin, but before she could, Maya grasped her hand. Looking up, Natalie realized everyone was holding hands. Gen reached across the table to take her right hand, and they all bowed their heads while Debbie offered a simple prayer of thanks for food, family and a new friend, which Natalie assumed meant her.

Afterward, Tanner filled their bowls with stew while Gen poured milk for the girls. "Water or milk?" Russ asked Natalie, holding a stoneware pitcher.

"Water, please." Natalie accepted the glass. Debbie held the breadbasket so that Evie could choose the slice she wanted. Maya asked Tanner for extra carrots. The scent of fresh-baked sourdough bread and rich stew filled the room. It was like being inside a Christmas commercial.

When Natalie was growing up, dinner was

usually whatever she heated up in the microwave when she got hungry. Occasionally, she and her mother would happen to eat at the same time, but Natalie wouldn't have called it dining together. Not like this.

The only times she'd experienced a big family dinner was as a guest at Brooke's house when her parents were still living in Anchorage. Brooke would be right at home at a table like this. Maybe this was going to work out okay for Brooke, after all. Natalie would love to be able to move to New Mexico without worrying that she was leaving Brooke without anyone to look after her.

Of course, the key was Dane. His family might be great, but Dane had assured Brooke he was coming back, and then disappeared without a word. It would be a shame if Brooke had managed to connect with the only jerk of the family. But there was bound to be one. Otherwise, this family was perfect. And perfect families didn't exist.

After dinner cleanup, Gen offered to make hot chocolate, a suggestion enthusiastically encouraged by her daughters. Tanner went outside to turn off the generator, leaving the cabin lit by battery lanterns and firelight. The whole family gathered around the fireplace. Natalie chose a rocker across from the leather sofa, where she could watch the fire. Debbie produced a plate of chocolate and vanilla pinwheel cookies, chocolate bars, and marshmallows, and the two girls immediately volunteered to make s'mores for everyone.

Russ supervised the marshmallow toasting, making the girls repeat his safety rules before skewering the marshmallows onto long forks for them to toast. Debbie hung a lantern on a stand beside the recliner and settled in, allowing the footrest to lift and support her legs. She picked up an embroidery hoop and began stitching. Tanner returned, shed his coat and took a tray from Gen to bring to the coffee table. He picked up one of the steaming mugs from the tray and handed it to Natalie. "Cocoa?"

"Yes, please."

"Marshmallows in that?"

Natalie laughed. "No thanks. I'll save it for my s'more."

"They'll be really good," Maya said. "I'm a good marshmallow cooker."

"I'll bet you are." As Natalie took the mug from Tanner's hand, their eyes met. Even in the dim lighting, she could see the joy he took in spending time with his family.

Since at least half of the marshmallows either burned to a crisp or fell into the fire before they could be claimed, dessert for the whole group took quite a while, but nobody seemed to mind. Maya brought Natalie one of the cookie sandwiches with melting marshmallow and chocolate in the middle. "We made these cookies," Maya informed Natalie. "Us and Mommy."

Natalie took a bite. "They're the most delicious cookies I've ever eaten."

Maya grinned and skipped back to the fireplace to start another marshmallow. Natalie's thoughts went back to a Christmas long ago, the only time she ever remembered baking cookies with her mother. On Christmas Day, Mom had unexpectedly produced one of those prefab cookie dough rolls with the shape of a Christmas tree in the center, and they'd spent the afternoon slicing and baking. Looking back, she realized the gesture was most likely driven by maternal guilt, since her only presents that year were new socks, a box of crayons and a coloring book, but at the time, she'd been thrilled. Funny how she'd forgotten all about that until today.

Once everyone had eaten their fill of the gooey goodness, Maya tugged on Tanner's shirt. "Read us a story, Uncle Tanner."

"Okay. You find a book," he told her. Maya and Evie scurried to a corner of the bookcase stocked with slim volumes, while Tanner fetched a headlamp from a shelf near the mantel. He'd barely settled on the sofa when the girls returned with an entire stack of books.

"We can't decide," Evie said, climbing onto Tanner's lap.

"We want all the stories," Maya explained, pushing her way onto his other knee.

"Well, let's start with this one tonight." Tanner reached for the top story and shifted the girls so that they were sitting on either side of him, leaving room in his lap for the large picture book. Tanner had a wonderful reading voice, smooth and melodious but with plenty of inflection and dramatic pauses. Even though Natalie knew the story, she found herself engrossed as Tanner told of the magical land with a special wizard and all his friends. Even more engrossing was the sight of the two girls cuddling close to their uncle, and the way he smiled at them.

Now that she knew he wasn't Dane, Natalie could admit to herself that she found Tanner attractive. He was easy to look at, funny and devoted to his family—a hard combination to resist. Not that it mattered. Natalie was heading off to a new life in a matter of days. The last thing she needed was any sort of romantic entanglement. But here in the cabin, gathered around the hearth, she couldn't help but wonder what it would be like to be part of a family like this. To be loved.

As the story continued, the girls' eyelids began to droop. Once Tanner reached the end of the story, Gen stood. "Bedtime."

"Not yet. We want another story," Evie protested.

"Tomorrow," their mother told them. "Say good night."

"Good night, Uncle Tanner." Maya gave him a hug. And then, having discovered a loophole, she proceeded to hug and say good night to every adult in the room, including Natalie. Evie did the same.

Even realizing it was more likely a bedtime stall than real affection, Natalie's heart melted when the two little girls put their arms around her neck and chanted, "Good night, Miss Natalie. Sleep tight."

"Good night, Evie. Good night, Maya. I'll see you in the morning."

"We'll get a Christmas tree tomorrow!" Evie said.

"I'll look forward to that. Good night." She watched as Gen herded the two girls off toward the second bedroom at the back of the cabin.

Russ put the toasting forks away and banked the fire. "I'm ready to turn in, as well."

Debbie yawned. "Me, too." When Natalie began to gather the empty cups, Debbie advised, "Just leave those for tomorrow. They're easier to wash when we can see."

"All right." Natalie set the tray on the kitchen worktable and followed Debbie toward the bedroom.

"You don't need to come to bed if you're not ready," Debbie told her. "You won't disturb me." She laughed. "Once I'm asleep it takes an earthquake to wake me up."

Natalie glanced across the room, where Tanner was still relaxing on the couch with his feet propped up on the trunk that served as a coffee table. This would be a good chance to be alone with him, to get more information about his cousin and what Brooke might be facing. But watching his face, profiled against the flickering firelight, she realized she didn't want to talk. She wanted to sit beside him on the couch, to gaze into the flames, perhaps to feel his arm around her.

Dangerous thoughts. She turned and padded across the room to join Debbie in the bedroom, not feeling safe until she'd drawn the curtain across the door.

"Feel free to use my dry shampoo or anything else you need," Debbie told her. "We do mostly sponge baths here in the winter. I can probably find you an extra toothbrush if you need one."

"I have one in my suitcase but thank you. You've been so kind."

"Not at all. We're delighted to have you here." Once they'd both gotten ready for bed, Debbie wished her a good night and turned out the lantern.

Natalie lay on the trundle bed, looking up into the darkness. Was it only this morning that she'd spotted Tanner in the post office and followed him to the train? How had she gone from stalker to pampered guest in his family's Christmastime celebration in one day?

Natalie closed her eyes, not expecting to get much sleep. She seldom slept well in a strange bed, much less in a strange house with a strange family, but the day's events must have worn her out, because that was her last thought of the night.

THE FAINT RUMBLE of an engine woke Natalie. She checked her watch. Almost seven in the morning. Tanner must have started the generator. The bed across the room was neatly made. She stretched under the heavy quilts.

She'd been surprised at how comfortable the bed was, and even more surprised at how comfortable she felt here in the cabin, with Tanner's family. Tanner would be an easy man to trust, but she needed to watch that tendency. His loyalties lay with his family, and he seemed very protective of his cousin. Natalie shouldn't let herself get too comfortable until she'd found Dane and made sure he would treat Brooke right.

The wind howled—no, not the wind, more like some kind of animal. She pushed open the window above her bed and peered out into the dark. Tanner was outside, the light from his headlamp playing over the logs under a lean-to near the shed. He seemed to be singing as he gathered a load of firewood. What song he was singing was harder to determine, because Vitus had decided to sing along making sounds somewhere between a howl and a gargle. Tanner laughed and ran his gloves over the big dog's head before picking up the bundle of logs and disappearing around the side of the cabin.

Natalie shut the window and pulled a sweater and jeans over the thermals she'd slept in. A quick check in the mirror over the washbasin showed some major bedhead. Natalie ran a brush through her hair and pulled it into a ponytail. She was just stepping out of the hallway when the front door opened and Vitus came running to meet her, tail wagging. "Aarrrr, aarrr."

"You're in a talkative mood this morning," she told the dog as she buried her hands in the cool mane of fur surrounding his head and rubbed his ears.

"He's happy to be home. How are you this morning?" Tanner asked as he fed the cooking stove. "Hungry?"

"Not especially. I usually just pick up a cappuccino on the way to work."

"Well, I can't offer you one of those, but I'll make coffee in a few minutes."

"Coffee sounds fabulous. What can I do to help?"

"Gen and the girls are collecting snow to melt." He reached for a cast-iron skillet hanging on the wall. "You could get the bacon and eggs from the ice chest if you'd like."

Russ climbed down the ladder from the loft. "Did I hear someone say bacon?"

"It's coming," Tanner said.

"Where's your mom?"

"Outside with Gen and the girls. They're supposed to be fetching snow for coffee, but Maya saw some moose tracks and she's convinced they belong to Santa's reindeer, so they had to stop and look for more." Tanner didn't seem the least bit put out at the delay.

By the time Debbie, Gen and the girls came inside, Tanner had fried up a generous pile of bacon. He took the pot from Gen and set it on the stove. "Thanks. Coffee should be ready in ten minutes or so." He cracked some eggs and looked toward Natalie. "Are you sure you don't want breakfast?" He winked. "It's included in the price."

The bacon did smell wonderful. "You've talked me into it. Thank you."

"Fried or scrambled?"

"Scrambled."

"Good, because my fried eggs usually end up scrambled anyway."

Fifteen minutes later, they'd once again gathered at the table. Maya gobbled up her bacon and eyed the strips on Evie's plate. Evie edged her plate farther from her sister. Maya turned to Tanner. "When can we get our Christmas tree?"

"After we've finished breakfast and cleaned up." He smiled. "Slow down and taste your food. The sun isn't even up yet."

"Okay, but hurry!" Maya wiggled in her seat waiting for the others to finish.

Gen finished her last bite. "Let's go brush your hair and find your snowsuits."

"Yay!" Maya and Evie jumped up from the table, dumped their plates on the kitchen worktable and ran to their bedroom. Gen followed at a more reasonable speed.

Natalie sipped her coffee, letting the caffeine wake her up enough to enjoy the delicious-looking breakfast in front of her. Vitus sat nearby, his attitude clearly stating, *I'm not begging, just making myself available*. Natalie took a bite of eggs, and then another and before she knew it the food was gone. When she rose to carry her plate to the kitchen, she "accidently" dropped a bit of bacon on the floor and Vitus immediately pounced on it.

Tanner, carrying his own plate, chuckled. "Now you've done it. He'll be sticking so close, you won't be able to turn around without bumping into him."

"I can think of worse fates." She smiled at the dog, now gazing at her with total devotion. "He's sweet."

"He is. Dane raised him from a pup. He was the runt of a large litter and not getting enough milk, so Dane took him in and bottle-fed him. Vitus always seems a little confused around other dogs. I suspect he thinks he's a furry person."

Natalie laughed. She looked over to see if Debbie or Russ were paying attention, but they were sipping coffee and talking quietly at the table. "I wonder if Brooke knows that story."

"Probably not. Dane isn't one to blow his own horn."

"Too bad I can't call her." Natalie pulled out her phone. Two bars flashed briefly before they disappeared. "Last time we talked, I still thought you were Dane. I need to let her know you'll give him the letter on the twenty-third."

"You can usually pick up a signal from the hilltop just south of here. If you want, we can snowshoe up once we've fetched the tree."

"That would be great. What's the deal with the tree?"

"We have ten acres, so we'll let the girls look around until they find the perfect spruce for our Christmas tree. Once we cut it and bring it home, I'll show you the hill. Deal?"

"Deal. Thanks."

"No problem." He poured warm water from the stove into a plastic dishpan and added a squirt of soap.

"You cooked. I'll wash," Natalie said.

"It's all part of the service."

"Not anymore. I want to do my share around here. You go get ready to take Evie and Maya tree hunting. I'll take care of these."

"Thank you." He paused, and a slow grin crossed his face.

"What?"

"I'm just surprised. For someone who tracked me down and followed me from the train, you're remarkably easy to get along with."

"Well, now that I know you weren't the one who left Brooke in the lurch, I'm feeling a little friendlier. Toward you, at least."

He raised an eyebrow. "I'm sure Dane has a good reason to have been gone so long."

She picked up a dish sponge. "I guess we'll find out."

Natalie would never admit it, but she rather liked washing dishes. Something about splashing around in warm suds while her mind wandered appealed to her. Debbie brought two more plates and grabbed a dish towel. "I see Tanner's put you to work."

"I volunteered."

"That's nice of you." She picked up a plate to dry. "So, you'd never met Tanner before you got off the train?"

"Well, um, we'd talked a little at lunch."

"Ah." Debbie nodded as though that confirmed something. "I'm glad you're making the best of being stuck here with us. I'm sure you had other plans with friends and family."

"Just a math department Christmas party."

"You teach at the university?"

"Yes." Natalie hadn't meant to let that slip, but it didn't really matter since at the end of the month, she would officially be off their employment rolls. Time to change the subject. "I do appreciate you taking me in until the next train. I know it must be a bother to have a stranger in the middle of your family gathering."

"Nonsense. Evie and Maya are always delighted to have a bigger audience, and the rest of us are enjoying your company."

"Well, I'm enjoying my time with them, as well. I don't get to spend much time around children. Evie and Maya are particularly charming."

Debbie smiled. "We think so." She stacked the last plate and set them on the shelf. "We always enjoy getting away to the cabin. It's like a trip back in time." As if to illustrate, Debbie pulled her needlework project from a basket.

Natalie had seen her working on it the night before, but she hadn't had a chance to look at it. Now she saw that the threads had formed a nativity scene in a lush blend of texture and color with subtle shading. Only a bit of a donkey was left unfinished. "This is beautiful. What do you call this sort of embroidery?"

"This is crewelwork, done in wool. I do counted cross-stitch, too."

"You're very talented."

"Thank you." Debbie crossed the room but before she'd settled into her recliner, Maya and Evie came running out, with their hair now braided and dressed in heavy sweaters.

"Grandma, are you coming with us to cut the tree?" Maya asked.

"Not this time, sweetie. I think I'll stay here. Maybe I'll hang the stockings while you're gone."

"Stockings!" the girls chanted.

Tanner climbed down the ladder from the loft. "Tree time! Who's going?"

"Me! Me!" the girls shouted.

He laid a hand on his mother's shoulder. "You okay?"

"I'm fine." She smiled at him. "I'll rest."

"Good. Gen, are you ready?"

Gen looked toward Natalie and back at Tanner. "You know, I have a few things to take care of. If Natalie doesn't mind going along to help supervise the girls, I might stay here with Mom."

"I've never, uh—" Natalie began.

"It's great fun," Gen assured her. "We always did it as kids. Tanner will do all the cutting."

"Please come, Miss Natalie," Evie said.

"It's our first time, too," Maya told her. "Pleeeeeease?"

Who could resist those faces? "Sure. Just let me get my boots."

"Yay!"

CHAPTER FIVE

IT TOOK ANOTHER twenty minutes and a couple of trips to the bathroom before Tanner had everyone prepared and bundled up, but eventually they made it out the door. The sun wasn't up yet, but the sky was light. Vitus plunged into the snow and ran in circles when he saw Tanner carrying his harness. Tanner laughed. "You've got to hold still so I can put this on."

Natalie stood with the girls, watching him buckle Vitus into his harness. Her cheeks glowed with almost as much excitement as theirs. Tanner had seen the way Gen looked between him and Natalie. He suspected she was doing a little matchmaking. She'd probably be less inclined if she knew the circumstances behind Natalie getting herself stranded, but Tanner didn't see the need to share that information. No use getting the whole family stirred up about Dane and this Brooke woman. And he couldn't blame Natalie for looking out for her friend.

Tanner hooked Vitus to the sled, added the

equipment and fastened on his snowshoes. "Everybody in."

Natalie went first, and with her help, Tanner got the girls settled in beside her. Soon they were gliding through the forest behind the house. "Keep an eye out for the perfect tree," Tanner told the girls.

"There's one," Maya said, before they'd even left the yard.

"Yeah, that one is right behind the house. Let's get out a little farther first." He took them down a trail into the forest.

"The one with the berries is pretty." Maya pointed at a mountain ash.

"It is," Tanner agreed. "But we probably want an evergreen for our Christmas tree."

"Yeah, Maya," Evie said. Maya pouted.

"But that doesn't mean we can't decorate with it," Natalie said. "Tanner, can we cut some of those mountain ash berries?"

"Sure." Tanner stopped the dog. Using the loppers he'd brought along, he cut a few clusters of the red berries and handed them to the girls. "Remember, these are not for eating."

"We know. Mom said never eat plants without asking," Evie answered.

They traveled a little farther into the woods when they came to a clearing with several small trees. "How about one of these?" Tanner asked, pointing at a nicely shaped four-foot tree.

"It's too little," Maya said. Evie nodded in agreement.

"Okay." Fifteen minutes later, he spotted a six-footer. "This one?"

"Bigger," Evie told him.

Tanner laughed. "Remember, it has to fit inside the cabin."

Natalie and the two girls grinned at each other. "Bigger," they said in unison.

They'd only gone a little farther when Maya squealed. "That one!"

Tanner stopped to examine the tree. It was probably nine feet tall, but it had been growing in the shade of bigger spruces, and the tiers of limbs had to be at least sixteen inches apart, with bare trunk in between. Some of the limbs had broken and regrown, creating an irregular pattern. "This one? Really?"

"It's perfect," Evie said. "It will go all the way to the roof."

"We could probably find a prettier tree. What do you think, Natalie?"

Natalie looked at the two girls' faces, and then she nodded. "I think we've found our tree. It just needs a little love. Right, girls?"

"Right! This tree." They all scrambled out of the sled and immediately sank into the snow.

When Natalie tried to pull Maya out, she fell over backward. Vitus yipped.

"Snow angels," Evie called and fell backward herself. Soon all three of them were waving their arms and legs.

Tanner laughed and unhooked the dog so he could play, too, while Tanner trimmed a dead branch at the bottom of the tree and then, using his bow saw, quickly cut through the spindly trunk. By the time he'd finished, Natalie had helped the girls up and the three of them were back in the sled, admiring their snow art. He loaded the tree into the sled, behind them, and inspected the shapes in the snow. "Very pretty."

"It's my very first snow angel," Natalie admitted.

"Really? You never made a snow angel before?" Evie's eyes went wide. "Not even when you were a little girl?"

"I don't think so. I don't know why." She put her arms around Evie's and Maya's shoulders and squeezed. "I guess I didn't have fun friends like you."

Tanner paused in tying the tree to the sled. There was something in her voice that made him suspect Natalie's childhood hadn't been the picnic his was. Maybe she didn't have a close family like his. Maybe, like Evie and

Maya, she'd lost her family in a divorce, which might explain some of her cynicism. The thought made him even more determined to make this Christmas special for his nieces. "Are we ready to take the tree home?"

"Yes!" Maya shouted.

Amid the giggles, Tanner hitched Vitus to the sled and got it turned around. "Vitus, hike!"

A STRAY TWIG from the spruce tree poked at Evie and made her squirm. Natalie pushed it away, accidently crushing a few needles and releasing the fresh scent of evergreen. Along the trail, a flock of chickadees skittered from one tree to the next. Natalie almost expected Santa's reindeer to appear.

As though she'd read Natalie's mind, Evie burst into "Rudolph the Red-Nosed Reindeer." Maya immediately joined in, and a couple of beats later, so did Tanner. Natalie added her voice, and they sang Christmas carols all the way back to the cabin.

Russ was in the back, collecting a load of firewood, when they came caroling into the yard. "Well, if this isn't a fine Christmas greeting," he said. "I see you found a tree."

"It's a good one," Maya told him. "Really tall. But it needs love."

"Ah, don't we all?" Russ agreed as he helped Tanner lift the tree from the sled. The two men exchanged wry smiles over the sparse branches, but the girls ran ahead, calling for their mom and grandmother to tell them all about the special tree. As soon as Vitus was unclipped, he ran off after them.

Tanner banged the trunk against the porch floor a few times to dislodge the snow before carrying it through the front door. A tree stand waited in front of the window, the table with the amaryllis now pushed to the side nearer the door. Once Tanner had shed his coat and boots, he lifted the tree into the stand. Debbie stood back, with a granddaughter on either side of her. "A little to the left. No, my left. And now forward toward me just a scooch. Perfect."

Gen crawled under to tighten the screws on the tree stand. Evie clapped her hands. "It's almost to the sky."

Debbie put her arms around the girls' shoulders and gave a squeeze. "Yes, I think we'll have just enough room for the angel on top. Nice work."

"Stockings!" Maya shouted.

Sure enough, a row of eight stockings now hung from the mantel. Each was a work of art, with a different Christmas scene embroidered on each one. Natalie went closer and discovered a name worked into the top of each scene. Tanner's had an old-fashioned red pickup truck carrying a Christmas tree. Gen's was dark blue, with intricate snowflakes on the upper stocking and a snowman scene across the foot. A sparrow carrying a sprig of holly decorated Dane's stocking. And then Natalie noticed that the last stocking, with a decorated Christmas tree viewed through the window of a log cabin, had a white cuff added to the top, with her name embroidered in script across it.

Maya tugged on Natalie's sleeve. "This one's mine." The red stocking featured a rocking horse, teddy bear and other classic toys.

"Mine has a puppy." Evie pointed.

"With a red bow," Natalie said. "These are beautiful. I'll bet your grandmother made them."

"Uh-huh. She sews pretty things. Did your grandma make you a stocking?"

"Um, no." Natalie had never met either of her grandmothers, but she didn't want to explain that to Evie and Maya. "You're lucky to have such a talented grandmother."

"Thank you," Debbie said, coming up behind them.

"That's so sweet that you made me a stocking."

"It was no trouble. I made that one for my mother-in-law. I just added your name for now."

"I won't be here for Christmas, though."

"Ah, but you're here now, and so you should have a stocking."

"Thank you." Natalie examined the fine stitches making up the pine wreath. "I'm in awe of all the detail in these. Just amazing."

"I enjoy it." Debbie gave a wry smile. "It gives me something to do with my hands when I'm sitting."

Tanner came over, carrying a half cookie in one hand and an open tin in the other. "Did you still want to make that call?" he asked, offering Natalie a cookie.

"Yes, if you don't mind showing me where I can get a signal."

"I'll get you some snowshoes." He laid a hand on his mother's arm. "We'll be back by lunchtime to help decorate the tree."

"Take your time," she told him. "We've got all day."

Tanner ducked into the back and returned carrying snowshoes and poles. "Have you snowshoed before?" he asked Natalie.

"A little. We used to ski and snowshoe sometimes in school." As she recalled, it was a lot of work, but if it meant she could call Brooke, it would be worth it.

"Good, then you know the basics."

"Can I come?" Maya asked.

"Not this time," Tanner replied as he pulled on his coat. "The hill is a little advanced for you and Evie. Maybe you can help Grandma dig out the ornaments for the tree, okay?"

Maya's lower lip started to sag, but her mother called from the kitchen area, "Maya, I need your help with this gingerbread house."

"Coming!" Snowshoeing was forgotten as she rushed to the kitchen. Natalie and Tanner finished bundling up and stepped outside, with Vitus close behind. Vitus leaped off the porch onto the snow and rolled onto his back, grunting happily as he twisted and turned.

Natalie laughed. "He gets such joy from life."

"Yes, dogs can teach us a lot about living in the moment." Tanner helped her attach the snowshoes to her boots before doing his. "It's this way." He moved toward a gap in the trees.

Natalie followed, careful to plant her feet far enough apart to avoid tripping herself. She'd done that more than once as a student. No one ever accused her of being overly coordinated. Vitus dashed ahead, made a lap around Tanner, and then ran back to her and gave a yip of encouragement. Tanner stopped and looked back.

"I'm coming," Natalie assured them, trying to increase her speed.

"I'm in no hurry." Tanner gazed up at the sky. "It's a beautiful day to be outside."

It was beautiful. The low winter sun glistened on the open snow around the cabin. A flock of tiny birds flitted between trees. Tanner slowed his pace, and Natalie was gratified to find she could stay just behind him along a relatively level trail through the woods and over a simple wooden bridge. A small stream of open water only a few inches wide gurgled down the center of the frozen creek.

On the other side of the bridge, the trail took a sharp turn uphill. After a few steps, Natalie started to slide. Tanner gripped her arm. "Kick into the snow with your toes for leverage." He demonstrated.

It worked. She followed him up the hill, but it was harder than the flat portion of the trail. Natalie's lungs began to burn, but she stayed with him, climbing just behind him, her breath condensing into clouds. Looking down at her feet, she bumped into Tanner, lost her balance and, before she knew what was happening, they tumbled together into the loose snow beside the trail. Vitus gave a yip and ran over to dogpile on top of them.

"Move." Natalie pushed the dog away and sat up, sucking in a lungful of frosty air. "I'm so sorry. Are you okay?"

He lay beside her, completely covered with snow. He shook his head vigorously, and a second later he sat up. When he wiped the snow from his face, a huge grin was revealed. "I'm fine. Are you?"

Thank goodness. She was afraid she'd hurt him. "Yes. What happened? Why did you fall?"

He laughed. "You stepped on my snowshoes."

"Oh, sorry. I didn't expect you to stop all of a sudden."

"I thought you might need a breather."

She sucked in another lungful. "I did, but next time throw on a brake light or something, okay?"

"I definitely will." He grabbed on to Vitus and scrambled to his feet before turning to offer her a hand. "Ready?"

She allowed him to pull her to her feet. He helped her dust the snow from her coat. It didn't take much longer to reach the top of the hill. A tree-covered valley spread out below them.

"Is your phone picking up a signal?"

She retrieved it from her pocket. "Looks like four bars."

"In that case, I'll leave you to talk with your friend. You can find your way back okay?"

"Sure. Just follow this trail across the bridge and then left to the cabin, right?"

"Right. Keep your weight on your heels going downhill. The dog can stay with you.

If you're not back in thirty minutes or so, I'll come looking, okay?"

"Sounds good. If I break a leg, I'll send Vitus home to do the 'Timmy's in the well' routine."

"Good luck with that." He chuckled. "Vitus would probably try to climb in the well with you, hoping for more bacon." He commanded the dog to stay and took off down the hill.

Natalie rubbed the dog's ears and watched Tanner's descent, graceful despite the clunky snowshoes. Maybe he was in a hurry to return to his family, but she got the idea he was purposely giving her privacy for the call. If so, it was thoughtful of him. She had to admit, he seemed to be a thoughtful sort of guy.

Brooke answered on the second ring. "Hi. I thought you were going to be away from civilization until the twenty-third."

"I am, but it turns out if I climb a hill, I can get a signal."

"So, you're still with Dane at his cabin?"

"I'm at his cabin, but it turns out I was never with Dane." Natalie explained about the mistaken identity.

"Dane's not there?"

"Just his family, but the good news is Dane is supposed to arrive here before Christmas. He'll get your letter then."

"Christmas. That's fantastic! I wish I could be there."

"Me, too. Say, maybe if Dane gets the letter and calls you on the twenty-third, you could come down on the train on the twenty-fourth." Or maybe that wasn't such a good idea. It all depended on Dane's response.

"I can't. I agreed to cover the desk on Christmas Day," Brooke told her, solving that dilemma. "But I'm sure as soon as Dane knows I want to see him about something important, he'll come to Fairbanks."

Natalie hoped so. "More good news—Dane isn't married."

"Of course not. I told you that already."

"You did, but I wasn't sure."

"I was. Dane isn't that kind of guy."

Everyone seemed to be eager to tell her about what kind of man Dane wasn't. Natalie hoped their faith wasn't misplaced. "Tanner says Dane is an artist."

"Yes, didn't I mention that? That's why he was here, in Fairbanks. He was part of an exhibit at one of the galleries downtown. He gave me that amazing birch bowl that's on my coffee table."

"It's lovely."

"I know. He's so talented. I hope this baby takes after his or her father."

"Speaking of the baby, how are you feeling?"

"Better. It's like once you told me you'd found Dane, the nausea disappeared."

Hmm. That sounded like Brooke hadn't been quite as confident as she'd pretended. "Well, I've found two cousins, his aunt, his father and two nieces, so it's only a matter of time before I find Dane."

"They're all at Dane's cabin?"

"It's a family cabin, but I guess Dane stays there the most. It's nice. Rustic, but comfortable. Like camping but with a decent mattress."

"That sounds great. Do you like his family?"

Natalie smiled. "I do. Especially the two girls. They're adorable."

"Did you tell them about the baby?"

"No, well except for Tanner. I had to explain why I was tailing him, but I made him promise not to tell Dane until you've had the chance to talk with him."

"What's he like? Do you think he'll keep the secret?"

"I do. Tanner is surprisingly nice, especially considering I was stalking him on the train."

"Nice, hmm? Is he cute?"

"Is that relevant?"

Brooke giggled. "You do think he's cute. I can tell."

Maybe, but Natalie wasn't going to give

Brooke the satisfaction by admitting it. "He looks enough like the picture you showed me that I thought he was Dane, so that should tell you something."

"Definitely. Are you interested in him?"

"Me? No way."

"Too bad. You could have married him and been my baby's, like, cousin-in-law or something."

"Nothing stopping that fantasy except my new job in another state, his lack of interest and the fact that I don't intend to marry anyone."

"Remember, you promised you'd start dating when you got to New Mexico. You'll change your mind when you meet the right man."

Natalie scoffed to herself. There was no such person as the "right man" for her. Just varying degrees of wrongness. But she had promised. "Yeah, well, until this hypothetical man comes along, I'll be just fine on my own. In the meantime, I'll be the cool aunt who sends presents and ignores all the rules when I babysit."

"How are you going to babysit from New Mexico?"

"I have summers off to come visit. And I figure around this time next year, you'll be ready to visit me and soak up some sunshine."

"That does sound nice." There was a short pause. "I'm going to miss you, Nat."

"I'll miss you, too. I'll call you from the train on the twenty-third, okay?"

"Yeah. In the meantime, enjoy your time with the cute cousin."

"I told you I'm not interested."

"That doesn't mean you can't enjoy the scenery."

Natalie rolled her eyes. "Goodbye, Brooke."

"Bye." Brooke giggled again. "Have fun."

Fun. Natalie hadn't chased a stranger onto a train for fun. She'd been determined to find Dane Rockford for Brooke before she left the state, and that was still her goal. She just needed to hang out with Tanner and the family until they could meet Dane's train and make sure he got that letter. Once she was sure everything was square between Dane and Brooke, she could concentrate on her new job in New Mexico.

She pocketed her phone and grabbed her ski poles. "Are you ready?" she asked Vitus, who wagged in response. She started down the hill, digging her heels into the snow as Tanner had reminded her. Vitus kept her company, running from here to there to sniff a bush or rock and then returning to escort her along the trail.

At the bridge, she stopped to catch her breath and watch two ravens quarrel over a bit of food. She'd forgotten how enjoyable a winter snowshoe trek could be. She and Vitus took the trail and continued toward the cabin. She'd almost reached the porch when something moved in the woods beyond.

The movement must have caught Vitus's eye, as well, because he ran toward it. A moose stepped out of the shadows, head lowered and ears flat against his head. Not good. An angry moose could do a number on a dog. "Vitus, come. Leave that moose alone!"

The dog ignored her, charging toward the big animal. "Vitus!" she hollered in her most commanding voice. "Come! Now!"

Vitus reached the moose and paused, as though he wasn't sure what to do now that he was there. The moose had no such hesitation and lashed out with a hoof in the dog's direction, only missing because the dog dodged at the last minute. Vitus, apparently deciding Natalie had the right idea after all, turned and ran toward her, with the moose in hot pursuit.

The door to the cabin opened and Tanner stepped out. Natalie made for the cabin, but in her panic, she'd forgotten she was wearing snowshoes and stumbled. Vitus whisked by her. Only a few strides behind the dog, the moose ran directly toward her.

Suddenly, Tanner dived from the porch and tackled her, pushing her out of the way as the moose sped by. They rolled as they dropped, and she ended up on top of him with his arms around her, half-buried in the snow. She released her snowshoes and scrambled to her knees in case the moose planned on making another pass, but she spotted him far down the trail still chasing the dog. Fortunately, Vitus seemed to have a substantial head start.

Tanner sat up, the snow clinging to his face. When he wiped it away, a grin appeared. "We seem to be making a habit of rolling in the snow together."

"Maybe I wasn't meant for snowshoes after all."

He looked down the trail where the moose was still watching them from a distance. "You shouldn't pick a fight with someone ten times your weight."

"Hey, it wasn't me. Your dog is the one who provoked the moose."

"Dane's dog, technically." He got to his feet and offered a hand up. Natalie allowed him to pull her to her feet and picked up the snowshoes.

When he climbed the porch steps, she realized he was in his stocking feet. "What happened to your boots?"

"I was in a hurry." Tanner whistled. "Vitus. Get back here."

A few minutes later, the dog galloped up

from a different direction than the one where they'd last seen him and sprinted to the porch. The moose had stopped about twenty feet from the cabin and snorted, obviously still ready for a fight. Tanner opened the door and urged everyone except the moose inside. "What did Dane tell you about chasing moose?" he scolded the dog.

Vitus turned away and busied himself biting the ice from the fur between his toes. Tanner shook his head and turned to Natalie. "I apologize for knocking you down. Are you okay?"

"I'm fine. Maybe a bruise or two, but nothing compared to what a moose could have done. Thank you for pushing me out of the way."

"I'm just sorry I got you into trouble. When I left Vitus with you, I didn't think about you running into a moose. Moose don't like dogs. They remind them of wolves."

"I know. And Vitus looks closer to a wolf than most dogs." At his name, the dog padded over to Natalie to lean against her. She tucked her hands in his soft fur. He closed his eyes and groaned in pleasure.

Tanner chuckled. "Yeah, he looks like a wolf, but he's really an overgrown lapdog who ought to know better."

Vitus opened his mouth in what looked like a

sheepish grin. Natalie stepped closer to help brush away the snow still clinging to Tanner's sweater.

"What happened?" Debbie came from the kitchen area.

"Vitus tangled with a moose and got Natalie involved," Tanner told her.

"Uh-oh." She looked over to where Gen and the girls were cementing candy onto graham cracker gingerbread houses. "Good thing the girls were in here. I'll warn them not to go outside until we give the all clear."

"Good idea," Tanner said. "Where's Russ?"

"He went for a ski. I'm sure he'll be keeping an eye out for moose."

"Yeah, he knows his way around. I'll go change into something dry."

"I'll build a fire so you can warm up," Debbie said.

"I'll do it," Natalie offered. Her snowshoeing might be a little rusty, but she was a whiz at fire-building.

"Thanks. Then I'll get back to the cookie houses."

"There's kindling in the basket by the stove," Tanner told Natalie before he padded toward the ladder.

Natalie slipped off her coat and peeked out the window. The moose was still there, closer now, nibbling on some twigs and keeping an eye on the cabin. Persistent fellow. She swung by to ooh and aah over the gingerbread houses and then went to lay the fire. She was opening the matchbox when Tanner came down the ladder and walked over, now wearing a red plaid shirt that emphasized the green in his eyes. Wonder if he knew how good he looked in red.

Not that she was looking. Natalie wasn't in the market. All her books and furniture were already in New Mexico, and soon she would be, too. Romance was the last thing on her mind. Even if the scenery was spectacular.

"I could use another cup of coffee," he announced. "Want some?"

"Sure." She struck a match and touched it to a strip of newspaper. The fire caught and flamed. She shook out the match and closed the fireplace screen. While she waited, she let her gaze wander over the books in the bookcase. A familiar volume caught her eye. Yes, it was the same one she'd seen on Dr. Waxman's desk. She leafed through the pages of brightly colored fishing flies until she came to a picture of Tanner holding a king salmon. Even in waders, the man looked good.

When she heard Tanner's footsteps behind her, she put the book away and moved her attention to a large collection of fiction on the next set of shelves.

"I think you'll find the K. Krisman books on the second shelf."

"Yours?"

"Yes. I usually pass them on to Dane when I finish." Tanner handed her a blue cup. "Milk and sugar, right?"

She tasted it. "Perfect." And it was. She'd never had anyone bother to memorize exactly how she liked her coffee before, especially after sharing breakfast only once. Tanner was either remarkably observant, or he was paying very close attention to her. She wasn't sure which explanation she preferred. "Thank you."

"You're welcome." He set his own cup on the mantel and held his hands with the palms facing the fire. Vitus, who had been lying on the rug, edged closer to rest his chin on one of Tanner's feet.

"So, you're working on a new book now?" Natalie asked, to make conversation.

"I'm done. All but one final pass before I turn it in to my editor."

"Congratulations."

"Thanks. Now I just need to finish tying all the sample flies for the photographer and my part will be finished."

"You tie all the flies yourself?"

"Sure. I've been tying flies since I was eight. My grandfather taught me the basics."

"Just you?"

"Mostly. We all loved fishing, but Gen wasn't interested in tying flies. Dane tried, but his flies tended to look like something a cat coughed up. Surprising, since he's the artistic one."

Natalie laughed. "Sounds like a fun childhood."

"I'll show you." He pulled a padded leather album from the lowest shelf and set it on the coffee table.

She drifted closer. "What's this?"

"Pictures." He sat down on the couch and opened it. The first photo showed an older man in a battered canvas hat surrounded by two boys and a girl. Each one held a fishing pole. Tanner pointed to the smaller boy. "This is Dane, fishing with our grandfather."

She sat down beside him so that she could study the picture. "Cute. How much younger than you is Dane?"

"Two years. A year older than Gen."

She turned the page to find another picture of the three kids climbing a tree. "Was it always the three of you?"

"Pretty much." He spoke in a low voice. "When Dane was seven, his mom bugged out, and—"

"Bugged out? What does that mean?"

"She left." He shrugged. "Decided that parenting was cramping her style. She used to send a postcard every year or so, but that was about it. Last I heard, she was in Mexico."

"Oh." Poor kid. At least Natalie's mother had stuck it out for eighteen years.

"Anyway, Russ works two and two on the North Slope, so after Dane's mom left, he stayed with us for two weeks out of every four when we were growing up. So we're close." He took another sip of coffee. "Dane really is a stand-up guy. If he's the father—"

"He is."

"Okay. Well, then your friend has nothing to worry about."

"Sorry if I seem doubtful, but I'd like to meet him myself before I form an opinion."

Tanner shook his head but smiled as he did it. "I think we've already established you're a skeptic."

"Realist."

"Whatever. I'd better get started on lunch." He stood and reached for the album, but Natalie stopped him.

"Do you mind if I look at the rest of the pictures?"

He shrugged. "Knock yourself out. It's just more of the same." He made his way into the kitchen.

Natalie turned the pages of the photo album, finding lots of action shots as well as family photos with the kids, their grandfather and a pleasant-faced older woman she assumed was their grandmother. Lots with Russ and Debbie, looking amazingly young, and another man who looked enough like Tanner to label him his father. One woman, a standout with black hair, pale skin and red lips appeared only two or three times, as part of a posed group photo when the kids were quite small. Dane's runaway mother perhaps?

Each year featured a group photo on the front porch of the cabin, documenting the growth and changes of the family. Even as gangly teenagers, the three of them seemed thrilled to spend time at the cabin with their grandparents. And judging by Tanner's easy relationship with his sister and his overprotective reaction to Dane's situation, the three were still close as adults.

Natalie had always suspected families like this existed only on old television series, but here was photographic proof. Maybe one day there would be pictures of Brooke's baby on the porch. Natalie smiled.

CHAPTER SIX

THE MOOSE HAD moved on by the time Russ returned for lunch. As soon as Evie and Maya had wolfed down their peanut butter-and-banana sandwiches with the crusts cut off, they clamored that it was time to decorate the tree.

"I left the decorations in the back closet," their grandmother told them. "Why don't you bring them in here while the rest of us finish eating?"

"Okay." Evie jumped up.

"After you take your dishes to the kitchen," Gen reminded them.

The two girls dutifully carried their plates and cups to the worktable before running into the back hallway. Maya's voice carried all the way to the dining area. "I want to carry the big box."

"No, I'm bigger, so I get to carry it," Evie insisted. "You carry this one."

"I'm gonna tell."

"Mom says Santa doesn't like whining."

Silence followed. Gen chuckled. "Too bad

Santa isn't around to monitor their behavior the rest of the year."

Maya marched across the living room with a red box. Evie followed, carrying a green box so big she could hardly get her arms around it. Maya swerved to avoid a purple snow boot that had somehow gotten kicked away from the door and into her path. Tanner realized Evie couldn't see her feet and started to call a warning, but it was too late. Evie tripped over the boot and the box went flying, the lid coming off in the process to spill Christmas ornaments across the floor. The lid hit the table holding the amaryllis, which rocked once, twice and then tipped over, dumping the flowerpot into the middle of the ornaments with a sickening crunch.

The adults all jumped up to run to Evie, but Natalie was closest. "Are you all right, sweetheart?" She helped Evie into a sitting position.

Tears fell as Evie took in the carnage. "I'm okay, but I broke all the ornaments."

"They're not all broken," Gen said. "See, here's the pine-cone reindeer you sent Grandma last year. It's fine."

"But all the pretty, shiny ones are gone." Evie sobbed. "And Grandma's flower is broken."

Maya came to lay a hand on her sister's shoulder, her eyes welling up, as well. "It's okay, Evie. You didn't break the or-ma-mints on purpose."

"But there won't be enough ornaments left to decorate the tree."

"Why don't we make new ones?" Natalie suggested.

"H-how?" Evie asked.

"Well—" Natalie tilted her head for a moment. "I took a class in origami once and learned how to fold cranes. If we have paper, we could make birds for the tree."

"And snowflakes." As usual, Mom had a solution. "We could cut paper snowflakes."

"And what about those mountain ash berries you gathered this morning?" Natalie reminded them. "They'd look pretty on the tree."

Maya opened her box. "We've still got these rope things, too."

"Garland," Gen said.

"Yeah, gardens. It'll be the prettiest tree ever, Evie. Promise." Maya nodded.

Tanner tried to think of other possibilities. "I've got some colored beads and things in my fly-tying kit. Maybe you can use them for ornaments."

"I'll bet we can," Natalie said. "And anyone who can make gingerbread houses as beautiful as you two did will make wonderful ornaments."

Tanner flashed Natalie a smile for her support. Neither of those gingerbread houses would have passed a building inspection after succumbing to the avalanche of icing and candy the girls had added, but Maya and Evie were proud of them.

Evie looked at her grandmother. "You're not mad I broke the ornaments?"

"Of course not." Mom stroked a hand over her back. "It was an accident. But we should be more careful about where we leave our shoes, right?"

Evie nodded and stood. "What about your flower?"

The fall had cracked the pot and dumped the soil, leaving the bulb exposed and the stem broken. Mom rescued the flowering stem. "It will be fine. We'll just put this in water. Russ, could you hand me that vase off the mantel?"

Evie stared at the wrecked decorations. "Is the angel okay?"

Tanner reached for the white-gowned figure, dusted off a bit of potting soil and straightened a wing. "She's just fine. I'll fetch a step stool, and we'll put her at the very top of that special tree you girls picked out. Okay?"

"Okay." Evie gave a brave smile.

"All right, then," Mom said briskly. "Tanner, bring a broom, as well, please. Everyone else, let's get those lunch dishes cleared from the table so we can start creating."

NATALIE'S ORIGAMI CRANES turned out to be a little advanced for the girls, but Maya and Evie were both quite good at paper fans. Mom had found some heavy wrapping paper with red-and-white stripes on one side and gold on the other. She cut them into long strips for the girls to fold. Meanwhile, Gen raided Dane's desk for white paper, glue, scissors and a stapler.

Mom folded the white paper in half, and then thirds, and showed the girls how they could cut notches and shapes into the sides and ends of the resulting triangles to form lacy snowflakes. "You know, they say no two snow-flakes are exactly the same. Just like people, each one is special."

"This one's special." Maya unfolded her masterpiece. "It's boo-tiful."

"Yes, it is." Mom gave Maya a hug.

Mom folded and the girls cut snowflakes until the pile of paper scraps under the table began to look like a real drift of snow. Mean-while, Natalie folded a few white cranes, and then came up with an idea for angels made from white paper fans for robes and wings. "But what can we use for the head? Tanner, do you have any big beads?"

"No, not that big." He thought for a moment as he sorted through his fly-tying supplies for inspiration. Then something in the kitchen caught his eye. "How about mini-marshmallows?"

"Marshmallows?" Mom laughed.

"Why not? We can replace them with wooden beads later, but for now it would work. I've got seed beads we can stick into the marshmallows for the eyes and mouth. Oh, and gold wire for a halo." He rummaged deeper. "I've got feathers, too, if you want to glue some onto the wings."

"Ooh, I want to make one," Maya said. "Are there pink feathers? My angel likes pink."

"Me, too." Evie grabbed a white sheet of paper and started folding.

"Me, three." Mom fetched the packet of marshmallows and chose shiny black beads for eyes and a bigger flat red bead to produce a round, singing mouth.

After they'd fashioned a dozen angels between them, Gen slipped into Mom's bedroom where Tanner knew she'd hidden the Christmas gifts. She returned with two cans, one of red and one of white modeling dough which Tanner recognized as part of an art pack Santa would be leaving under the tree in a few nights. "Look, we can roll the dough into ropes, twist them together and make candy canes. Once they've dried overnight, we can hang them on the tree."

While the girls worked their dough, Tanner clipped the barbs off the ends of a few hooks and used them to tie some big, flashy dragon-fly patterns. As far as he knew, dragonflies weren't a traditional Christmas theme, but he thought the gossamer wings and sparkly bodies would fit right in with angels and snowflakes.

"Oh, I've got an idea." Tanner opened his satchel and pulled out a pad of yellow sticky notes. Using the scissors from his fly-tying kit, he cut a strip from the end of a paper square, formed it into a circle and pressed the sticky part together. Then he did it a few more times, interconnecting the strips to form a paper chain. "We can drape this over the windows."

"I want to help." Maya came to sit beside him. Tanner cut strips and she stuck them together until they'd completed yards and yards of yellow garland.

A few stars made from twigs that Tanner wired together at the points completed their efforts. They worked all afternoon, only stopping when Mom announced that the roasted chicken and vegetables were ready. After dinner they decorated the tree. Tanner had to admit that once the spindly spruce had been draped in miles of sparkling silver garland and hung with their homemade ornaments, it was a beautiful sight. And that didn't even include the dough candy canes that were currently drying near the fire.

Unlike the artificial tree he'd put up a month ago in his house in Anchorage, this one didn't have twinkling electric lights, but the moonlight bouncing off the snow and through the window behind it made it glow sort of from within. The two girls sat on pillows on the floor in front of the tree, gazing into the branches. Maybe it was better that the ornaments had broken, giving them an opportunity to create their own old-fashioned Christmas.

Tanner's gaze rested on Natalie, laughing at something Gen was saying as they put away empty boxes. If she hadn't followed him off the train, thinking he was Dane, Natalie wouldn't be here, coming up with ideas and making everything better. Some of the best things in life happened when plans went awry.

THE NEXT MORNING, Tanner's mom announced that they had been invited to the Wellington Christmas brunch. The Wellingtons and the Rockfords had been neighbors since before Granddad built the second cabin in the fifties, and Russ and Mom always enjoyed visiting with them. With lots of kids expected at the party, Maya and Evie were jumping up and down with excitement. Evie was in fact named for Evelyn, the matriarch of the family.

Gen was eager to go, as well, to catch up with the three daughters she'd played with often as a child. Tanner and Dane had mostly steered clear of the bossy Wellington girls, and Tanner had no burning desire to spend time with them now. "Thanks, but I have flies to tie."

"Oh, come on." Gen smirked at him. "I'm sure Helena won't try to make you play spin the bottle this time."

"Nevertheless, I'm going to pass. You all have fun." Tanner loved his family, but a little quiet time alone wouldn't go amiss. He climbed the ladder to the loft for the list of flies he still needed to complete and waited until he heard the door shut behind them before climbing back down.

He'd just set up his vise on the table when he heard footsteps and Natalie appeared from the back bedroom. "Oh, hi. I thought you went with the others to the party."

"No, I've done enough party-crashing this week." She held up her book. "I thought I'd spend a little time reading instead. Do you mind having me here? I'll try not to disturb you."

"No, that's fine. Make yourself at home." He watched her settle into the rocker next to the fire and then turned his attention to the flies.

Sometime later, Tanner cut a thread, daubed the knot with head lacquer and reached for a magnifying glass to examine his latest fly. Even wraps, good proportions in the thorax, but the wings were a little uneven. A snip of the scissors, and the fly achieved camera-ready status. That made thirty-nine of the forty-three flies featured in his book ready for the photographer. The others would require supplies he'd let the girls use up on their angels, so those would have to wait until he got home.

The low sun cast a glow through the south window. The family must be having a good time at the party, to be staying so long. Across the room, Natalie added another log to the fire. Tanner had half expected to have to entertain her, but she'd been entirely undemanding. In fact, she'd volunteered to make sandwiches for lunch and fetched a load of wood so that he could work uninterrupted. Now and then, he'd looked up to watch her curled up with her book, the low sun reflecting off her shiny dark hair. It felt oddly companionable.

Now she made her way to the kitchen, giving him a little smile as she passed. "I'm getting some water. Want some?"

"Sure, thanks."

She set his cup on the table beside him and nodded at the fly still clamped into the vise. "That looks exactly like a mosquito."

"It's supposed to. I call it the Seductive Skeeter."

She laughed. "At least it doesn't suck blood. I was looking at your book. I didn't realize how complicated fly-tying is."

"It doesn't have to be. The San Juan Worm is just a piece of red yarn tied to a hook. This mosquito pattern is a little more complex, but you just do it one step at a time. Want to try it?"

"I don't want to waste your time."

"I'm done for now." He stood. "Here, have a seat."

She hesitated briefly but took the chair. Tanner demonstrated how to release his fly from the vise and set a new hook in place. "Okay, we'll start with this brown thread. Wrap it smoothly front to back until we've covered about half the hook." Tanner reached around her to demonstrate. She pushed her hair behind her shoulders, releasing the sweet scent of violets. Nice. He would have expected something dark and mysterious from her cloak-and-dagger moves on the train.

"Like this?" Natalie had completed a few wraps, not perfectly smooth but good enough. The fish wouldn't care.

"Yes, just like that. Keep going for another few wraps. Okay, stop. Now we let the bobbin dangle to hold the thread in place while we add a clump of grizzly feather fibers to form the tail."

"Interesting. Who plucks these feathered grizzlies?"

He laughed. "Okay, technically grizzled rooster tail feathers. Gather up a clump of twenty or so fibers and hold them here. Now continue wrapping and once you get to the curve of the hook, reverse direction and wrap forward to about a quarter of the distance from the eye of the hook." He pointed.

Natalie continued to wrap, slowly but smoothly. "How long have you been in the fly-tying business?"

"For ten years now. When my grandfather died, he left his savings to the three grandkids. I used mine as start-up. At first, I sold hand-tied flies locally and taught classes through some of the sporting goods stores. I started putting together kits they could buy. Okay, stop wrapping." He snipped off the extra fibers. "Now we're going to add two grizzly tips to make wings. It can get a little tricky to make them stand up." He partially stripped the tiny feathers and held them in place while she wrapped the thread to hold them.

"Like this?"

"Almost. This one's a little crooked." He pulled it into place. "Now wrap tight." Once she had the feathers in place, he snipped off a couple of loose ends.

"Wow, it does look like wings. What now?"

"Now we build up the body. We take a long quill. I've soaked these in warm water to make them more flexible. Use thread to wrap this one to the back of the hook, and then I'll show you how to build up the body."

While she wrapped, she asked, "How did you get from teaching local classes to writing books published by one of the major publishing houses?"

Interesting that she'd noticed the publisher. But then, she was an academic. "Rob Bakersfield, who had started several businesses in his life, moved to Alaska and decided to take one of my classes. Afterward, he approached me about partnering up to mass-produce the kits and sell them through the national chains. It's worked out well. Rob handles the manufacturing and distribution, and I design the kits and make instructional videos, as well as write books. Give that thread an extra couple of wraps to make sure the quill is secure and I'll show you how to wrap the quill to form the back half. Then we'll use a long hackle feather to form a fuzzy middle."

"Fuzzy middle. That sounds like a bar drink."

"It does." Tanner chuckled. "But then, the Seductive Skeeter does, too." He showed her how to use the hackle pliers to wrap the feather into place. "Now we whip finish the end, using this tool to make a knot. Cut the thread. And paint on a little head cement which makes the fly more durable and gives it that buggy look." He removed it from the vise and handed it to her. "There you go. Your first fly."

"Beautiful."

"It is. A fish would definitely go for this one."

She grinned. "It's too pretty to fish with. I may have to frame it."

He laughed. "You do that."

Footsteps on the porch announced that the family was back. The door burst open and Maya ran in, tracking snow across the floor. "Uncle Tanner! Miss Natalie! Look! We made more or-ma-mints for the tree!" She held up a paper reindeer with antlers the size and shape of her hands and a red pom-pom nose.

Evie toed off her boots and followed, showing off a heart formed from two candy canes and a star made of Popsicle sticks and glitter.

"Wow, those are nice," Natalie said.

"Looks like you had fun at the party." Tanner grabbed a broom to sweep out the snow before it melted into a slick puddle.

Mom and Gen came through the door together. Mom was holding on to Gen's arm, but she shot a smile at Tanner. "It was great. You should have come."

"I got a lot done here, but I'm glad you had a good time." He went to her. "Are you okay?"

"I'm fine. I just need to put my feet up for a little while. You don't need to hover."

He did, though. Mom always put on a brave face, but sometimes she pushed past her limits. "Just watch the floor here where the snow got tracked in."

"I see it." She made her way to the recliner in the living area. "Ah, the fire feels good."

Tanner stood, considering whether he should ask if Mom needed a pain pill or anything. Natalie came over carrying two cups with paper tags hanging over the sides. "I saw the cinnamon spice tea bags. Hope it's okay that I used them." She set one of the cups on the table next to Mom's chair.

"Of course. Thank you. That's just what I need." She smiled at Natalie, ignoring Tanner. "Sit down and tell me what you've been doing this afternoon."

Natalie settled into the closest rocker. "I've been reading and exploring your shelves. I see lots of board games."

"Do you like board games? We can play this evening." She shook her finger at Tanner. "No Scrabble."

Tanner laughed. "Aw, come on."

"Nope." Mom turned to Natalie. "Nobody will play Scrabble with Tanner anymore. He's too good."

"That's a shame. I like a good game of Scrabble myself," Natalie said.

"There you go, Tanner. A challenger."

"Interesting." Tanner stood. "But right now, I'd better help Gen get dinner together."

"Can I help?" Natalie started to put her cup down, but Tanner shook his head.

"Stay and drink your tea. We've got it." Tanner moved to the worktable, where Gen was busy peeling potatoes. He grabbed one and started peeling. "Mom seems tired."

"She was on her feet a lot at the party, but she did fine snowshoeing home." Gen cut a potato into chunks and dropped it in a pan of water. "You worry too much."

"I don't know. I think she overdoes it."

"Everybody overdoes once in a while. It's part of living. And Mom lives her life well."

"That's true."

Gen reached for another potato. "Speaking of living life, I may have a line on a job in Anchorage."

"Oh yeah? What kind of job?"

"Receptionist in a law office."

"Receptionist?" Tanner frowned. "If you wanted to be a receptionist, you could work for Rob and me."

"And put Peggy out on the street?"

"You could be her assistant. I'm sure she could keep you busy."

"I don't want busywork. I want a real job."

"As a receptionist? You have a college degree."

"Yeah, in psychology. Unfortunately, I didn't realize that psychology was one of the lowest-paid degrees I could get. And on top of that, I've been out of the workforce for five years."

"Still, you're smart and reliable. And those psychology classes mean you know how to deal with people, which is an important part of every job. I think you should keep looking."

"Tanner, I need to work now. I need to get out of your house and support myself and my children."

"I like having you and the girls around."

She shot him a look of exasperation. "We like you, too, but I can't keep living like this.

I feel like a sponge." She unwrapped a package of moose steaks.

"You're not a sponge. You're raising two daughters and doing an amazing job of it. August after next, they'll both be in school."

"I can't wait a year and a half for a job."

"Gen—"

His sister grabbed a meat mallet and started pounding, efficiently putting an end to the discussion. Tanner took the hint and set the potatoes on the stove to cook before moving away to set the table. He could understand Gen's need to feel self-sufficient, but why rush it? He was her brother, and in a position to help. Why not wait until the girls were in school, or at least until a better job came along?

The pounding slowed. When he looked over, Gen gave a little smile and a shrug. Good, at least she wasn't still mad at him. He'd leave it alone for now. They had come to the cabin to give the girls the best Christmas possible, and that's what they'd do. They could talk about Gen's future career after the holidays.

CHAPTER SEVEN

Russ discarded a tiger card. Natalie couldn't use it. She played her last card, and Evie cheered. She snatched up Natalie's whale card, discarded an elephant and laid down a four-some of whales. "Did I win?"

"You did," Tanner confirmed, marking the win on a notepad. "That's two for Evie, two for Grandma, one for Maya and one for Russ."

"Let's play again," Maya urged.

"It's bedtime for you two," Gen said, gathering up the cards.

"Awwww." Maya slumped. "I don't wanna—"

"Santa," Tanner mumbled, half covering it with a cough.

Maya immediately straightened and set her expression to angelic. "Can we have a story before bed, please?"

"One story," Gen told her.

Evie chose a book from the stack on the trunk. "Miss Natalie, can you read to us tonight?"

"Um, sure. What do you have here?" Natalie took the book with a picture of animals and a white mitten in a snowy scene. "This looks interesting."

"You have to sit on the couch to read." Maya tugged on her hand. Tanner handed her a headlamp.

Natalie allowed herself to be led to the couch and sat back while the two girls parked themselves on either side of her. She passed a hand over Maya's soft hair as she wiggled into place. Natalie tried to remember if she'd ever read to a child before. She didn't think so, and yet it felt perfectly natural to snuggle in, open the book and start reading all about the adventures of a lost mitten.

When she reached the end of the book, Evie sighed happily. Maya yawned and snuggled closer. For a few minutes, the whole family just sat, listening to the crackle of the fire, watching the dancing shadows. The silhouette of the Christmas tree against the window contrasted with the snowy scene outside. A pile of presents had mysteriously appeared underneath. A warm sense of contentment flowed around the room and settled somewhere inside Natalie's chest. Peace.

She looked down to see Maya's eyes drooping shut. Gen must have noticed, too. "Come on," she whispered and took Evie's hand. "Bedtime."

Natalie picked up Maya and followed Gen and Evie into the bedroom. Maya's eyes opened briefly when she laid her on the bed. "G'night, Miss Natalie."

"Good night, Maya. Good night, Evie."

"Good night, Natalie," Gen whispered. "Thanks."

When Natalie returned to the living room, Russ and Debbie were making moves toward their beds. Only Tanner was left on the couch, picking up the children's cards and packing them into their box. "I guess all that partying wore everyone out," he commented to Natalie. "Are you tired?"

"Not especially." She stood in front of the fire, letting it warm her back. "Tomorrow is the twenty-third, when your cousin arrives and I catch the train for Fairbanks."

"I guess it is. Time flies."

"I won't have time to talk to him before I get on the train." She sat on the other end of the couch and leaned toward Tanner, watching his face. "Will you promise to give him Brooke's letter immediately?"

"Of course."

"And you won't tell him about the baby."

"No, I'll let her do that."

"But you'll make sure he understands how important it is that he contact her right away."

He raised an eyebrow. "Can you say *micromanage*?"

"Brooke is important to me."

"Right. I'll make sure he contacts her." He tilted his head. "What are your plans for Christmas?"

"Um, I was going to have Christmas dinner in Anchorage with someone I knew from work, but since the train on the twenty-third is going to Fairbanks, I'll probably cancel and spend it with Brooke, although she's working on Christmas. Why?"

"You could stay here one more night and catch the train back to Anchorage on the twenty-fourth. That would give you a day to spend some time with Dane, and you can see exactly how he reacts to the letter. I think once you get to know him, you'll feel better."

Natalie was tempted. It would give her a chance to size up Brooke's mystery man, and she had to admit she was enjoying her time here. But no. She'd already intruded on them under false circumstances. "I can't impose on your family for any longer."

Tanner laughed. "Evie and Maya didn't seem to think you were imposing when you read them their bedtime story. Nobody's going to mind if you stay an extra day. In fact, stay through Christmas, and catch the train next week with the rest of us."

"No, definitely not." She got up and stood by the fireplace.

"But you're thinking about catching the train on Christmas Eve instead of tomorrow?"

"It would mean an extra trip to the train station for you."

"Hey, now that I've finished all the flies, I have nothing but time."

"Let me think about it." She picked up the girls' game off the coffee table and returned it to the shelf. "In the meantime, how about a game of Scrabble?"

Tanner chuckled. "You know you're talking to the reigning Scrabble champion of this cabin."

"So I've heard."

"You don't look scared."

"Not in the least."

"Then let's make it interesting. If I can beat you at Scrabble two games out of three, you stay over Christmas."

"Why do you want me to stay longer?"

"You've been pretty skeptical about Dane. Sometimes he's hard to warm up to right away. I want you to have enough time to really get to know him."

He had a point. Natalie would sleep better

after the move if she felt like Brooke's man was dependable. And if he wasn't, she needed to know that, too. "Okay, if you win, I'll stay until after Christmas, as long as your family is good with that. If I win, I catch the Christmas Eve train to Anchorage. I'll hike up and call Brooke tomorrow to let her know." She grinned. "Good thing I never lose at Scrabble."

"We shall see."

"Indeed."

"TRIPLE SCORE, ONE *Z* on a double letter square, a blank tile for the other *Z*, makes a score of sixty-nine which puts me ahead by thirty-two points." Natalie smiled in triumph.

"Izzle?" Tanner raised an eyebrow.

"Sure. It was added to the official Scrabble dictionary about the time they added 'frenemy' and 'wingnut.' Weren't you paying attention?"

"Are you making this up?"

"Do you want to challenge?"

"Hmm, I suppose since the dictionary here is at least fifty years old, challenging would involve a hike to the top of the hill to get a cell signal. So no, I won't challenge." Tanner laid *O*, *N*, and *S* after the *I*. "Four points, and that's all my letters. What did I catch you with?"

"Not enough. Two *E*s and a *T*." She got up

and gave a little shimmy. "Say hello to the new reigning Scrabble champion of this cabin."

Tanner laughed. "I don't suppose you'd like to make it best three out of five?"

"No, I'm going to quit while I'm ahead. Besides, it's getting late. What time will the train be through tomorrow?"

"Between ten and ten fifteen. It takes around half an hour to get to the tracks. I'll probably have Dane back here about eleven."

"I'll look forward to meeting him." Together they packed away the game pieces. While Tanner returned the game to the bookshelf, Natalie stretched her arms over her head and groaned. "Ugh. I expected to have sore legs from snowshoeing, but I didn't know it would get to my shoulders."

"Climbing takes a lot of pole work." Tanner came up behind her and rubbed her shoulders.

Natalie's first impulse was to move away, but it felt too good. "Mmm." She closed her eyes and let his strong hands work the soreness from her muscles for several minutes. When he stopped, she opened them. "Thank you."

"You're welcome."

"Not just for the massage, but for letting me stay with you, especially after you figured out why I was here."

"I couldn't very well leave you to freeze to

death. Besides, you're just trying to help your friend, and Dane does need to know what's going on."

"All the same, you could have made it very uncomfortable for me, and instead you and your family have gone out of your way to make me feel at home."

"Honestly, I've enjoyed the company."

"Even though I beat you at Scrabble?"

"Especially because you beat me at Scrabble."

"I'm glad." She picked up a stray mug and carried it to the kitchen. "Good night, then." She stopped to pet Vitus and wish him sweet dreams before she headed for the bedroom. "See you in the morning."

"Good night, Natalie. Sleep well."

THE NEXT MORNING was bustling. As the girls hung their now-dry candy cane ornaments on the tree, Gen attempted to create a wreath for the door from twigs and spruce cuttings, and Russ and Tanner prepared to make the trek to the railroad to pick up Dane.

No one seemed the least upset, or even surprised, when Tanner mentioned that Natalie would be staying another day so that she could take the train to Anchorage. Natalie and Debbie were washing the breakfast dishes when an unexpected sound rang through the room. A cell phone.

Tanner hurried over to grab his phone off the shelf and answered. "Oh, hi. What's up?" There was a short pause before Tanner spoke again. "I understand, but I really need to talk to you about something. Where are you?… Dane?… Can you hear me?… Listen, if you can hear me, stay at this number. I'm going to climb the hill and call you back."

He slipped the phone into his shirt pocket and reached for his coat. "Dane said he was tied up and couldn't make it for Christmas, after all."

Debbie sighed. "That's a shame. We haven't seen him since Thanksgiving."

"He said he tried to call you but couldn't get through," Tanner told Russ. "He left a voice mail."

"My phone's dead, but I'll charge it and climb the hill to check the message later," Russ replied. "I wish I knew what he's been doing all this time."

"Did he say when he'd be back?" Natalie asked.

"No." Tanner stepped into his boots. "The call dropped before he could say much of anything. I'm going to try to call him back."

Tanner sprinted up the hill as quickly as his

snowshoes could carry him. He didn't like to hang over Dane's shoulder, but it was time he found out what was keeping his cousin so busy he couldn't even get home for Christmas, besides getting him the message that Brooke needed to see him. When Dane dropped off the dog not long after Thanksgiving, Tanner had assumed Dane might be working on getting his art into more galleries, or possibly that art auction website, but he'd been gone too long for that.

Tanner reached the top of the hill and dialed. A woman's voice answered. "Hello?" Voices sounded in the background.

"Hi. This is Tanner Rockford. My cousin, Dane, called me from this number about fifteen minutes ago."

"Yeah."

"But the call got dropped. Is he still there?"

"No."

"Do you know where he is, or if he's coming back?"

"Hang on." He could hear her asking someone if they needed a refill. Must be a restaurant or bar somewhere. Someone ordered a Rusty Anchor, whatever that was. Finally she returned. "Hey, the guy said he needed to make a call, so I loaned him my phone. I don't know anything else, and I'm kind of busy here, okay?"

"Okay, but if he comes back in—" The call ended.

Great. Tanner redialed. "I'm sorry. I know you're busy, but it's very important that I speak to my cousin—"

"This is what I get for being nice. He's not here. Don't call back. I'm blocking this number right now."

"Wait. Where are—" Dead air.

Tanner huffed. Not for the first time, Dane's refusal to live in the twenty-first century was turning out to be highly inconvenient. Trouble was, Dane wasn't the one being inconvenienced.

Tanner made his way back to the cabin. Natalie must have been watching out the window, because she slipped out on the porch to talk privately before he spoke to the others. "Did you reach him?"

Tanner shook his head. "He'd already gone, and the woman whose phone he borrowed didn't know anything."

"Where was he calling from?"

"She wouldn't say. And she blocked my number."

"Blocked it? Why? What did you say?"

Tanner explained. "All I know is it sounded

like a busy place. I could hear people talking and plates rattling."

"But you have no idea where?"

"The number has a 907 area code, so he's still in the state. I assumed whatever business he's conducting had to do with his artwork, which would limit it to towns big enough to have art galleries, but I'm beginning to think it may be something entirely different."

"What exactly did he say?"

"That he's not done with his business yet and did I mind keeping Vitus a little longer. And to wish everyone a Merry Christmas and tell them he'd see them soon."

"A little longer. Does that mean a few days or a few weeks?"

"Your guess is as good as mine."

"I fly out on New Year's Day."

"I promise I'll give him Brooke's letter as soon as I see him."

"I'd really like to meet him before I go."

"Size him up you mean?"

"Okay, yes. Size him up. I want to know Brooke will be okay. If you find out where he is, tell me and I'll go there."

"If he calls again before January first, I'll do whatever I can to make him stay in one place long enough for us to catch up with him."

"Us?"

"Us." He grinned. "I'm not sure I can trust you alone with Dane. After all, you cheat at Scrabble."

"Are you saying you want a rematch?"

"That's what I'm saying."

"You got it. Tonight, after everyone goes to bed, I'll show you what a real Scrabble player looks like."

"We'll see about that." He winked. "I'm feeling lucky."

NATALIE WAS FEELING pretty lucky, too, that evening. Since Dane wasn't coming, she'd considered trying to catch the train to Fairbanks and spending Christmas with Brooke, but she'd decided to hang around for one more day, hoping for more information about Dane's whereabouts once Russ retrieved his message. Unfortunately, Dane had simply told his dad to wish everyone a Merry Christmas and said he'd see him soon.

And yet the day wasn't wasted. Natalie and the girls cut more snowflakes and stapled them together to create garlands they strung across the ceiling. Then they all snowshoed out to cut more mountain ash berries for Gen's wreath. The hardest part of the day was calling Brooke to let her know Dane was still AWOL, but Brooke, as usual, put a positive spin on the news. Another family game night followed after dinner, this time a trivia game with child and adult questions. Debbie excelled at anything to do with music or art, and Russ didn't miss a history question all night.

That night, Russ read the bedtime story. He'd been so unobtrusive over the last few days that Natalie almost wondered if he was avoiding her, but she'd come to realize he was simply shy. And yet he willingly read aloud because the girls had asked him to. This man would be a wonderful grandfather for Brooke's baby. Natalie only hoped his son would be as good a father.

Once everyone else turned in, Tanner and Natalie dug out the Scrabble tiles. He pretended to gloat when he won the first game, but he just grinned when she clobbered him in the second. Now once again they were neck and neck, and it was Tanner's turn. He studied his letters, frowning. She smiled and rearranged her tiles. Unless he covered the *D*, she was going to win. She hadn't had this much fun in ages.

Sharing a dorm room with Brooke had sparked Natalie's love of board games. Brooke liked to set up a game, microwave a big bowl of popcorn and play with whoever wandered in. It was a great way to meet people, and Natalie's game skills helped make up for her lack of social skills. Gradually, she'd gained confidence. And self-confidence was only one of the many gifts Brooke had given her. She owed Brooke so much. Hopefully, she could repay her by finding Dane.

Tanner laid down his letters. Natalie studied them. "Adze?"

Tanner looked up before marking his score. "Care to challenge?"

"Um…no. You look too confident." He'd ruined her plans for that *D*, forcing her to settle for adding a single *I* before an *S*.

Tanner pounced and played his final three letters. "What have you got?"

"A *U* and a *Q*, unfortunately. That brings my score to three ninety-five. What have you got?"

"Four hundred and one."

"I bow to the king."

Tanner smirked. "As well you should."

Natalie laughed. "Hang on a minute." She took the score sheet, folded in the corners, turned it over and continued to fold and tuck until she'd created a tiny crown. She stood and placed it on his head and gave a mock curtsy. "Your Majesty."

"You won yesterday," he reminded her. "Aren't you going to make a crown for yourself?"

"I don't think so."

He winked. "Well, you won by a bigger margin, so I think you should wear the crown." He removed it from his head and set it on hers. "I'm going to take Vitus outside and grab another load of wood."

"I'll clean up the game while you're gone."

He followed the dog out and closed the door, only to open it again almost immediately. "The northern lights are out."

"Are they?" Natalie grabbed her coat and pulled on her boots. The aurora borealis weren't easy to see in Anchorage because of the competition from the streetlights. She'd been lucky enough to catch some good ones in Fairbanks, but here, away from the city, they would be brighter. She hurried down the steps, slipping her hands into her mittens at the same time as she looked up at the wave of green flickering above the trees. In her haste, she stumbled and pitched forward.

Tanner gripped her hand to steady her. Once she'd recovered her balance, she expected him to let go, but he kept her hand in his and led her farther from the cabin to the center of the clearing. They stood close together, watching the green light splash across the skies, brighter than she'd ever seen them before.

Natalie knew that green aurora borealis were simply oxygen atoms in the middle atmosphere excited by high energy particles, the same phenomenon as a neon sign, but they still seemed magical to her, like a celestial artist painting the skies with light. As they watched, the single brushstroke separated into two dancing lines. Natalie sighed with pleasure.

The green splash grew dimmer. Suddenly, at the very top of the green lights, a line of pink appeared, flickering along the border just before the colors faded away, leaving just a crescent moon and stars twinkling between the scattered clouds.

Such beauty. She turned to say so but stopped when she saw Tanner's face. He was watching her, his expression intense and yet soft. He reached up to smooth a lock of hair away from her cheek, his glove brushing against her chin, and she knew he wanted to kiss her. He was giving her the chance to draw away, but distance was the very last thing she wanted.

Instead, she eased closer to him. He brushed her lips with his, testing, and seemed to like what he found because he wrapped his arms around her waist and did it again, a long and lingering kiss. She slid her hand behind his neck and slanted her head to bring them closer together. His lips moved to caress her cheek, her chin and the tip of her nose before returning to her lips for another kiss. Afterward, he pressed his forehead against hers. "Natalie," he whispered.

"Yes?"

"Nothing. I just like saying your name."

She stood on tiptoe to kiss him once again. "I like hearing you say it."

Suddenly, Vitus was back from wherever he'd been, pushing between them. Natalie laughed. "Hey. What's your deal?"

"He's just jealous. He thinks all affection should be directed his way."

Natalie dropped to her knees and wrapped her arms around the furry dog. "You are a handsome thing, Vitus, and a good boy in spite of wanting to hog all the hugs." Vitus wagged and wiggled.

Tanner chuckled. "You go ahead and take him inside. I'll get the wood and be right in."

"Okay." Natalie returned to the cabin, turned on a battery lantern and switched off the electric lights in readiness. She set the game back on the shelf and looked around for any other tasks she needed to complete, but they'd already left the cozy cabin neat and tidy. She was going to miss this place.

Not just this place. This family. She'd gotten on that train to follow who she thought was a two-timing sleaze, determined to hold him responsible for his actions. Instead she'd found a funny, thoughtful, family-oriented man who made her feel as though she belonged. And when he kissed her, she'd never wanted it to end.

She looked toward the door. In a few minutes Tanner would come through it and they would, what? Kiss again? Not a good idea. Tomorrow, she was taking the train to Anchorage. In just over a week, she was leaving Alaska. The last thing she needed was an entanglement.

She left the lantern in the living area for Tanner, brushed her teeth in the kitchen and was about to head to the bedroom when she heard the front door close. "Natalie?"

"I'm going to bed. Good night," she whispered.

"Good night," he whispered back. "Sweet dreams."

CHAPTER EIGHT

SWEET DREAMS? NATALIE rolled to her side, trying not to make any noise that might wake Debbie. Maybe if she could get to sleep, she would have some, but she'd been lying there for hours, possibly years, and sleep had never seemed so far away.

She'd heard Tanner puttering around, banking the fire in the stove, filling the pot with snow for tomorrow's warm water. He'd eventually climbed the ladder, leaving the cabin silent and dark, and leaving her alone with her thoughts.

She'd kissed him! Okay, he started it, but she'd been a full participant. Why? Was it the forced proximity of the cabin that engendered a false sense of intimacy? The romance of the northern lights? Or did he simply send out the right mix of pheromones? Whatever it was, it was a mistake. She'd only met him three days ago. Three days wasn't enough time to assess someone's character. Eighteen years hadn't been enough to discern her own father's true colors.

Maybe she was making too much of this. A kiss was just a kiss, not a lifetime commitment. She should be making plans for the next few days. Tomorrow, Christmas Eve, she'd catch the train to Anchorage and arrive in the evening. Despite the constant Christmas music and hoopla in Fairbanks, Natalie had been too busy finishing up her degree and then staking out the post office to focus on the holiday. She'd wrapped and left a couple of nice surprises for Brooke under the tree she'd helped her set up and decorate, but somehow the reality of Christmas hadn't set in.

Natalie had never been a big Christmas person. Her mom wasn't the type to create an over-the-top Christmas experience for her only child, but she'd tried. They had had a small tree, a fake one, decorated with some red plastic balls and a few craft ornaments that Natalie had brought home from school. There would be a gift or two for Natalie to unwrap and a bag of candy. They'd have turkey at the diner near their apartment. It had been fine.

Natalie suspected Christmas with her fellow instructor Marianne Carson, her husband and their three kids would be filled to overflowing with tinsel and music and wonderful food.

They'd never been close outside of work, but when Marianne heard Natalie was giving up her apartment early, she'd tried to convince her to stay with them over Christmas break. When Natalie had declined, she'd insisted on at least having her for Christmas dinner. Natalie could only hope her new coworkers would be as kind as Marianne had always been. She made a mental note to pick up a nice bouquet of flowers or a fruit basket or something tomorrow before the stores closed.

Natalie hated to leave the state until everything was settled with Dane and Brooke. Surely Dane would call again after Christmas when the family was back in Anchorage so that she and Tanner could find him.

She checked the time on her phone. Three fifteen. Maybe a cup of something warm would help her sleep. She'd seen some cocoamix packets and had finally gotten the hang of working the burners on the wood-burning stove. As quietly as she could, she slipped out into the kitchen. By the faint moonlight, she could see the vague shape of the dog stretched out on the floor near the fireplace, his white tail waving gently.

A creak on the ladder made her realize she wasn't the only one awake. "Natalie, is that you?" Tanner asked softly as he reached the hallway.

"It's me," she answered. "I was just about to make some cocoa. Want some?" She lit a battery lantern and hung it from a hook. Suddenly, Vitus sat up and let out a howl. "Shh, Vitus. It's just me. Don't wake everyone up." But then she heard it: a distant rumbling, like a train. Wind gust or earthquake?

The overhead light began to sway, and then the first shock hit, sending her stumbling toward the kitchen table, her heart pounding. Living in Anchorage all her life, she'd experienced many earthquakes, but never one large enough to knock her off her feet. She gripped the edge of the table as the cabin continued to shake. The vase in the center of the table holding the amaryllis blooms fell over. The slap of a book hitting the floor sent Vitus scrambling away from the fireplace. The Scrabble box followed, scattering tiles across the floor.

Tanner swooped toward her and wrapped her in his arms. "We need to get under a beam." He guided her to the doorway into the hall and whistled. "Vitus. Come!"

The dog yipped and scurried to them, burying his head against Tanner's leg, as though Tanner represented the only port of safety in the room. Natalie knew how he felt. Tanner held her tight against his bare chest, his arms wrapped protectively around her. When another shock rolled through, he braced his legs and held firm even while the floor under their feet pitched and rolled.

Dishes crashed onto the floor. The Christmas tree swayed and then fell. A cry came from the girls' bedroom. "Under the bed!" Gen's voice commanded. The stockpot rattled across the stove, edging closer and closer to the lip. The cabin groaned as the logs shifted against each other. Vitus whimpered. But through it all, Tanner's arms kept her warm and safe.

Another tremor, but weaker this time. The shaking subsided and finally stopped. Natalie held her breath, listening for the telltale rumble of another wave, but the earth was blessedly silent. Tanner hugged her and then let her go. "I think it's over."

She blew out her breath and sucked in another, unimaginably grateful that her body was still functioning. "That was a big one."

"Biggest I've ever experienced," Tanner agreed and called out, "Mom, Gen, Russ. Is everyone okay?"

"I'm fine," Debbie said.

"The pitcher is broken, but everything else is okay up here," Russ called.

"Wow, that was wild," Natalie added. Gen and the girls came from the bedroom.

"Uncle Tanner, did you feel that?" Evie cried. "My whole bed bounced up and down like a trampoline."

"I know." He crouched down to massage Vitus's massive head. "Good thing we had a brave malamute to protect us." Vitus's tail wag seemed a little sheepish, as though he knew Tanner was teasing him. Tanner shoved the pot back to the center of the stove. "I guess we'd better see where we stand. I'll go check on the generator."

"I'll come with you," Natalie said quickly. After that shaking, she didn't want to get far from him. She noticed Vitus was sticking very close to Tanner, as well.

They pulled on their coats. The front door squealed as it rubbed against the door frame. Tanner flipped a couple of switches before pulling it shut behind them. One of the moose antlers that had decorated the gable over the porch was now lying on the steps. Big, wet snowflakes drifted from the sky. At least it felt warmer, probably just below freezing. They made their way to the back, where the generator seemed undamaged. Natalie held the lantern while Tanner got it running, and a floodlight lit up the back of the cabin.

Tanner ran his eyes over the wall. "We got lucky. Other than a scrape where some ice fell off the roof, the walls seem fine. I think the logs flexed with the quake." By the time they'd circled the cabin and found almost no damage, Natalie was feeling better about going inside.

Another tremor hit, this one without warning, but almost before they'd registered it, it was gone. "Aftershock," Natalie whispered.

Tanner nodded. "I'm sure there will be plenty yet to come. Shall we go in and survey the damage?"

Inside, everyone had gathered in the kitchen, where someone had put a kettle on to boil. The destruction wasn't as bad as Natalie had expected from the sounds. Several games and books had fallen to the floor. Three plates and two bowls had smashed, but the rest of the crockery had survived the fall. Someone had righted the vase, and the four red saucer-sized amaryllis flowers bloomed bravely. One windowpane had cracked. Overall, the log cabin had endured the intense shaking with minimal consequences.

Even the Christmas tree was fine, once it was set upright and a few ornaments rehung. Natalie hoped the earthquake had been centered very close by, because if it was that strong on the outskirts and the center was close to Anchorage or Fairbanks, the effect might be devastating. Were Marianne and Brooke okay? She took her phone from her pocket. No signal, of course.

Tanner looked around for his own phone and found it where it had fallen under the kitchen table. "Looks like it cracked the screen, but it still works." He laid a hand on Natalie's shoulder. "Once it's light we can hike over to make some calls and check in with everyone. Assuming the tower is functioning." His voice sounded calm, but from the wrinkle between his eyebrows, Natalie could tell he was worried.

"Good idea, but for now, let's get this place cleaned up," Debbie suggested. "Girls, put on some shoes before you go dashing around."

Natalie reached for a broom. "I'll sweep up this broken china."

Soft, fresh snow compressed under their feet, and the light from their headlamps overlapped to form a snowflake-filled cocoon as Natalie and Tanner made their way up the hill. Vitus crashed through the brush somewhere to their right. Natalie concentrated on the snow directly in front of her. Tanner had warned it would be harder going in the dark, but neither of them could bear to wait any longer to try their phones.

Once they reached the crest, Tanner fished his phone from his pocket. "Good. The tower must have survived the quake undamaged."

Thank goodness. Natalie closed her eyes in relief while she caught her breath. Tanner passed his hand over her back before he moved a little distance away to make his call. His voice carried across the snow. "Hi, how are you? We're okay…"

Brooke picked up on the second ring. "Nat? Are you all right?"

"Yes. Are you? Did the earthquake hit there?"

"We felt it, but they said it was centered about halfway between Hurricane Gulch and Anchorage. A big one—seven point two magnitude. Did you have damage?"

"Only minor breakage. Everyone's fine, including the cabin."

"The news is showing a collapsed overpass in Anchorage. No injuries reported, thank goodness. Have you heard from Dane?"

"Sorry, no. Not since he sent word that he wouldn't make the train yesterday."

"Oh," Brooke sounded momentarily deflated, but immediately perked up. "I'm sure he's fine. Were the little girls scared in the earthquake?"

"We all were, but they recovered quickly. I think they're taking their cue from the adults around them…" Natalie chatted with Brooke for a few more minutes and then called Marianne. "Is everything okay there?"

"We're fine," Marianne assured her. "But we lost heat. The earthquake knocked the baseboard system loose, and of course nobody is available to work on it for a few days. We're relocating to our friends' reindeer farm for Christmas. Are you still riding the train in this evening?"

"Yes, but—"

"I'll pick you up at the station and bring you to the reindeer farm. They won't mind an extra guest."

"Thank you, Marianne, but that's not necessary."

"You can't be alone on Christmas." Marianne sounded horrified at the very idea.

"I'll be fine. I've been invited to celebrate Christmas with another friend." It was half-true. Tanner had invited her to stay with the family over Christmas. The fact that she was choosing to get on the train instead wasn't relevant.

"Are you sure? It's a big farmhouse, and

they're all about Christmas out on the reindeer farm. I'm sure you'll be welcome."

"I'm sure, but thanks. Good luck getting that heating system fixed. How are you going to keep your pipes thawed?"

"Portable electric heaters. They got the power restored within two hours of the earthquake."

In the background, something rattled and a baby gave a happy squeal. "Got to go," Marianne told her. "Marshall is playing with the dog's food again."

"Okay. Merry Christmas, Marianne, to you and your family. I hope you have a wonderful time at the reindeer farm, and a happy new year."

"Merry Christmas. Oh, wait. Jackson just told me the railroad has suspended service until they have time to check the tracks. You might want to call before you go to the station."

"Oh." Natalie had forgotten she'd let Marianne believe she was still in Fairbanks. "I'll do that."

"Good luck down in New Mexico. Keep in touch."

"I will. Merry Christmas, Marianne." Natalie ended the call. No train? Too bad she'd decided to wait for the Anchorage-bound train today. If she'd taken yesterday's train, she'd be in Fairbanks with Brooke. Now there was no telling when she might get out. What if she missed her flight on New Year's Day? She made her way toward Tanner.

"I'll bet he was scared. Is he okay now? Sure, I'll hold." He lowered the phone and turned to Natalie. "Is everyone okay?"

"Yes. How about you?"

"Fine. My neighbor got some minor drywall cracks and his wife says their cat is still hiding under the bed. He's checking out my house right now—the neighbor, not the cat, obviously. But anyway, they say the train—"

"I heard. What—"

"Tanner." A low voice came through his phone.

"Yeah, Brad? That's good to hear. I appreciate you going over there. Did you set up— oh, good. The girls will be thrilled. I'll help you fix that drywall if you want." He laughed. "Good point, better hire an expert. Thanks again. Bye." He pocketed his phone and faced Natalie. "I gather you heard about the train?"

"Just that it's not running today."

"I asked Brad to check their website. They've not had any reports of damage, but the railroad is inspecting the tracks today. If they pass inspection, they'll run a train on the twenty-sixth."

"Do you think they will?"

"No way to know. That was a pretty big shaker last night, but if the cabin wasn't damaged, I don't see why the tracks would be. We'll just have to wait and see."

Natalie nodded. Her flight was on the first, but classes didn't start until the fifteenth, so she had some wiggle room.

Tanner grinned. "Well, despite your Scrabble win, it looks like we'll be spending Christmas together after all."

"I guess we will." For reasons she didn't want to examine too closely, the thought made Natalie smile. "I guess it's only fair, since you should have been the winner of the first Scrabble game."

Tanner clasped his hand to his chest. "Are you telling me 'izzle' isn't a word? I'm shocked."

"I'll bet you are. At least I get to hang out with Evie and Maya on Christmas morning."

"Yeah, that should be fun. It's my first Christmas with them, too."

"Oh?"

"Yeah. They moved from Florida a month ago." Tanner knelt down to adjust his snowshoe. "Gen just went through an ugly divorce, and she's trying to get her feet under her. It's the girls' first Christmas without their dad around."

"They're not going to see their father over the holidays?" Natalie could remember wondering if her dad might show up on Christmas the first year after her parents divorced. He never did.

"He has other priorities. He quit his job and moved in with his girlfriend to pursue a career in comedy." For the first time, she detected a bitter note in Tanner's voice. But then, he was close to his sister, and divorce was never pretty. "But you don't want to hear about my family's problems. I just hope the railroad employees don't find any major problems on the tracks."

"Me, too." She drew in a breath. "But I guess there's nothing we can do about that. We might as well make the most of today and tomorrow. It's Christmas Eve, after all. We can worry about the railroad later."

"Agreed." Tanner whistled. "Come on, Vitus. We're going home."

CHAPTER NINE

THE SKY WAS growing light over the mountains by the time they'd made their way down the hill and across the bridge. But outside the cabin, Tanner paused and reached down to scoop up some of the fresh snow.

"What are you doing?" Natalie asked, standing on the porch. Vitus scratched on the door and whined.

"You'll see. Go on in. I'll be just a second."

Inside, no one would have been able to tell that the cabin had recently been through an earthquake. The scent of bacon permeated the air, drawing Vitus to the kitchen like he was being pulled by a rope. At the stove, Russ expertly flipped a pancake.

Debbie, Gen and the girls emerged from the back, dressed for the day. Debbie smiled at Natalie. "You made it. Did you reach your friends?"

"I did, and they're fine. One had some trouble with her heating system, but she says it's not too bad."

Tanner came through the door, holding something in his hand. "Evie, Maya, come look."

The girls ran to him. "It's a snowball."

"A snowball you say." Russ poured pancake batter into the skillet before coming to see. He took the ball from Tanner's glove and tossed it back and forth between his hands a few times before handing it back. "Perfect." He grinned at the girls. "Do you know what this means?"

They both shook their heads.

"This is snowman-building snow."

Evie gasped. "I've wanted to build a snowman ever since we got to Alaska, but the snow wouldn't stay together."

"That's because all the snow we've had this winter has been powder snow, until now. This is what we've been waiting for," Russ said, rubbing his hands together.

"Yay!" Maya grabbed her boots.

"Wait. Breakfast first. Then snowmen," Gen insisted. With a huge sigh, Maya abandoned her boots and came to sit at the table.

"Look at this." Debbie set pancakes on the girls' plates. Russ had poured the batter so that two small and one smaller cake had fused together. The smallest circle contained two raisins for eyes. "Uncle Russ made you snowman pancakes. Do you want syrup or jelly?"

"Syrup," Maya told her. As soon as the syrup was poured, she dug in. "Yummy. Snowmen taste good."

Evie chose jelly and spread the raspberry preserves into a red jacket for her snowman and added bacon for arms. She wouldn't take a bite until everyone had admired her food art.

Natalie poured syrup and bit into her pancakes. "These are really good."

"Sourdough," Russ told her, as he sat down at the table. "It makes the best pancakes."

"Ah, the famous family sourdough starter. I heard about that, how it's the same starter as your grandmother had."

Russ nodded. "I think about a dozen people now have some from that original starter, so if someone forgets to maintain it, we have backup."

"The great thing about sourdough starter as a family heirloom is the more you share, the more you have," Natalie observed.

Russ smiled his approval. "Exactly what I've always thought."

Over breakfast, Tanner reported that he'd called various neighbors and that all their houses appeared to be undamaged. "The newspaper says they have no reports of serious injury due to the earthquake. No messages from Dane, but I guess no news is good news."

Russ shook his head. "Once I catch up with him, we're going to have a talk about getting him a cell phone. It's one thing when he was spending most of his time here at the cabin, but if he's going to be traveling around the state, we need a way to reach him."

"He didn't give you any indication of what this business he's handling is about?" Tanner asked Russ.

"No. I thought it might be related to negotiating a new outlet for his art. Remember he said he was talking to someone about featuring his bowls on that auction site? But I can't imagine why that would be taking this long."

Maya finished her pancake and wriggled in her seat. "Aren't you done yet, Uncle Russ?"

"Almost." He crammed the last bite of pancake into his mouth and picked up his plate and mug.

"Leave them," Debbie said. "You and the girls go on outside. We'll clean up and be out to help build snowmen in a little while."

Evie, Maya and Russ were dressed and outside in a flash. Tanner was only a few steps behind. "It's so nice and quiet in here." Gen reached for the coffeepot. "We may as well enjoy a second cup while we have the chance."

From her chair, Natalie could see through the window. Vitus indulged in a vigorous roll in the snow. Meanwhile, Tanner huddled with the girls as though he was sharing some secret plan. From their eager nods, they liked what they heard. Russ gathered a snowball together and then showed the girls how to push the ball on the ground, collecting more snow as it rolled. Soon the ball was so big Tanner had to help them push. Together they moved it to a spot just off the porch.

Russ went to work patting snow around the ball to flatten the top, forming a platform about eighteen inches high while Tanner and the girls formed smaller snowballs and packed them in a straight line across one edge of the platform. It didn't look like any snowman Natalie had ever seen. What were they up to?

Natalie finished her coffee. In her hurry to call Brooke and Marianne this morning, she'd thrown clothes on over her pajamas and hadn't even bothered to brush her hair. "Excuse me. I'm going to wash up and change."

"The water I put on the stove should be hot," Debbie said.

Before Natalie could fetch the pitcher from the bedroom to fill with warm water, Evie opened the front door. "Grandma, come outside. We have a surprise for you."

Debbie raised her eyebrows. "For me? Whatever could it be?"

Maya popped in. "Hurry, Grandma. Put on your coat and boots. Don't look, though. It's a surprise."

Debbie obediently bundled up. Evie helped with her boots and then took her hand. Maya took the other one. "Come outside but close your eyes."

Gen and Natalie followed as the girls led their grandmother onto the porch. "Okay, open your eyes. Look, we made you a throne!"

"You're the queen!" Maya exclaimed.

They had indeed formed a high-backed arm-chair out of snow and added a cushion from the porch rocker to the seat. "See, you can sit in the chair and watch while we make snow people."

"I do see. That's lovely. Thank you."

Natalie suspected this was Tanner's idea to keep his mother from overexerting. Judging from the amused smile Debbie tossed his way, she knew it, too, but she played along. With great ceremony, she settled regally on the snow throne. "I'll need a scepter."

"What's that?" Evie asked.

"It's like a special stick that royal people hold while they rule," Gen explained.

"I know." Maya ran to the porch and chose a walking stick. "Here's your skepper, Grandma."

"Perfect." Debbie held up the walking stick.

"And now, my two princesses, why don't you build some snow people for my court?"

The girls jumped right in, rolling snowballs with Russ and Tanner. Gen put on her coat and boots and went to help. Natalie went to her room to brush her hair and wash her face. A glance in the mirror confirmed that, despite using Debbie's dry shampoo, her hair could use a wash, as well, but while the basin in the bedroom might have worked for Debbie's short curls, it wasn't big enough to rinse her long hair.

When she returned to the kitchen to look for something suitable, Tanner was digging through the ice chest. When he straightened, he held up a bunch of carrots. "The queen has declared that today carrots will be used as noses, rather than food."

"A wise decision," Natalie agreed. "Say, I wanted to wash my hair. Is it okay to use one of the cooking pots for a catch basin?"

"You could, but we have something better. Let me deliver these snowman noses, and I'll set you up." A few minutes later he appeared with an old-fashioned galvanized washtub and a couple of towels. He set another pot of snow on the stove and turned up the heat.

Natalie grinned. "Why do I feel like the comic relief in an old Western?"

"Hey, it works." Tanner set the tub on the floor and leaned a cushion against it. "You just lean back on the pillow with your head over the tub and I'll pour the water for you."

"Don't you need to be building snowmen with your nieces?"

"Mom, Russ and Gen have it covered. They won't miss me for a while."

Rinsing her hair would be a lot easier with help. "I— Okay, if you don't mind."

"I'll get the shampoo."

Once the water was warm, Natalie sat on the floor and leaned back against the pillow, letting her hair dangle into the tub. It was actually not too different from the shampoo sink at the hair salon. She closed her eyes and let Tanner empty a pitcher over her head.

The warm water felt lovely trailing down her scalp. He walked to the stove to refill the pitcher. She squeezed her hair to wring out the drips and started to sit up, but Tanner stopped her. "Just stay where you are." He pulled over a kitchen chair and picked up the shampoo bottle. "Close your eyes."

"Why?"

He squirted shampoo into his palm. "So you don't get soap in them."

"You're going to wash my hair?"

"Well, I'd call in a professional, but none of

them make house calls on Christmas Eve. Just relax." His strong fingers massaged her scalp and worked almond-scented lather through the strands. So relaxing.

"That smells nice."

"Glad you like it. It's Gen's. She said you could use it." After a few minutes, he poured another pitcher of warm water over her head with one hand while working it through with the other.

"Thank you." She reached back to squeeze the excess water from her hair.

"Oh, you're not done yet. Lather, rinse, repeat, right? Plus, there's conditioner if you want it."

"Conditioner, you say. This is a full-service salon."

Tanner grinned. "Maybe tonight we could all give each other facials."

"Facials." Natalie laughed. "What do you know about facials?"

"Don't they consist of rubbing mud on your face? There might be some dirt in the cellar."

"I think I'll skip the facial." Natalie lay back and allowed Tanner to pamper her. At one point, she opened her eyes to see him looking down at her while he worked the conditioner through her hair. The soft expression on his face looked a lot like just before he'd kissed her under the northern lights.

She closed her eyes again quickly before he could see the answering desire in them. More kisses would be a bad idea, especially with his family running in and out. When he'd rinsed the last of the conditioner from her hair, he wrapped a towel around her head and helped her sit up.

"There you go."

"Thank you. It feels good to be clean." Natalie went to her room, combed her hair and changed from her damp shirt into a soft sweater.

When she returned, Tanner had picked up the tub and was carrying it toward the door. Natalie went to hold it for him, but as she opened it, Maya ran inside. "Gotta go potty." Tanner jerked to a stop to avoid running into her, and the water sloshed out of the tub and drenched his sweatshirt. Maya stopped. "Oops. Sorry, Uncle Tanner."

"It's okay. Go on back but be careful of the wet floor."

"I'll get a mop." Natalie found a bucket and mop in the back closet. When she returned, Tanner was shirtless, drying off with the spare towel she'd left behind. It was obvious the man was no stranger to the gym. Tearing her eyes away, she set the bucket on the floor and began mopping.

Tanner grinned at her. "Dishes, mopping, sweeping—you've probably done more house-work in the last couple of days than Cinderella."

Natalie wrung out the mop. "I'd rather be here than at a royal ball."

"Oh, really?"

"Absolutely." She pointed to her wool socks. "Glass slippers would be murder on my feet."

He laughed. "I'll just grab a dry shirt and be right back."

Too bad. She was enjoying the scenery. Natalie smiled to herself. "I'll be here."

Tanner returned, wearing a dry fleece pull-over. Natalie had finished mopping and guided Maya around the damp floor and back outside, where three life-size snowmen were in prog-ress. "It looks like everyone's having a good time out there."

"It does," he agreed, standing beside her to look out the window.

"I'll go help once my hair dries." Natalie watched Debbie in her snow chair laughing and throwing out compliments. "You sug-gested the snow throne so that your mom would rest, didn't you?"

"Uh-huh," he admitted. "Standing around is harder on her than walking, but I knew as long as the girls were having fun, she'd stay out there with them. It's too bad my dad isn't here. He loved to build snowmen even more than Uncle Russ does. He was a mechanical engineer and took snow structure seriously. One Christmas break when we got a big snow, he organized Gen, Dane, me and all the kids in the neighborhood into work teams and we built a twenty-foot snowman in our front yard. People were coming from all over town to see it."

"Wow." It would never have occurred to Natalie's mom to take an interest in playing with children, especially other people's. "You were a lucky kid."

"I was," Tanner agreed. "My dad was big on family time, especially outdoors. The whole family would come out here in the summer. We'd pitch tents all around the cabin. Because of my mom's mobility issues, Dad used to carry her down the bank to the river so the whole family could fish together."

"Good memories."

"The best. It's been three years but sometimes I think about something I want to ask my dad, before I remember he's gone."

"Does your mother live alone now?"

"Yes." Tanner blew out a breath of frustration. "She shouldn't. Not that she's helpless." Tanner laughed. "She's the dead opposite of helpless, in fact, but if she were to fall or something…" He shook his head. "I got her one of those alarm things, but I'm not sure she actually wears it."

"And I imagine the more you nag her about it, the less likely she is to wear it?"

"Bingo. How did you know?"

"Because that's exactly how I'd react."

"I believe it." He laughed. "You know, if my mom happened to be tailing someone to help a friend, she probably would have gotten off that train, too."

"So, you're saying I remind you of your mother?" She raised her eyebrows.

"Only in the sense that you're both strong, determined women."

"Darn right." She reached up to fluff her hair and encourage drying. "You know there are a lot of people who would give anything for a family like yours."

"I know." Evie spotted them at the window and waved. Tanner waved back. "I'm grateful."

CHAPTER TEN

TANNER SPENT MOST of Christmas Eve helping
Evie and Maya build snowmen, but when they
went inside for a hot chocolate break, he took
the opportunity for a visit to Dane's workshop.
Inside, he pawed through a box of bits and
scraps left over from Dane's projects until he
located what he was looking for: a branch of
mountain ash.

Tanner wasn't an artist like Dane, but Granddad had taught them all how to whittle when
they were kids. He found a pencil, sketched a
design on the surface and picked up a blade.
Twenty minutes later, he'd finished the carving. He was out of practice and it wasn't as
even as he'd hoped, but it would do.

He locked up the shop and went into the
cabin. The girls had gotten distracted cutting more snowflakes with Natalie, as though
the fifty thousand already on display weren't
enough, but they were having fun. Tanner
grabbed his fly-tying toolbox and carried it

up into the loft where he could work in relative privacy.

The light in the loft wasn't great, but then he wasn't trying to create a work of art, just a little keepsake. After studying the crescent-shaped piece of wood, he selected some copper wire and glass beads from his supply chest and wound them around the wooden shape. The ends of the wire curled into swirls and spirals. A loop of clear fishing line formed a hanger. He lifted it and examined the result. After tightening the wire and repositioning a bead or two, he was satisfied.

He went to look over the railing at his family below. Natalie and Gen were showing the girls how to fold paper back and forth to cut long strings of paper dolls. Russ and Mom were in the kitchen together, peeling potatoes for the clam chowder they always had on Christmas Eve. Vitus lay stretched out full length on the floor beside the Christmas tree. He thought of other Christmases, with his grandparents. With his own dad. And with Dane.

This was the first Christmas Dane had ever missed spending with the family. And while it was true Dane wasn't a fan of crowds, he'd always loved family Christmas. Tanner couldn't imagine what business Dane might have that was so important it kept him away from his family right now. Hopefully he wasn't in some kind of trouble.

Tanner sighed. If Dane was in trouble, he would be there to help. Just as he was there for his mom, and for Gen and the girls. Tanner's dad had always put family first, and Tanner was trying to follow in his footsteps as best he could. Because nothing was more important than family.

THAT EVENING, THE girls spent a good ten minutes debating whether Santa would prefer sugar cookies or chocolate pinwheels, but eventually decided to leave one of each. They carefully arranged the cookies on a plate on the trunk in front of the fireplace, along with a glass of milk. Meanwhile, all the adults gathered round the hearth. Natalie found herself on the couch, between Gen and Tanner. Debbie brought out an old leather-bound book and clipped a book light to the cover. Once she settled into her recliner, the girls crowded close to her. "What's this book, Grandma?"

"It's our Christmas book." She opened the cover, adjusted the light and pointed to some handwritten words. "The first year your great-grandmother moved into this cabin, she wrote down how they celebrated and had everyone who was there sign the book. Look, here's your great-great-grandmother's name. And here's your grandpa. We've kept track of Christmases at the cabin every year since."

Both girls touched the book reverently. "Where's your name, Grandma?"

She flipped some pages until she was in about the middle of the book. "I'm right here. Deborah Elaine Coalson Rockford, married to Benjamin on Christmas Eve, 1979. Ah, that was a beautiful day." Debbie smiled at something in the distance only she could see.

Gen let out a sigh and looked down at her lap. When she looked up again, the book light reflected off unshed tears in her eyes. Natalie guessed she was remembering her own marriage, but unlike her parents', Gen's hadn't lasted. Natalie reached over to give her hand a squeeze. Gen managed a sad smile.

Debbie opened the book to a place she'd bookmarked. "I've already written for this year, about the tree, and the earthquake, and the snowmen and how we've been getting ready for Christmas. Now it's time to sign the book. Can you write your name here, Maya?" Debbie handed her a pen.

The tip of Maya's tongue showed at the corner of her mouth as the little girl concentrated on printing her name. Then it was Evie's turn.

They passed the book from person to person until Tanner signed and handed it to Natalie.

Natalie started to pass it on to Gen, but Debbie stopped her. "You didn't sign."

"I didn't think you'd want me in your Christmas book. I'm not supposed to be here."

Debbie chuckled. "Oh, you're exactly where you're supposed to be, in my opinion. Won't you please sign it?"

Natalie opened the book, took the pen and signed her name just below Tanner's neat autograph. It felt official, as though she was now a permanent part of the history of this cabin. Of this family.

She passed it on to Gen, who wrote her name and gave it back to Debbie. Debbie signed at the bottom with a flourish, closed the book and began to sing. "Silent night..."

The others joined in, even Natalie, who would have sworn she didn't know the words to most of the carols. Yet somehow, they must have seeped into her brain, because there she was, singing along as though she'd done it all her life. After several songs, Russ turned on a headlamp and opened a book. He cleared his throat and began, "'Twas the night before Christmas..."

Maya and Evie exchanged grins, and then listened wide-eyed as he read the classic poem in his rich, deep voice. Natalie felt Tanner reach for her hand. She let him take it and leaned against his shoulder as she listened. Russ reached the end of the story, closed the book and looked up toward the ceiling. "Did you hear that?"

"What?" Evie asked.

"That sound. Didn't you hear it? I think it came from the roof."

Maya gasped. "Reindeer?"

"I don't know," Russ told them. "But I know two little girls who need to go to bed before Santa can visit."

Evie jumped up and grabbed her sister's hand. "Come on, Maya. If he sees us, Santa won't stay."

Maya gestured toward the fireplace. "But what if Santa comes down the chimney and gets burned?"

"Don't worry," Russ assured them. "We'll take care of the fire. Besides Santa's magic protects him from things like that. Now, you'd better skedaddle."

Together the two girls galloped toward the back of the house.

Gen flashed a grin toward Russ. "Nicely done."

He shrugged. "It always worked with Dane."

Gen chuckled as she followed the girls to

their bedroom. Tanner leaned forward to snag a cookie from Santa's plate, but his mother slapped his hand. "Not yet," she whispered. "They may take a while to get to sleep."

"Okay." Tanner made a trip to the kitchen and returned with a cookie tin. He took a cookie and passed the tin around.

Natalie took a chocolate cookie. "So, what happens now?"

"We wait until Gen is sure they're both asleep, and then Santa will leave their gifts under the tree," Debbie said.

Tanner finished his cookie. "In the meantime, how about a game of—"

"Not Scrabble," Debbie warned.

Tanner exchanged glances with Natalie, who tried not to laugh remembering their hard-fought Scrabble competitions. "All right. What would you like to play?"

"Let's see." Debbie went to the shelf to look through the games. Eventually, she held up a wooden box. "Dominoes? We could play a train game."

"I'm in," Russ affirmed.

And so they played. Natalie had never tried dominoes before, but the game they explained wasn't hard to grasp. Gen returned before long and joined in. It was funny how, despite the earthquake, despite not knowing for sure when they'd be able to ride the train out, despite personal hardships and setbacks, the Rockfords all seemed to find such joy in simple things. Even more unusual was how their joy spread and made its way inside Natalie, leaving her feeling secure and content, two emotions that had been in short supply most her life.

At the end of the game, Russ was in the lead and Gen had fallen to the back of the pack, but no one cared. Gen tiptoed into her bedroom and reported that both girls were sound asleep. Tanner and Debbie brought in a couple boxes full of goodies, and they filled the girls' stockings, bit into Santa's cookies and spread an assortment of gifts under the Christmas tree.

"You guys are spoiling them," Gen exclaimed, looking at all the packages. "Especially Mom and Tanner."

"That's a grandma's job," Debbie declared.

"I might have gotten a little carried away," Tanner admitted. "But it was fun finding all the stuff on their lists."

"And a lot more, it looks like." Gen blinked rapidly. "I do appreciate it, Tanner. I don't know what the girls and I would have done if I didn't have you—"

"But you do." Tanner slung an arm around his sister's shoulders. "Always."

She favored him with a watery smile.

"Thanks." She checked her watch. "I'd better get to bed. Tomorrow will be an early morning. Good night."

Shortly afterward, they all decided to turn in. Debbie fell asleep almost immediately, but Natalie lay wrapped in quilts, looking up at the dark ceiling and listening to Debbie's even breathing. The cabin creaked, and then was still, truly a silent night. Natalie closed her eyes and slept.

CHRISTMAS MORNING, NATALIE was awakened by squeals of delight. Darn, she wished she'd been there to see their faces when the girls discovered Santa had come. But it didn't look like she'd missed much when she stepped into the living room. The girls had dumped their stockings on the coffee table trunk and were exclaiming to their mom over every treasure they discovered. They hadn't even noticed the presents under the tree yet. Gen looked happy, too.

Debbie came into the room and moved some dough she'd left in a cool spot near the window to a shelf over the stove to rise. She chuckled, watching the girls. "Nothing like kids to make Christmas complete."

A few weeks ago, Natalie would have disagreed, but now she was picturing future

Christmas breaks with Brooke, watching her baby grow and change. Before they knew it, the baby would be as old as Maya was now.

Russ and Tanner climbed down from the loft. "Did Santa come?" Tanner asked in an innocent voice.

"He did! Look!" Evie pointed at everything that had come out of her stocking.

"How about that. And look, the other stockings aren't empty either." He lifted the stockings from their hooks and passed them to their owners. He smiled when he handed Natalie her borrowed stocking.

"But how? I wasn't even supposed to be here."

He winked. "Santa magic."

Natalie reached into the stocking to pull out a pair of red-and-green-striped socks, a tube of lip balm, a few foil-wrapped chocolate truffles and a small box tied shut with a red ribbon. Maya came running over. "Miss Natalie, did you get something good?"

"I sure did." Natalie turned to catch Tanner's eye. "Best Christmas presents ever."

"Come see what me and Evie got."

"Okay." Natalie tucked the box into her pocket, but before she allowed herself to be dragged across the room, she looked back at Tanner to whisper, "Thank you."

"You're welcome," he mouthed.

An hour later, the girls had opened, examined and enthusiastically approved all their Santa presents including brand-new sleds. A note signed by Santa mentioned another surprise was waiting for them when they got home to Anchorage. Maya was playing with her unicorn family, while Evie was busy using fabric markers to color the animals on a printed pillowcase.

Debbie pulled a braided loaf filled with dried cherries and nuts from the oven. "It's a little too brown on the bottom. The oven must have been hotter than I thought."

"It smells wonderful," Natalie said as she poured a second cup of coffee.

"Let me get the icing on, and we can munch on slices while we open presents."

They gathered around the tree. Maya dived underneath to pull out an oddly shaped package covered with crumpled wrapping paper and tied with enough red ribbon for a dozen packages. Evie tugged on one end of the package. "It's from me, too!"

"I know. Don't tear it." Both still holding on to the package, they presented it to Tanner. "It's from both of us," Maya announced.

"I wonder what it is." Tanner pulled Evie and the package into his lap while Maya stood at his knee. "Want to help me unwrap it?" Maya eagerly unwound the ribbon and Evie tore off the wrapping paper, revealing a fish-shaped object completely covered with sequins, buttons and colorful beads.

"We made it. See? We knew you liked fish, so we made a real pretty fish for you."

"Wow. I do like fish, and this is by far the fanciest fish I have ever seen. Thank you." He wrapped an arm around each of the girls and gave them each a loud kiss on the cheek. "That was so nice of you."

Looking over the girls' shoulders, he winked at Gen. She snickered. "The girls thought you might like to hang it in your office."

"Absolutely. Once we get home, it's going on the wall."

"Ms. Natalie, we made something for you for Christmas, too."

"Really?" Natalie said. "That's very thoughtful. What did you make?"

They each presented her with a piece of paper. Evie had drawn a picture of a Christmas tree with piles of squares she assumed were gifts underneath. Two smiling people held more boxes. Lots of colorful circles decorated the tree. Maya's drawing was more abstract, but Natalie detected lots of snowflakes and thought the black-and-white shape in the middle might be a dog. Or possibly an amoeba. Anyway, it had been colored with enthusiasm.

"Wow! These are beautiful. Thank you so much."

"We didn't want you to feel left out," Maya explained. "Because Uncle Tanner got a present and you didn't."

"You're very sweet. Can I give you hugs?"

Both girls jumped into her lap, narrowly missing crushing the drawings, and put their arms around her. She gave them both a squeeze. "Thank you for drawing these for me."

"You're welcome."

They distributed the other gifts from under the tree. Framed family photos for Debbie, a new fishing reel for Ross, a gorgeous cashmere sweater for Gen and many other things, but nothing as precious as the drawings Natalie held on her lap.

Once they'd finished with the gifts, Gen began collecting wrapping paper, Russ went to tend the fire and Debbie said something about starting lunch. The girls were busy building something from snap-together blocks under the tree.

Natalie started to follow Debbie to the kitchen when Tanner laid a hand on her arm. "Did you open the box in your stocking?"

"Oh, I forgot." She pulled it from her pocket and untied the ribbon. "I can't imagine what it would be." She opened the box and gasped. "It's a crescent moon. Like the one we saw in the sky with the auroras." She stroked her finger along the wire. "And the beads are green just like the northern lights." She looked up at Tanner. "It's wonderful!"

"It's made of mountain ash, or rowan as they call it in Europe. I think rowan is supposed to bring good luck, or ward off evil spirits, or something like that."

"You made this?"

"I did."

"I love it." Natalie held the carving by the string and let it rock back and forth so that the beads caught the early morning light from the window.

"I'm glad."

"I wish I had something for you."

"You've helped make Maya and Evie's Christmas a good one. That's the best present you could have given me."

"I'm kind of glad the train didn't run on Christmas Eve," she admitted.

He smiled. "Me, too."

AFTER LUNCH, TANNER, Natalie, Gen and the girls dressed for sledding, except that Maya couldn't find her left mitten and refused to wear her "old" mittens because she'd gotten a new pair for Christmas. A scavenger hunt ensued. Along the way, Gen discovered a forgotten dog toy shoved under a chair to Vitus's great joy, and Maya found a partially eaten candy cane between the couch cushions. Fortunately, her mother was able to snatch away the lint-covered candy before she stuck it in her mouth. Eventually Tanner discovered the wayward mitten under the bed and the sledding expedition could begin.

Between several passes with the snow machine and a couple on snowshoes, the trail was packed enough to walk without snowshoes, even with yesterday's fresh snow. Vitus leaped ahead. They followed, but hadn't gone more than twenty steps from the front door when Maya suddenly stopped. "I have to go potty."

"Really?" Gen asked her.

Maya nodded her head urgently.

Gen shrugged and looked at Tanner. "You and Natalie go ahead. We'll catch up."

"Okay." He took Maya's sled, stacked it on top of Dane's toboggan that he'd been dragging and reached for Evie's. "I'll take these."

"I want to pull mine," Evie protested.

"Okay. See you in a few minutes."

He led Natalie along the path until they

reached the intersection with a more traveled trail and a short walk to a hill. Tanner dragged the sleds to the top and gestured toward the long wooden toboggan. "Ladies first."

"Are you sure this is a good idea?" Natalie gripped the edges of the sled and gazed down at the steep slope. "It's a long way to the bottom."

"You went down a bigger hill than this on the utility sled when we were walking from the tracks," Tanner pointed out.

"True, but then I didn't have time to think about it first."

"So, stop thinking." Tanner pushed her three steps forward and, at the last second, jumped onto the sled behind her.

Natalie shrieked as their combined weight sent the sled shooting down the hill, but within a few feet the deep snow slowed their descent until they came to a stop halfway down the hill where the slope leveled off briefly before increasing again. Vitus sped after them. When the sled stopped, he licked Natalie's cheek, approvingly.

Tanner hopped out and grabbed the towrope, pulling her along. "It's going to take a few runs before we can really get up more speed."

"And more speed is what we're after?"

"Absolutely." He dragged her over the hump

and sent her sliding down the bottom half of the hill, creating a chute in the snow. She scrambled to her feet, and they trudged to the top of the hill for a second run. "This time will be faster," Tanner predicted.

"Then you go alone. I want to watch first."

"All right." Tanner jumped onto the sled and it shot forward at a much higher speed than before. He rode it all the way to the bottom and only stopped by veering off to the side. He shook the snow off and waved. "Much better," he called.

He returned the sled to the top. Vitus followed, but halfway up he took off to investigate the bushes to the edge of the slope. Tanner positioned the sled for Natalie. "Your turn."

"Here goes." Natalie plopped onto the sled and Tanner gave a push, launching her downward. Cool air rushed past her face and lifted her hair from her shoulders. As she reached the middle where the slope changed, a dark shape came rushing from the left and knocked her into the snow. She raised her head to see that Vitus had commandeered the sled and was surfing to the bottom of the hill, his tongue hanging out and blowing back away from his face. She laughed.

Tanner came running toward her but lost his footing on the steep slope. He fell backward and skidded the rest of the way on his back, making her laugh even more. He sat up. "Are you okay?"

Natalie was laughing too hard to catch her breath. She gave him a thumbs-up, instead. "You?" she managed to choke out.

Tanner nodded, laughing along with her. When they looked down the hill, Vitus had reached the bottom and was trotting toward them, the towrope from the wooden sled in his mouth.

"Did you teach him that?" Natalie was finally able to ask.

"Not me. It must have been Dane," Tanner answered.

When Vitus reached them, he approached Tanner and offered the rope, but when Tanner went for it, he turned his head away, keeping the rope just out of his reach. After falling for Vitus's fake twice, Tanner grabbed the rope nearer the sled. "Drop," he ordered.

Vitus spit out the rope and opened his mouth in a doggy grin. "Yes, very funny," Tanner told the dog. "But no more sled-jacking. Got it?"

Vitus looked away and Natalie could have sworn the dog shrugged. All three of them climbed to the top of the hill once again. This time when Natalie climbed onto the sled, Vitus jumped on behind her in a sitting position before Tanner could give her a push. He started to order the dog out, but Natalie stopped him. "Let him ride."

"Sounds like the name of a song," Tanner said, as he pushed the sled forward, sending Natalie hurtling down the hill with a furry head beside hers. Vitus stayed pressed against her back for the entire run, but when they reached the bottom, he hopped out of the sled and grabbed the rope in his mouth, dragging it up the hill with her on it. In harness, he'd have been able to do it easily, but concerned for his teeth, Natalie scrambled out of the sled to let him tow it.

Gen and the girls came into view. As soon as she spotted them, Evie charged up the hill, dragging her sled behind her. Not to be outdone, Maya scrambled up after her. Gen stayed where she was, watching. Once the girls reached the top, Evie jumped onto her sled. "I'm ready."

"Don't you want Maya to go with you?" Tanner asked.

"No, I wanna go by myself."

"I wanna go, too." Maya's lower lip trembled.

"I'll go with you on your sled," Natalie offered. "Two people go faster."

"Go faster!" Maya jumped into her sled and

Natalie had to grab it to keep from starting down the hill without her. While she climbed into Maya's plastic sled, Tanner gave Evie a push. She took off down the side of the slope, shrieking happily. The sled veered off into the deeper snow and tipped, landing Evie on her side in the snow. Vitus ran to her and licked her face. She got to her feet. "Again!"

"Come on up beside the run," Tanner said to her. "It's Maya and Natalie's turn." As soon as she was out of the way, he gave their sled a push. The sled eased forward and then took off down the slope, the polished surface carrying them at high speed to the bottom of the hill where Gen waited.

Maya giggled. "We goed fast!"

"We sure did."

"Faster than Evie."

"Faster than Evie," Natalie agreed. "Want to go again?"

"Again!"

Gen walked with them to the top of the hill. After seeing how fast Maya and Natalie's ride had been, Evie demanded that Gen ride down with her. The next time, the two girls went together, but since they were so much lighter, the sled didn't gain as much speed.

It didn't take Evie long to figure out the correlation. "Bigger people go faster. Uncle Tanner, you and Miss Natalie go together and see how fast you go."

"That's okay. We came to bring you girls sledding."

"I wanna see you go fast," Maya said.

"I'd like to see that myself," Gen said.

With a little more urging, Natalie and Tanner got together on the sled. Gen gave them a shove, and off they went, streaking down the hill much faster than they had earlier. They flew over the first rise, into the dip, and their momentum carried them over another small hill and down the other side. At the base of this hill was a mostly frozen pond, but at the opening where the creek ran in, a flock of mallards swam in the open water.

Natalie swallowed as she tried to calculate whether their current trajectory would miss the open water or land them on the ice. And just how thick was that ice, anyway? Tanner must have decided he didn't want to find out, because just before they reached the pond, he rocked to the side and dumped them both into a deep drift of snow.

"Sorry." Tanner brushed a clump of snow away from her face. "Somehow I keep landing you in the snow."

"I'm not. I'm just glad you had the presence of mind to stop us." Natalie smiled at him.

His glove stilled against her cheek. His mouth curved into an amused smile, just inches away. Without giving herself time to analyze it, she leaned forward to press her lips to his. His hand slid behind her neck, pulling her closer, extending the kiss. Warmth spread through her body.

"Uncle Tanner?" The two girls were calling from the top of the hill. "Miss Natalie? Where'd you go?"

Tanner broke the kiss with a smile of regret. "We're here," he called to the girls. "Stay where you are. We'll be right there." Tanner struggled to his feet and offered his hand to Natalie. "That was unexpected."

"I know." Natalie allowed him to pull her up. "It didn't even occur to me that we could end up in the lake. Maybe someone should put up some snow fencing or something, in case any of the kids get this far. Or at least a sign warning about the danger."

"I wasn't talking about the sled ride." Tanner straightened the pom-pom on her hat and grinned. "But you might be right about the danger."

CHAPTER ELEVEN

IT WASN'T EASY to shift gears the day after Christmas. After a trip to the hill for cell phone coverage, Tanner confirmed with the railroad station that the train from Fairbanks to Anchorage would run that afternoon. All of them except Russ had originally planned to stay until the next weekend, but after the earthquake they'd decided that if the train ran on the twenty-sixth, they should take it and get back to town. Which meant packing, cleaning and transporting everyone to the tracks.

Tanner stomped the snow from his boots and followed Vitus into the cabin. The Christmas tree was gone. Natalie was the only one in the living room, taking down the snowflakes and paper chains. "The train is coming," he told her. "It's on the usual schedule, which means we need to be at the tracks by four."

"All right." Natalie set the crushed paper in the kindling box. "No earthquake damage to the tracks?"

"No, the rep I talked to said the full route has been inspected and cleared."

"Good. I've finished packing." Her tone was businesslike, as though in her mind, she'd already left this cabin and Tanner behind and moved on to her upcoming job. Which was a shame, because he'd have loved to spend more time with her.

Not that Tanner was looking to add a woman into his life right now. Between his business, his mom, and Gen and the girls, he had quite enough on his plate, which might be part of the reason his romantic relationships never seemed to last. The most recent had ended about six months ago, when he'd first gotten wind of Gen's upcoming divorce. When he had mentioned his plans to invite his sister and nieces to live with him, Stephanie had called it quits. Tanner had gotten the impression she'd planned on being the one to move in.

They'd met in the parking lot of a home improvement store, when Stephanie was attempting to load a stack of lumber into the back of her tiny car. Tanner had offered to help, and somehow found himself not only delivering the load of lumber to her house but using it to rebuild the fence that had blown down during the last chinook windstorm.

She'd been grateful. She had always been

grateful for his assistance in the various home improvement projects she was so good at starting and inept at finishing, until it had finally dawned on him that Stephanie's helplessness grew in inverse proportion to any demands in his life that didn't center around her. Anyway, last he'd heard, Stephanie had reconciled with an ex.

Gen claimed Tanner had a white-knight complex, that he rode around looking for damsels in distress. Of course, she'd said that during the conversation when he'd invited her to stay with him. He'd laughed and assured her he'd never even ridden a horse, but she might have a point. Most of the women he'd dated seemed to be looking for someone to take care of them. Natalie, on the other hand, valued her independence to the point she had practically been ready to dig a snow cave before she'd agreed to come to the cabin with him.

"What else do we need to do before we leave?" Natalie asked, as she pulled down the last of the snowflakes. "Do you have a checklist?"

"No." Tanner almost wished he did, just to satisfy her obvious need to feel in control by checking off boxes. She was systematically obliterating every sign of their Christmas together.

Hard to believe this was the same woman who had made decorations, read stories and sung Christmas carols. The woman with whom he'd shared a kiss under the northern lights and another yesterday in the snow. As her barriers had come down, he'd begun to catch a glimpse of the warm and funny woman inside, a woman he'd very much like to spend more time with. But now the barriers were up once again.

Mom walked in from the bedroom. "Is the train running?"

"It is," Tanner told her. "On the usual schedule."

"Good. I went ahead and packed, assuming it would be. Thank you, Natalie, for taking down the tree and decorations. That's always the saddest part of the holiday for me."

"Glad I could help."

Gathering the stuff and packing it up didn't leave time for much of anything else. Evie and Maya bickered more than usual, a predictable response to the letdown of Christmas being over, but they perked up when Tanner reminded them that Santa said another surprise waited at home.

It took three trips pulling the utility sled behind the snow machine to get all the people, equipment and baggage to the tracks. Tanner left the sled, the dog and everyone else at Red's store and took Dane's snow machine back to the cabin. He went inside for a final sweep before locking up. Something near the window caught the light.

A silver earring shaped like a teardrop. It was one of the pair he'd noticed the first time he spotted Natalie watching him on the train, when she thought he was Dane and intended to follow him home.

Tanner needed to find Dane, give him that letter and find out the real story. After spending several days with Natalie, he trusted her, but that trust didn't necessarily extend to Brooke. Cynical though she was, Natalie's loyalty to her friend was clear, and sometimes loyalty could be misplaced. Some might see Dane as an easy mark—and they might very well be right. Tanner needed to keep an eye on the situation.

He pocketed the earring, locked up, strapped on his snowshoes and started for the tracks. Christmas was over. It was time to move on.

THE TRAIN WAS right on time. The brakes squealed, bringing the train to a stop. Tanner and Russ helped load the luggage and the dog and then went to locate the family all together in one of the passenger cars. Mom sat in one row with Maya beside her at the window. Gen was in a different row beside Evie. Either they'd separated the girls for fighting or they'd both demanded a window seat. Tanner didn't expect much trouble from them. Judging by the way she was leaning against Mom's shoulder, Maya was practically asleep already. Russ dropped into the seat in front of Mom's.

Natalie sat in the row behind Gen, next to the window. Was Tanner imagining the regret on her face as she looked out over the area they were leaving behind, or was he projecting his own feelings on her? Perhaps she'd found some of the peace and contentment he always experienced at the cabin. He hoped so.

The whistle blew and the train started forward. Tanner settled into the chair beside Natalie and dug the earring from his pocket. "You dropped something."

She touched her ear. "Oh, I'm so glad you found it. These were a gift from Brooke." She threaded the earring through the piercing in her earlobe. "Thank you."

"No problem."

"Before I forget." She pulled a wallet from her bag, but before she could open it, Tanner put a hand over hers.

"We're not going to accept payment. You were our guest."

"But I said I would."

He smiled. "That was when you were staying with strangers. Now we're friends. And we don't charge friends."

She hesitated for a long moment before she slipped the wallet back into her bag. "Thank you."

"You're welcome." He waited for her to say more, but she just gave a polite smile and looked out the window again. Clearly, she wasn't interested in talking.

Which was fine. Now that they were no longer stranded, he needed to get down to the business of locating his cousin. Sure, Dane had said he'd see them soon, but who knew what that meant? Tanner took out his phone and looked up the number from which Dane had made the last call. As he'd noted, it was an Alaskan area code.

"Is that the mystery number your cousin called from?" Natalie asked.

"Yeah. I was just trying to figure out if it gives us a clue to the location. It's an Alaska area code, but are different towns assigned different prefixes?"

"I don't think so," Natalie answered, "but I'm not sure."

Gen's head popped up over the seat in front

of them. "What's going on? Are you trying to track Dane down?"

Tanner sighed. He hadn't wanted to drag the whole family into this. "Yeah. I was trying to figure out what town he might have called from."

"Why?"

"I, uh, picked up his mail."

"So? If the mail has been sitting there for a month, why the sudden rush to get it to him? Was there some urgent-looking letter?"

"You could say that." He and Natalie exchanged glances.

"I want to see this letter," Gen demanded.

"Why?"

"Because you and Natalie are hiding something, and it has to do with Dane. He's my cousin, too."

"It's just a letter," Tanner said.

"From who?"

Tanner gave up. "A woman."

"A woman?" Gen's eyebrows shot up.

"What woman?" Now Mom was leaning in from across the aisle.

"I think we're going to have to tell them," Tanner said to Natalie.

She nodded. "Fine, but remember, Brooke gets to tell Dane."

"Tell Dane what?" Russ was standing at Tanner's shoulder.

Tanner nodded to Natalie to go ahead. She licked her lips. "The letter is from my friend, Brooke Jenkins. She lives in Fairbanks. About two months ago, she and Dane spent two weeks together. And now she's, she's pregnant."

"Pregnant?" Gen blinked.

"Dane is going to be a father?" Mom's eyes lit up.

"Wow." Russ smiled, but then his eyebrows drew together. "But they haven't seen each other in two months? What happened?"

"That's what I'm trying to find out," Natalie said. "Dane told Brooke he'd be back, but she hasn't heard anything since. She wrote him a letter saying she has something important to talk with him about."

"Wait a minute," Gen said. "You and Tanner said you didn't know each other. You just accidently got off the train at Hurricane Gulch."

"That was true," Natalie said. "Well, except for the accidently part. I, uh, actually followed Tanner onto the train and got off when he did on purpose."

"You were following Tanner?" his mom asked. "Why?"

With a little help from Tanner, Natalie gave them the whole story.

Mom was shaking her head in bewilderment. "You thought Tanner was Dane? And you tailed him onto the train? All this for your friend?"

"Brooke and I go back a long way," Natalie said. "She's always been there for me. On January first, I'm supposed to be on a flight to my new job in New Mexico, but I can't go until I'm sure this is settled between Brooke and Dane."

Gen looked dismayed, but before she could say anything Mom said, "Tell me about the young woman who's going to be part of our family."

"Brooke and Dane only spent two weeks together," Tanner protested. "I don't know that she's necessarily part of the family."

"If she's the mother of Dane's child, she's family," Mom insisted. "And I want to know all about her. Does she have family close by?"

"You'll like her," Natalie told her. "Brooke is a sweetheart. Her parents are in Africa right now, on a three-year assignment. But they plan to return to Alaska."

"It must be hard for her, not to have support from her parents right now. I hope you can find Dane quickly." She gave a fond smile. "He's always been hard to keep track of. I remember once, when he was about six, he was staying with us and one day he just disappeared. I looked everywhere, walking through the neighborhood calling his name. Eventually I had the whole neighborhood out looking for him. I think Tanner was the one who found him. Dane had climbed into my husband's drift boat and fallen asleep. He was one of those kids who could sleep through anything."

"That wasn't the only time he disappeared," Russ said. "Remember when he was fourteen and left a note that he'd gone camping for the weekend? He was away for two days and I had absolutely no idea where he was. Scared the life out of me. When he got back, I grounded him for a month and we had a long talk about keeping people informed of his whereabouts." He shook his head. "Apparently, the lesson didn't stick. Where did you say he called from, Tanner?"

"He didn't say. All I know is the woman he borrowed a phone from was in a busy place, and in the background, someone ordered a Rusty Anchor."

"It sounds vaguely familiar," Gen mused. "Do you remember exactly what they said?"

Tanner tried to think back. "Let's see, she asked someone about a refill and then talked to me for a second, like she may have gone to a different table, and then asked if they were ready to order. Somebody asked for something I couldn't understand, and a man ordered a 'Rusty Anchor, large.'"

"Large." Natalie nodded. "You don't specify large or small for a cocktail. Coffee maybe, but not a bar drink."

"I guess it could have been a coffee bar," Tanner mused. He tapped his phone. "Maybe if I search for coffee bar menus in Alaska and look for the word 'anchor.'"

"Wait, I think I've got it!" Gen's eyes lit up. "Pizza. Remember three summers ago when I came up for my high school reunion and went RVing with friends around the Kenai Peninsula? We found this great wood-fired pizza place and I'm almost sure one of the pizzas was called the Rusty Anchor. I think it had halibut cheeks and seaweed on it or something."

"Fish pizza?" Tanner wrinkled his nose.

"That's what I thought when I saw it, but after tasting the Mount Fuji pizza with Kobe beef and teriyaki sauce, I'd try anything on the menu there."

"So where was this pizza place?"

"Let's see. We were all over the Kenai on that trip. I'm thinking it started with an *S*. Soldotna or Seward maybe?"

Tanner did a search on his phone. "Besides chains, there's a place called Soldotna Pizza."

"Doesn't ring a bell."

"Also, Pat's Pizza in Soldotna, and a place called Fireside Pizza in Seward."

"Fireside Pizza. That's the one!"

"Let me see if the menu is online." Natalie fiddled with her phone and pulled something up. "Bingo! The Rusty Anchor with halibut cheeks, seaweed and sun-dried tomatoes. So, if we're right, your cousin is in Seward."

"Or at least he was three days ago," Tanner said.

"You think he might've moved on?"

"I hope not. He did say he had to finish up some business and that's why he couldn't be home for Christmas. Unless we hear from him in the meantime, I'll head to Seward tomorrow."

"You mean we'll head to Seward," Natalie said.

"We?"

"Yes, we. I want to meet this cousin of yours and make sure he understands how important it is that he contact Brooke right away." She frowned. "But there's no reason you have to go. I can deliver the letter myself."

"Oh, I'm going." And if that meant he needed to spend another day or two in Natalie's company, he wouldn't complain.

"Well, if you find him, tell him to call his dad," Russ said.

"Remember—" Natalie waggled her index finger "—nobody tells Dane about the baby. It's important to Brooke."

"Fine." Russ nodded. "But soon, we need to have a father-son talk."

"The train gets in at seven. We could drive down tonight," Natalie suggested.

"Let's make it tomorrow. Why don't you stay at my house tonight, so we can get an early start in the morning?"

"That's not necessary. I can get a hotel."

"It would be easier all around if you stay with us."

She hesitated. "If you're sure…"

"He's sure," Gen said. "There's an empty bed in my room. We'll have a slumber party." She winked. "I'll paint your nails."

Natalie laughed. "Then I accept. Thank you."

IT WAS DARK when they reached the station in Anchorage. Rows of icicle lights outlined the platform. It took a while to collect the dog and the luggage, but in the meantime, Gen and Debbie took the girls and went to bring their cars from the parking lot to the depot.

As soon as Tanner removed the dog's muzzle, Vitus pressed his head against Natalie's hand. Smiling, she fondled the dog's ears. Good to know someone in Tanner's household liked her, even after she'd confessed that she had been tailing Tanner and hunting for Dane. The others didn't seem upset, but she wasn't so sure she would be quick to forgive someone who infiltrated her household under false pretenses.

Tanner, Russ and Natalie managed to move all the baggage to the curb. Debbie pulled up in a red SUV, with a green minivan right behind it. Russ loaded several bags and boxes into the SUV. "I'll drop your mom at home," he told Tanner and then turned to Natalie. "It was good to meet you. I'm heading to the slope day after tomorrow, but I'll call Tanner if Dane gets in touch with me."

"I'll do the same," Tanner promised.

After ordering the dog into the back of the minivan, Tanner started loading the bags and motioned Natalie toward the passenger door. "Get in out of the cold. I'll be right there."

Gen looked up from her phone. "I was debating whether we should pick up something for dinner on the way home or thaw the batch of chili I left in the freezer."

"Let's go home and see what Santa left," Evie voted.

"Santa," Maya echoed.

"Chili sounds great to me," Natalie said.

Tanner slid into the back seat beside the girls. "I don't know what we're talking about, but I never say no to chili."

"Chili at home, or takeout."

"Home, James," Tanner ordered.

Gen smiled and started forward. They drove through the downtown area past the shops still dressed in their holiday finery. On the mountain to the northeast, the Anchorage star glowed, reminding Natalie of the twig stars Tanner had created.

Natalie had seen professionally decorated trees, theme trees and floral trees. Once, at a Christmas party at the head of the department's home, she'd seen an enormous tree covered with valuable antique baubles that made her wince each time someone got too close. But she'd never seen a tree with as much heart as the spindly spruce in the cabin.

"I'm still thinking about Dane," Gen said to Natalie as she drove. "And what he could possibly be doing all this time. I started to say I'm shocked he didn't make it for Christmas, but that's not true. He's never missed Christmas before that I'm aware, but Dane has always been single-minded. What surprises me is that, if he's in the middle of some project, he had the presence of mind to call Tanner and let him know he wouldn't make it."

"Kind of the absentminded professor type, huh?" Natalie made a mental note to pass that information on to Brooke, just in case she had ideas about sharing custody with someone who might forget he had a baby in the car.

"Natalie is a professor," Tanner volunteered from the back seat, apparently overhearing part of the conversation. "She teaches math."

"At UAA?" Gen asked.

"I did. But I'm starting an associate professorship in New Mexico next semester."

"I've always wanted to see New Mexico. Santa Fe is supposed to be so cool. Are you close to there?"

"No. More South Central. But I flew into Albuquerque and took a weekend in Santa Fe when I was interviewing. The missions were lovely."

"I loved visiting old missions when we lived in Florida." Gen's expression darkened for a moment, but then she flashed a smile in Natalie's direction. "We're home."

Gen turned the van into the driveway of the two-story timber-framed home. Bright, flashing Christmas lights hung from the gabled front roofline and framed each of the doors and windows including a long row of glass doors looking out over the second story deck. An almost life-size moose figure covered with white Christmas lights stood in the yard. A slightly smaller but similar reindeer with a red shiny nose appeared ready to take flight from the balcony railing.

"Oops, I meant to turn off the light timer while we were out of town," Tanner said. "But it is a nice welcome home."

Once they'd parked in the garage the girls and Vitus spilled out of the car and dashed into the house. "Let's go see what Santa brought!" Evie called.

Tanner exchanged grins with Gen, and they all followed the squeals to find the girls exploring the biggest dollhouse Natalie had ever seen.

"Look, Mommy. It's three stories tall," Evie exclaimed. "It has a sunroom and a bedroom and a kitchen and two cars—"

"One's purple," Maya volunteered.

"On the purple car, the top folds down." Evie demonstrated.

"Oh, a convertible?" Tanner asked. "I've always wanted a convertible."

"That explains a lot," Gen mumbled under her breath. She excused herself to start warming the chili while the girls showed Natalie and Tanner every detail. Vitus regarded the dollhouse briefly before following Gen toward the kitchen.

Tanner chuckled. "Vitus never gets too far away when there's kitchen activity. It's high opportunity time for scraps."

While the girls continued to ooh and aah over each feature of the dollhouse, Tanner plugged in the artificial Christmas tree. In a way, this tree was the exact opposite of the tree at the cabin, large, full and covered with hundreds of twinkling colored lights, but there were also Popsicle-stick decorations and candy canes and globs of ornaments on the lower half of the tree that had obviously been hung by Maya and Evie. Like the cabin tree, it had heart.

By the end of dinner, Maya and Evie were fading fast, much as they'd like to have denied it. Tanner shooed them out of the kitchen. "Let's go brush teeth, and then I'll read you a story."

"Can I have the purple car in my bed?" Maya asked as they walked.

Natalie couldn't hear Tanner's answer, but she suspected that any wish of Maya's that was within Tanner's power to fulfill would get an affirmative answer.

Gen carried the girls' bowls to the sink to

rinse. "Can you believe the size of that doll-house?"

"You didn't know about it?" Natalie brought the rest of the dishes to the sink.

Gen shook her head. "Tanner told me he was hiding a dollhouse at a neighbor's house until Christmas. I had no idea it would be that big."

"It's nice, though."

"Very nice. And way too expensive. I'm not sure I want Evie and Maya getting used to…" Gen trailed off as she bent over to stack the bowls in the dishwasher.

Natalie could see her point. Kids needed boundaries. She'd dealt with more than a few college students who seemed unable to grasp that they couldn't always have exactly what they wanted whenever they wanted it. Including grades. On the other hand, she knew that Tanner just wanted to make this Christmas the best possible for them after they'd been uprooted.

She was debating whether to mention that when Tanner reappeared, carrying the sparkly fish they'd given him for Christmas. "They're almost asleep. You'd better go kiss good-night." He held up the fish. "Natalie, how about helping me find a place to hang this in my office?"

"Okay." Natalie put the cloth away and followed, curious to see his work space.

The room was Tanner all over. In the center of the room, a large worktable held two fly-tying vises and numerous tools and supplies, all neatly organized. The corner contained a computer desk with a large monitor. An attractive grouping of art hung above rows of small oak drawers lining most of one wall. Each drawer had a metal frame holding a paper tag. "Are these old library card catalogs?" Natalie asked.

He nodded. "I use them to organize supplies."

Natalie moved closer to read the labels. Peacock herl. Guinea feathers—yellow. Ostrich plume. She turned to smile at him. "All these pretty feathers would go well with your fancy fish."

"Don't give Evie and Maya any ideas." He removed a watercolor of a rainbow trout from the wall and hung the sparkly fish his nieces had made in its place. "What do you think?"

"Perfect." And she meant it. The fact that his niece's feelings were more important to him than the tasteful surroundings he'd created said volumes. She walked to a bookshelf that held multiple copies of books similar to the one she'd seen at the cabin. "You wrote all of these?"

"I did. This was the first." He pulled out the thinnest book and opened it to a random page labeled Damselfly. The iridescent fishing fly in the photo was a work of art.

She turned a few pages to see more colorful flies and then looked up at him. "These are so lifelike."

"Well, thank you, but what matters is if the fish like them. Dane helps me test them. Amazing fisherman. I think he could set a fly in a teaspoon from twenty yards away. Together, we've come up with some original techniques."

"Do you think we have a chance of finding him in Seward tomorrow?"

He shrugged. "Seward isn't that big of a town, especially in the winter. If he's there—"

"Tanner?" Gen stuck her head into the room. "Oh, here you are. Wow, you really did hang the sparkle fish in your office." She laughed. "The girls will be so excited. I'm starting a load of sheets from the cabin," Gen told Natalie. "Do you have any laundry you'd like me to throw in with them?"

"That would be great. Tanner, we can talk later."

"Morning is plenty of time. I put your stuff in Gen's room, by the way."

"Thanks." Natalie followed Gen down the hall to a generously sized bedroom. Her suitcase stood at the foot of one of the twin beds.

Through an open doorway, she could see an attached bathroom.

"There's tons of hot water," Gen told her, "so don't be afraid to take a shower while I do laundry. I know cabin life with no shower can be kind of stressful if you're not used to it."

"You know, it was kind of the opposite." Natalie sorted through her suitcase, tossing several items into the laundry basket Gen had produced. "I am looking forward to a shower, but I really didn't mind the cabin. It was restful. No electronics, no crowds, no distractions. Well, except the earthquake."

"Yeah, that was unanticipated." Gen picked up the laundry basket. "You never mentioned at the cabin that you were about to move away."

"I guess it never came up."

"Hmm. Well, here's a spare robe if you need it. I'll get these into the washer. Enjoy your shower."

"I will."

CHAPTER TWELVE

"I STILL CAN'T believe Dane has a girlfriend."

After Natalie showered, she'd pulled on Gen's robe and returned to the living room to find Tanner and Gen talking.

"I don't know if you could call her a girlfriend," Tanner said, scooting over on the couch to make room for Natalie. "They only spent two weeks together."

"Maybe the amount of time doesn't matter as much as the quality of the time. Let's see." Gen counted on her fingers. "They would have met in early November. I thought Dane seemed particularly happy at Thanksgiving. Remember, Tanner?"

Tanner shrugged. "Dane's always happy."

"Yeah, but he actually talked to people. Remember, he was asking Mom about her friend who used to run a backcountry lodge? And he was giving you suggestions for the series you're filming next summer."

"What series?" Natalie asked.

Tanner fiddled with his mug. "It's no big deal."

"It is, too." Gen threw a grin Tanner's way. "Tanner and Dane are starring in a six-episode television series on fly-fishing in Alaska."

"Wow," Natalie said. "Television stars."

Tanner scoffed. "Don't be too impressed. It's a minor cable channel."

"Still. I want your autograph before I go to New Mexico."

"You got Maya's and Evie's signatures on your drawings. I'm sure they're more valuable than anything from me."

"Probably true." Natalie smirked. "Judging by the fish in your study, they are going to be famous artists one day."

"Not the starving kind, I hope." Gen laughed. "But back to Dane. How are you going to find him? Just walk around town looking for him? Seward isn't that big, but still."

"I thought we might try lodgings."

"Knowing Dane, he's probably not at any of the main hotels," Gen mused. "He might even be camping."

"Then we'll check the campgrounds, too." Tanner grabbed a walnut and cracker from the bowl on the table. "I've been gone awhile. Is everything okay here? Anything I need to fix before we go?"

"We're fine." Gen turned to Natalie. "He always does this. He thinks nobody can get along without him for more than a few days. Drives Mom crazy."

"Hey, Mom loves me." Tanner cracked the nut and offered half to Natalie. She accepted.

"Of course, she does. She's your mom," Gen said. "She appreciates all the help, too. She just doesn't appreciate the implication that she can't manage on her own."

"Well, despite what she says, she really can't. Dad used to—"

"Dad's been gone for three years now. She's adapted. She can ask for help when she needs it."

"The place could be falling down around her before she'd ask for my help. She needs to move out of that house."

"You're preaching to the choir," Gen said. "I've told her the same thing, but she's an adult. We have to respect her wishes."

"What's wrong with her house?" Natalie wasn't sure she should be getting into the middle of this family discussion, but she was curious.

"First of all, it's a split-level," Tanner said. "She can't go anywhere without negotiating stairs, and sometimes her leg makes that difficult. The laundry is on the bottom level and the main living area is upstairs, so she can't carry laundry baskets up and down, but she keeps trying."

"I did her laundry just before we left for the cabin, so she should be fine for a while."

"Good. Thank you." Tanner turned to Natalie. "Second, it needs remodeling. The windows are drafty. The kitchen isn't efficient. The bathroom doors aren't wide enough to accommodate a wheelchair if she gets to the point where she needs one."

"She says that won't happen," Gen said.

"Her doctor says it will, eventually. There's a fine line between having an independent spirit and just being stubborn."

"Yeah." Gen sighed. "But it's hard, giving up your pride."

"I know," Tanner said softly.

The sudden look of understanding that passed between the siblings led Natalie to believe they weren't talking about their mother anymore. Maybe they needed some time alone. She finished the nut and stood. "Bedtime for me. I'll see you in the morning."

"I folded your clothes," Gen told her. "They're in the basket beside the bedroom door."

"Thanks. Good night." Natalie found not

only clothes in the basket, but an extra quilt for her bed if she needed it. Gen was so thoughtful.

But then, thoughtfulness seemed to run in this family. They all seemed to genuinely care about each other. The little girls obviously felt secure in the love from their mother and their uncle. Tanner had said he was worried that their first Christmas away from their home and father would be hard, but from what she could tell, they seemed content. Maybe happy families really did exist.

"WHAT DID YOU think of the dollhouse?" Tanner had noticed Gen hadn't looked thrilled when she spotted it and now that Natalie was gone, he wanted to feel her out. "The girls seemed to like it."

"Of course, they did," Gen replied. "What little girl wouldn't? But they didn't need anything this fancy. You'll spoil them."

"I just wanted their first Christmas in Alaska to be a good one, you know."

"I know." She sighed.

"Did their dad call before they left?"

Gen shook her head. "No, despite my emails telling him when we were leaving for the cabin, he called on Christmas and left a message. I listened to it just before I dished out the chili. He said he'd mailed them presents but they might not arrive for a few days."

"How did the girls seem?"

"Fine. Not particularly interested. But then, why would they be?" Gen shrugged. "I tried to ignore it, but the truth is their dad has been slowly drifting out of our lives for a couple of years. He hasn't really engaged with them for a long time now."

"So you think—"

"Yes, he's been having affairs for years. I was just too blind—well, maybe not blind. Maybe just too scared to look. You know?"

"I'm sorry."

"Don't be sorry. Gah, if you weren't here—"

"I'll always be here for you."

"Thanks. But it's ridiculous. I'm a grown woman. I have a college degree. They're my kids. My brother shouldn't be the one putting a roof over their heads and buying their presents from Santa. I need to stand on my own two feet."

"You will."

"You say that like you believe it."

"I do. You're amazing and talented. You just need some time to find the lucky employer who will recognize those talents. But most importantly, you're a great mom. And in the meantime, I like having the girls around and listening to them when they play. It's fun."

She gave him an appraising look. "Maybe you should think about getting a couple of your own."

"Yeah, well, ideally that would involve finding a wife."

"What ever happened to that woman you were dating last summer?"

"She went back to her ex."

Gen nodded as if she'd seen that coming. She probably had. Everyone seemed to see these things before he did. "You know what your problem is?"

"Please enlighten me."

"You always have to be the savior. Sure, women are grateful when you help them out of a jam, but it gets old, being grateful all the time. I can attest to that."

"Come on, Gen. Nobody's asking for your gratitude. I'd be happy to have you and the girls stay here until they go off to college, if that's what you need. You're family, and family helps each other. You'd do the same for me if our positions were reversed."

"But they're not, are they? You're always the one who does the helping." She gave her head a shake. "Anyway, we were talking about your love life. The problem with always being the hero is that you either end up with someone who will use you and move on as soon as the crisis is over, or the clingy kind who wants to create lots of drama and have you swoop in and save them over and over."

Tanner considered that. When he thought back to his last few relationships, he could categorize almost all of them as one or the other. And, as Gen had suggested, either they'd moved on quickly, or he'd grown tired of their manufactured crises and broken off the relationship. "You may be right."

"You did it again with Natalie at the cabin, but she doesn't seem like the clingy type."

"No." He smiled, remembering how insistent she'd been, once she realized she was stranded, that she'd pay for her lodging. "She's definitely not."

"From the way you were looking at her earlier—"

"Let it go, Gen. It's not going to happen."

"I'm just saying she seems smart and independent. Someone who could be a real partner to you. You're going to be spending the next couple of days together looking for Dane. Why not pursue the relationship and see where it goes?"

"She's moving to New Mexico next week to start a new job."

Gen cracked an almond and chewed it contemplatively. "And a long-distance relationship is out of the question?"

He gave a wry smile. "As you've so eloquently pointed out, I can't seem to maintain even a short-distance relationship."

"Because you haven't found the right woman."

"How do you know if it's right?"

Gen laughed, but it wasn't a happy sound. "I'm the wrong person to ask. I thought I knew who I was marrying, but clearly, I was seeing qualities that weren't there. Like trustworthiness." She rubbed her forehead. "How could I have been so stupid for so long?"

"Hey, this is on him, not you. You're supposed to trust the people you love. We grew up seeing Mom and Dad, and Grandma and Granddad, and we thought all marriages were like theirs. Russ's broke up before we were old enough to understand. You had no frame of reference to recognize a liar and cheat."

"But I recognized early that our relationship wasn't close like theirs was. We never really seemed to laugh at the same things. I thought we'd get closer once we had kids, but it seemed to push us farther apart instead of bringing us together. Stupid, stupid, stupid." She stood and walked to the window, staring out at the darkness and trying to surreptitiously wipe at her cheeks.

Tanner tried to think of the right words to comfort his sister, but grabbed a tissue and handed it to her. When she turned, he pulled her into a hug. "I'm sorry. I wish I could fix this for you."

That was the best he could come up with. The little smile she managed as she dabbed at her cheeks told him it was enough. "You can't fix everything," she whispered. "But I love that you try."

THE NEXT MORNING, Natalie rose early, but the other bed was already empty. Last night, Natalie had feigned sleep when Gen walked into the room but watched her from under her lashes. The light from the hallway illuminated telltale tear marks running down Gen's cheeks. That must have been some talk she and Tanner had had last night.

Natalie padded barefoot into the kitchen and found Gen and Tanner there. One would never know, from the cheerful smile Gen flashed her way, that she'd experienced a single unhappy moment in her life. "Good morning. Tanner tells me you're a cappuccino fan." She opened the doors to one of the lower cabinets in the kitchen island. "I thought so. Tanner probably hasn't touched this espresso machine since Mom gave it to him for Christmas three years ago."

"That's not true. I use it now and then." Tanner lifted the shiny contraption onto the counter.

"Like when Mom drops in for breakfast?"

"Exactly."

"I would love a cappuccino," Natalie admitted. "How do you work the machine?"

"The way I work it is let Gen or my mom handle it." Tanner produced a bag of some sort of gourmet coffee and handed it to his sister.

Gen went to work brewing, steaming and stirring. A few minutes later, she handed Natalie a cup with a creamy heart floating on the top. Natalie blew on the surface to cool it and took her first sip. "It's perfect. How do you do that?"

"Practice. I worked as a barista all through college."

Natalie tried another sip. "I'll bet you made good tips. This is wonderful."

"Thank you." Gen seemed pleased at the compliment.

"No. Thank you." Natalie let out a happy sigh. "The cabin was nice, but this setup has its perks."

"Perks?" Tanner laughed. "I see what you did there." Natalie smiled.

"I don't get it," Gen said.

"Perks. Coffee." Tanner hinted.

"Oh. Right. Obviously, I need caffeine." Gen started another cup.

"So what's the plan? When are we heading to Seward?"

"Soon, I thought, once I've checked in with my mom."

Small feet pattered in the hallway. "Good, you're still here." Maya came right up to them, with her sister at her heels. "Uncle Tanner, do you think you can take us sledding before you go?"

He threw a questioning glance at Natalie. "Do you mind?"

Evie turned to Natalie. "Please, Miss Natalie. Can you take us sledding? The park with the sledding hill is only three blocks away, but we're not allowed to go unless a grown-up goes with us."

Natalie shrugged. "It's only two and a half hours to Seward. I suppose we can fit in some sledding."

"Yay!" Evie shouted as both girls jumped up and down. "I'll get the sleds."

"You're still in your pajamas," Gen pointed out. "And so are Tanner and Natalie. Sit down and eat some cereal and give them a chance to drink their coffee. Then everyone can get dressed. And then you can get the sleds."

"I get dibs on the purple one," Maya called.

"Purple's mine," Evie declared.

"Remember how we talked about sharing?" Gen set two cereal bowls on the table. "Anyone else?"

"I'll take a bowl," Tanner said.

THE SLEDDING WAS FUN, even if the small hill in the neighborhood park wasn't as thrilling as the big one near the cabin. Vitus frolicked in the snow, but he made no move to steal the girls' sleds. Maybe it was only Dane's sled he tried to claim. After an hour the girls were ready to leave.

Tanner would have thought they would be worn out from all that climbing and sledding, but once Evie and Maya reached the cul-de-sac, they ran ahead shouting something about hot chocolate. Vitus ran with them, leaving Natalie and Tanner to follow along behind, pulling the sleds. Which was fine with him. He reached for Natalie's hand. Even through heavy gloves, it felt good to touch her, especially when she squeezed his hand.

There was something between them, something indefinable, but real. That little kiss the last time they went sledding was no big deal, except it was. There was something different about it, something different about her. She was like those chocolate Santas in the girls' stockings: a hard chocolate shell on the outside, but with a gooey marshmallow center. Intriguing. Just his luck he'd lived in the same city as this woman all his life and never met her until she was on her way out.

He opened the front door for Natalie and almost bumped into Gen, who was hanging Evie's coat in the closet. "Put your hat in the bin, Maya. You, too, Evie. We can't have our hot treats until we've finished picking up."

Tanner smiled. Gen probably could have picked it up all herself in half the time, but she was determined to teach her daughters good habits. Maya and Evie were lucky to have her as their mom. Too bad he couldn't say the same for their dad.

Gen closed the closet door. "Mom called."

Tanner nodded. "I'm heading over there now. Was there something special she needed?"

"I don't think so, but she invited you both for an early lunch."

"Lunch?" That would delay them even more. He turned to Natalie. "Do you mind? I know you're in a hurry to get to Seward."

"It's fine," Natalie told him. "I know you worry."

Gen shook her head. "He worries about everybody. If he were a dog, Tanner would be a border collie."

"That would imply that the people I care about are sheep." Tanner laughed. "Can you imagine anyone less sheep-like than Mom?"

"I can think of a few," Gen said, looking at Natalie, who had picked up Maya so she could reach high enough to hang her own coat in the closet.

Natalie set Maya back on her own feet and turned to Tanner. "Give me a few minutes to change and I'll be ready to go."

"Take your time. I need to throw a few things in a bag. We may have to stay in Seward for a day or two if we don't find him right away."

Ten minutes later they were at the door. "Thank you," Natalie told Gen. "You've done so much for me. I wish I knew how to repay you."

"What, for doing a little laundry?"

"That, and sharing your bedroom, and your daughters, and your family's cabin. You've been great. Is there anything I can do for you?"

"Natalie doesn't like to owe anyone," Tanner told his sister.

"You don't owe me anything," Gen assured her. "We like having you here. Don't we, girls?"

On cue, Evie put her arms around Natalie's waist. Not to be outdone, Maya hugged her leg. "Don't go, Natalie."

"She has to, sweetie," Gen explained. "Natalie has things to do."

Natalie's eyes seemed unusually bright as she hugged the girls back. Maya was getting that mutinous look that Tanner had found often predicted a meltdown. He scooped her up and set her on his shoulders. "Do you want to go see where I hung the fish you gave me?"

Maya giggled. "Ride horsie."

"I wanna ride," Evie begged.

"The next turn is all yours. Let's go see the fish."

Natalie mouthed, "Thank you," as he passed. He winked at her and followed Evie down the hall to his office, ducking low under the door frame to avoid bumping Maya's head.

Although they were pleased to see their art on the wall, the girls were more interested in piggyback rides. He'd given them two apiece while packing his bag by the time Gen lured them into the kitchen for hot chocolate. While they were busy bickering over whose cup contained the most marshmallows, Tanner and Natalie were able to slip out with only token resistance. Tanner dropped a kiss on each girl's head and snapped the leash on the dog. "Bye," he called on the way out the door. "Love you."

"Love you, too," Gen replied, and the girls echoed her.

"Bye," Maya called. "Love you, Natalie."

CHAPTER THIRTEEN

NATALIE FOLLOWED TANNER into the garage, to a dark blue SUV. She could never tell one brand of car from another, but this one looked expensive. He opened the passenger door for her. "Here, let me take your bag."

"Thanks." Natalie waited until he'd put Vitus into the back seat, stashed the luggage and backed out of the garage. "Evie and Maya are so cute."

His face softened with affection. "Yeah, they are. Thank you for going sledding with us this morning. The girls loved that."

"So did I," Natalie replied.

"I could tell. Maybe that's part of the reason they like you so much." Tanner adjusted the controls so that warm air blew on Natalie's feet. "To be honest, I was a little surprised that Maya warmed up to you so quickly at the cabin. Evie loves everyone, but Maya is usually suspicious of strangers."

"I'm honored." Natalie was surprised at the warm glow she felt at his words. Why should it matter to her if a four-year-old liked her? She was never too concerned about her popularity among her students as long as they learned, but for some reason, Maya's opinion did matter.

A few minutes later, Tanner pulled up in front of a yellow split-level house. White lights wrapped around the pillars on the porch, and a Christmas tree twinkled in the bay window. Tanner opened the back door to allow Vitus to jump out and run up the sloping driveway. Natalie and Tanner followed. Tanner stopped and rested a hand on her back to urge her up the six porch steps ahead of him.

The front door opened, and Debbie stepped out and ran a hand over the dog's head. "You made it."

"We did." Tanner kissed his mother's cheek.

"Natalie, come in. You can leave your coat here." Debbie gestured to a row of hooks on the landing and turned to grip the stair banister. Only when she slowed to swing her right foot up to the first step did Natalie remember Tanner's concerns.

They made slow progress up the stairs, but once Debbie reached the second level, she almost sprinted across the living room. "I hope you like halibut. It's one of Tanner's favorites."

"I do," Natalie confirmed.

"The kind with the crab stuffing?" Tanner asked eagerly.

"Of course."

Debbie led them to a table set with red place mats and holly-bordered plates. Green napkins folded into the shape of a Christmas tree rested in the center of each plate. "We're still in the twelve days of Christmas, you know."

"Everything looks so nice." Natalie contrasted the manger scene on the mantel, wreaths in every window and an elaborate Christmas village arranged on the buffet with the tabletop tree and generic ornaments she usually added to her own apartment as a nod to the season. And this year, she hadn't even done that.

On closer examination, Natalie realized most of the houses in the Christmas village were painted wooden birdhouses. Three of them seemed to have been crafted from round sticks. Debbie saw her interest. "Tanner, Gen and Dane made those for me one Christmas when they were kids. Aren't they cute?"

"They are. Like little log cabins." Natalie knew she would never see a picture or model of a cabin again without remembering Christmas in the Rockford cabin.

"Sit down. Everything's ready. I know you're in a hurry to head for Seward and find Dane."

Debbie had them all hold hands while she said grace. At the *amen*, Tanner gave Natalie's hand a squeeze before he released it.

"Do you really think Dane is still in Seward?" Debbie asked as she passed Natalie a bread-basket.

"I hope so. If he's there, we'll find him." Tanner sounded confident. Natalie wasn't so sure. Seward was a small town, but that didn't mean they could search every last inch of it.

"When you do, give him this." Debbie reached behind her for a small wrapped package and handed it to Tanner. "I was going through some of the boxes in the basement and found your grandfather's pocketknife. I thought Dane would like to have it."

"He'll love it." Tanner put the package into his shirt pocket. "He taught us all to whittle with that knife when we were kids," Tanner told Natalie.

"And then Dane grew up to be a sculptor." The idea of a skill handed down from genera-tion to generation seemed so foreign to Natalie. "That's wonderful."

"So, I want to know more about the newest member of our family," Debbie said to Nata-lie. "Tell me all about Brooke."

"Well, she has a degree in hospitality and

works as an assistant manager at a big resort in Fairbanks."

"Impressive. But tell me about her as a person. If she was able to see past Dane's shyness to his big heart, I would guess she has a lot of heart herself."

"You would be right." Natalie smiled. She still had some doubts about this hermit/artist as a father, but she couldn't find any fault with his extended family. "Brooke is the most giving person I know. We were college roommates, and she's the best friend I ever had."

Debbie chuckled. "Considering how you came to be stranded with Tanner at the cabin, I'd say you're a good friend to her, as well."

Natalie shrugged. "I was just looking out for her. Sometimes Brooke can be a little… optimistic."

"Is that a bad thing?" Debbie asked.

"Maybe idealistic is the better term."

"Whereas Natalie is a skeptic," Tanner volunteered. "She assumed Dane was married and going by an alias. That's why she was tailing him."

Debbie looked aghast. "You thought Dane lied to your friend?"

"Well, I didn't have the full picture. He didn't give Brooke a phone number where she could reach him, or—"

"All right," Debbie nodded. "I'll give you the benefit of the doubt because you've never met him. But I assure you, my nephew is not a liar."

"I'm glad to hear that," Natalie said. "Now if we can just find him and give him Brooke's letter, they can get in touch."

"Then let's have dessert so you can be on your way."

Natalie couldn't turn down the fruit salad and homemade sugar cookies. Once they'd finished, Tanner and Natalie started to clear the table, but Debbie shooed them away. "Go on and find Dane."

"Is there anything you need before I go?" Tanner asked.

"Well, if you have a minute, the lamp beside my bed is flickering."

"I'll check it." Tanner strode out of the room.

Debbie gave Natalie a conspiratorial smile. "Don't worry, it won't take long. It's just a loose light bulb. I know because I loosened it myself."

"Why?"

"Because Tanner is never happy until he's helped me with something."

Natalie laughed. "I imagine that could get annoying."

"A little." Debbie smiled. "He worries. When his dad died, Tanner appointed himself my caretaker, whether I need one or not. He asked me to move in with him. I told him he's too old to live with his mother."

"What did he say to that?"

"He suggested I might enjoy senior community housing."

"And you're not interested in moving?"

"I might be," Debbie admitted. "If he stopped pushing so hard."

"So, you're just hesitating to spite him?"

"Maybe." Debbie grinned. "Wouldn't you?"

"Probably," Natalie admitted.

"Okay, the lamp is working now," Tanner announced as he walked into the room. "It was just a loose bulb, but I checked the cord just in case." He leaned over to kiss his mother's cheek. "Thanks for lunch. I love you."

"I love you, too." Debbie put her arms around her son. "Call me when you find Dane."

"I will." Tanner stepped back and suddenly Natalie found herself pulled into a soft hug. After recovering from her surprise, Natalie found she was enjoying it. When was the last time she'd been engulfed in a motherly embrace?

Debbie released Natalie from the hug but held on to her hands for a moment more. "It was so good to spend time with you, Natalie. I hope we meet again." It was an ordinary sentiment, but Debbie said it with an expression of absolute sincerity. Debbie turned to Tanner. "Drive safely. Text me when you arrive."

"I always do." After one last smile for his mother, Tanner laid a hand on Natalie's back to guide her out the door.

"Sorry that took so long," Tanner said as he pulled his SUV onto the street.

"No problem." Natalie smiled. "I enjoyed it. Your mom is..." She paused to find the right word.

"I know." Tanner grinned. "She absolutely is."

They drove along in companionable silence for a while. When they reached the water's edge, Natalie looked out across Cook Inlet at the snow-covered mountains on the other side. This might very well be the last time she ever saw them. Today, the water lay in a smooth plane with only the faintest ripples shimmering on the surface. Floating chunks of ice congregated at the edges.

"It's always changing, isn't it?" Tanner commented. "The seasons, the angle and intensity of the light, the tides, even the direction of the wind make a difference."

"Not to mention birds and whales and people. I used to drive this stretch several times a week, and each day the water looked different."

"To ski at Alyeska?"

"No. I've never been skiing."

"Never?"

"Not downhill skiing, anyway. We used to cross-country ski in PE class in elementary school. I liked it. I've thought of taking it up again, but I never seem to find the time or money."

"Well, if you weren't driving to the ski area, why were you on this road so often?"

"I drove a bus shuttling tourists from the airport to Girdwood."

"Bus driver to math professor? Interesting career path."

"Oh, I've had lots of jobs. You know those people who stand at the front of construction zones with a Slow sign? I did that one summer."

"I can't imagine that's the most intellectually challenging job you've ever had."

"No, but it paid fairly well. Besides teaching, I've done housecleaning, waitressing, retail. Once I tried my hand at commercial fishing, but it turns out I get seasick when the waves get big. Too bad, because I might have been able to earn enough in the summer that I could have gone to school full-time and finished sooner."

"You worked your way through school?"

She shrugged. "Loans weren't an option."

"Oh? Why not?"

"My credit was already maxed out. My father used my social security number to apply for a bunch of credit cards in my name and ran up the balances."

A deep frown passed over Tanner's face. When he spoke, his voice was controlled, but she could sense the anger underneath. "Your father stole your identity?"

"Yes. His credit was shot, so he used mine."

"Couldn't you prove the identity theft and get it straightened out with the credit bureaus?"

"Maybe I could have." Natalie sighed. "But then my father might have gone to jail for fraud."

"For stealing your credit."

"I owed him. If he hadn't let me live with him, I couldn't have finished my senior year of high school."

"I guess... I can understand that," Tanner said slowly. "Did you file bankruptcy to clear his debt?"

"No, I paid it off over time."

Tanner flashed her an incredulous look before returning his eyes to the road. "You paid it off. Your father didn't even help?"

"No, but he had a good excuse. I can't remember what it was, but he always had a good excuse."

"You paid off your father's debts after he stole your identity, and you put yourself through college at the same time? While maintaining high enough grades to get yourself into graduate programs?" Tanner shook his head. "Incredible."

"Not that incredible. It took me fourteen years to finish what should have taken eight, but I'm done. I have my doctorate, I'm debt-free and I have a job waiting. I've finally reached my goal."

"I stand by my statement." He flashed another look at her. "You, Natalie Weiss, are incredible."

Natalie felt her cheeks growing warm. Some of her instructors were understanding, even complimentary, but other than Brooke, no one in her life had ever seemed to consider her journey anything special or acknowledged the effort she'd put in. It felt good. Especially coming from Tanner.

A FEW MILES after taking the turnoff to Seward, Tanner spotted a sign for a bed-and-breakfast inn, and something clicked. They were still ten miles or so from Seward, but Dane had to be staying somewhere, and knowing him, it wouldn't be in the middle of town if he had other options. Tanner turned in. "Let's start here."

"We can check out the main hotels and eliminate a lot more rooms in a lot less time than if we stop at every little B&B," Natalie pointed out.

"True, but I have a feeling that, given a choice, Dane would stay someplace with fewer people."

"All right. You know your cousin."

The inn was a charming cedar building, set back from the road. An evergreen wreath with a big red bow hung on the front door. Leaving Vitus in the car, they stepped inside the door, slipped off their shoes and added them to the row of discarded ones already lined up in the entryway.

A black-and-white pit bull slept out on a rug in front of a fire in the great room. When they closed the door behind them, she rolled to her feet, let out a half-hearted "woof" and ambled over to sniff Tanner's leg. On the other side of the dining area, a woman appeared through the door. "Welcome to The Forget-Me-Not. I'm Ursula Macleod."

Tanner took the lead. "Hello. I'm Tanner Rockford. I'm looking for my cousin, Dane Rockford. I thought he might be staying here."

Ursula's eyes rested on the row of shoes beside the door before returning to Tanner's face. "I'm sorry. I don't give out information on my guests." She paused, briefly. "I do have rooms available if you'd like to stay."

Tanner glanced at the shoes and noticed a familiar pair of worn brown snow mocs. "I understand. Yes, two rooms, please." Natalie shot him a look of confusion. He laid a hand on her arm to reassure her that he knew what he was doing and nodded toward the dining area. "I assume everyone gathers for breakfast together?"

"Yes." Ursula gave him the same sort of smile his fourth-grade teacher used to give when he answered a difficult question correctly. "Although I only have one other guest at the moment, and he's spending tonight away, so it would just be the two of you for breakfast in the morning."

"But your guest plans to return?"

"Yes, he left most of his things in his room. A very nice gentleman, rather quiet."

"Good, good. Oh, I should have asked. We have a dog with us. Is that all right?"

"You brought the dog?" Ursula's smile widened. "Of course, he's welcome. We'll put a large dog bed in your room. Let me just get the registration papers."

As soon as she was out of earshot, Natalie leaned closer and asked, "Why are we checking in?"

"Dane is staying here."

"How do you know? She wouldn't give us names."

"She said her guest was quiet."

Natalie shook her head. "Lots of people are quiet. She probably meant he wouldn't disturb us."

"She also said she'd bring a large dog bed without asking what kind of dog we have. Dane must have told her about Vitus."

"Or she looked out the window and saw him in the car."

Tanner grinned and nodded toward the doorway. "I recognized his shoes."

"Well, you could have led with that!" Natalie's face brightened, but then she frowned. "But she said her guest was away for the night. You do think he's coming back?"

"I'm sure he is." Tanner chuckled. "Those are his favorite shoes."

Ursula returned with registration cards and a portable card reader. Natalie handed Ursula her credit card. Tanner pulled out his wallet, but Natalie shook her head. "I've got this."

"You don't need to—"

"I said I've got it," she hissed. "This time, you're my guest."

One look at her determined face, and Tanner knew she wasn't backing down. He nodded. "Thank you."

Ursula ran the card and collected their information. "If you'd like to bring in your luggage, I'll get your room keys."

They returned to the car. Tanner opened the door to let Vitus jump down. "I think the innkeeper knows where Dane is."

"Maybe, but she seems pretty adamant that she doesn't give out information on her guests."

"True, but she purposely directed my attention toward the shoes. If we chat with her, she might give us more hints."

When they returned to the lobby, Ursula and the dog had disappeared. A man who looked to be in his fifties carried a thick dog bed across the great room toward a hallway. "I'm Mac Macleod, Ursula's husband. She's putting you in rooms in the west wing. I'll show you."

The door opened into the dining room, and a young girl with pale blond hair ran through it, the black-and-white pit bull at her heels. Vitus stiffened when he spotted the other dog.

"Blossom, down," Mac commanded, and the dog dropped to the floor.

The girl hurried toward Vitus, but before she got there, Mac rested a hand on her shoulder. "Rory, remember the rule?"

"I have to ask first," the girl recited with a sigh. "Can I pet your dog, please?" she asked Natalie. "He's a malamute, right?"

"Right." After a glance at Tanner to affirm it was all right, Natalie nodded her permission. "Go ahead and pet him. His name is Vitus, this is Tanner and I'm Natalie."

"I'm Rory." While Rory was occupying Mac's attention, the pit bull, while maintaining the down position, was slowly creeping closer to Vitus. Tanner chuckled, and Vitus wagged his tail as though he was amused, as well.

The girl looked toward her dog and laughed. "Blossom just wants to play. She likes other dogs. Some people are scared of her, but she's real nice."

"I think they'll be okay together," Tanner said. "Vitus gets along with other dogs."

"All right." Mac gave the pit bull permission and she sprung to her feet and dashed forward. She and Vitus sniffed each other, tails wagging.

Rory petted a dog with each hand. "I never met a dog named Vitus before."

"He was named after Vitus Bering, an explorer."

"Vitus has a lot of fur," Rory said to Natalie. "I bet he likes to play outside. Are you staying here tonight?"

"Yes, they are." Mac told her and gestured for them to follow him down a hallway. Rory and the dogs tagged along.

"We're gonna go skiing," Rory told Natalie as she skipped along beside her. "Do you want to come?"

"We didn't bring skis," Natalie replied.

"We've got lots of skis in the shed. It's fun. The dogs can come, too."

"You're welcome to come along with us if you'd like," Mac affirmed. "We do have extra skis and boots."

"What do you think?" Tanner asked Natalie. "One last ski before you leave Alaska?"

"I don't know. It's been so long since I've skied," Natalie said.

Mac reached an open doorway and laid the dog cushion at the foot of a quilt-covered bed. "I'm a beginner myself. Ursula and Rory are experts, but you can stick with me and we'll take it slow."

"The Rose Room is ready." Ursula came from the room across the hall. "And I see Mac has your dog bed in place. Thank you, sweetheart." She brushed a kiss on Mac's cheek before turning to Natalie and Tanner. "Is there anything else you need to be comfortable?"

"They're considering going skiing with us," Mac told Ursula. "But they didn't bring their equipment."

"I'm sure we can outfit you," Ursula said. "The groomer just set track today, and he said snow conditions are excellent."

"It sounds like we can't find Dane before tomorrow anyway," Tanner whispered to Natalie. "We might as well enjoy ourselves this evening."

"It does sound like fun," Natalie agreed.

"Great. I have your keys." When Ursula reached out, Vitus nudged her hand. She stopped to rub his ears. "Well, hello there."

"His name is Vitus," Rory reported. "He's a malamute. He's twice as big as Blossom."

"At least." Ursula gave Vitus a final pat and turned to hand room keys to Natalie. "We'll leave you to get settled. If you two can be ready to ski in twenty minutes or so, that will give us time to organize."

"We'll be there," Natalie replied.

Funny, now that she'd paid for their rooms, Natalie seemed comfortable speaking for both herself and Tanner, as though they were a couple. Oddly, Tanner found he didn't mind at all.

THE MOUNTAIN TO the south of the inn blocked the low winter sun, but the reflection off the snow provided plenty of illumination for skiing. Natalie discovered that once she was standing on the borrowed skis, the long-dormant skills she'd learned as a child returned. She should really send a thank-you note to Mr. Becker, her elementary school PE teacher, for insisting that all the kids in her school learn to ski and snowshoe.

Natalie was breathing hard but not out of control as she followed Mac up a hill. Behind her, she could hear the woosh of Tanner's skis. In school, Natalie had been an average skier. Some in her class had been pretty good, although nothing like the little girl they skied with today. Rory was literally skiing circles around them, racing ahead and then zipping back to drop a word of encouragement. "You're almost to the top. Wait until you get to the downhill. It's so fun!"

Natalie wasn't sure how Rory was related to the couple from the inn. They were about the right age to be her grandparents, although she called them by their first names. Whatever it was, the encouraging comments, fond smiles, and occasional hugs and pats on the head made it clear they loved each other. And somehow that circle of love seemed to expand

and warm everyone around them as they all skied together.

Vitus and Blossom were included, too, as they cavorted alongside the trail, taking turns chasing squirrels and each other. Once, Blossom dashed underneath Vitus's belly to pounce on a blowing leaf on the other side. Vitus almost turned a somersault in his attempt to see what she was up to.

Natalie finally reached the crest of the hill, where Ursula and Mac were waiting. A forest of stark spruce trees frosted with clumps of marshmallow snow stretched out below them. Here and there, clusters of birch broke up the forest, their bark pale against the dark spruce. Rory was already flying downhill along the trail, her hair a blond flag behind her.

Tanner came to rest beside Natalie and flashed her a smile. She smiled back. On the trail below, Rory hit a bump and caught some air, and her exuberant laughter spilled through the forest. Ursula chuckled. "I suppose I'd better at least try to keep her in sight." She poled forward. "Rory, wait up!"

Mac turned to smile at Natalie. "You're doing very well. I'll leave you to catch your breath. When you pass the gate in a little while, follow the signpost to the Fireweed trail. It's an up-and-back, so you'll run into us either coming or going. Enjoy."

"We will. Thank you." Tanner transferred both of his poles to one hand and put an arm around Natalie's waist. She edged closer, content to lean on his strength.

"Having fun?" Tanner asked, once Mac was a little way down the trail.

"I am. I'd forgotten how much I like skiing. I should have started up again years ago, but it was faster and cheaper just to exercise at the university gym."

"I get the feeling you sacrificed a lot of things to get where you are."

"Maybe." Natalie considered. "But I'm where I want to be now. Or at least I will be, next week when I arrive at my new home."

"Yeah." Tanner's expression was thoughtful. "I just wish…" He didn't finish the thought.

"What?"

"Never mind. Are you ready to go?"

"All right." Natalie moved into the tracks, but before she pushed off, she looked back to see Tanner watching her with an expression on his face she couldn't quite read. She'd almost call it…wistful.

Natalie enjoyed the rest of the ski outing. Eventually, they returned to the inn. She'd worked up an appetite. Tanner must have, as well, because once they'd put away their skis, his first question to Ursula was about restaurants. "I believe there's a place here that serves a pizza called the Rusty Anchor. Is that right?"

"Oh, you mean Fireside Pizza. They're a few blocks up the street from the SeaLife Center. Amazing pizza combinations. I believe the Rusty Anchor is smoked seafood with sun-dried tomatoes. It's delicious."

"Personally, I'd recommend the five-cheese pizza," Mac declared. "But it's hard to go wrong at Fireside."

"Here, I have a card with the address." Ursula crossed to a display of tourist-related business cards and selected one.

"Thanks." Tanner took the card. "By the way, do you have any idea when your other guest is expected back tomorrow?"

"Not until later in the day. Do you like sled dogs? You might want to talk with Barb Unitak tomorrow." Ursula handed over another business card with a picture of a husky. "She does mushing tours."

"Thanks." Tanner exchanged glances with Natalie. Was this a hint about Dane's whereabouts? Tanner seemed to think so. And if it wasn't, they'd get to hang out with sled dogs, so Natalie couldn't see a downside.

"We'll definitely check it out," Natalie said.

THE RESTAURANT WAS BUSY. "Sit wherever you want," a waitress called as she passed by carrying two large pizzas. "I'll be right with you."

They found an unoccupied table with four chairs in the corner. Natalie chose a seat facing into the restaurant. Rather than sitting across the table, Tanner sat down beside her. He pulled out his phone and paged down until he'd found a number under recent calls. "This was the call from Dane." He laid his phone on the table with the number in clear view.

The waitress hurried over with menus. "Sorry you had to wait. We've been swamped. I'm Cindy, and I'll be your—" She noticed the phone and frowned. "How did you get that number?"

"My cousin, Dane, called me from this number just before Christmas."

"Oh, yeah," Cindy said slowly. "I remember."

"I apologize if I was a nuisance," Tanner told her. "I'll delete the number now." He pushed some buttons and made the listing disappear as she watched. "I'm just trying to find my cousin."

"Why? Is he in trouble?" she asked, suspicion written in her frown.

"Not at all," Natalie interjected. "Tanner's just concerned because his cousin missed

Christmas with the family. And we have some important news he'll want to hear."

Cindy appeared to be reassured by Natalie's statement. "Okay. I probably shouldn't have blocked you, but you kept calling and I was dealing with three big groups that night. You know, everybody home for Christmas and they bring all the kids and old people and in-laws and outlaws, and everybody wants something different. It was chaos. Anyway, the last time I saw your cousin was when he stopped in for dinner about three days ago."

"And he didn't mention where he was going?"

"No. He didn't talk much." Cindy grinned. "Good tipper, though."

"It runs in the family." Tanner winked. "Thanks for the info. I'm glad to hear he's still in the area. Now, what's the special tonight?"

"The North Pole." Cindy pointed to a blackboard near the entrance. "We're out of roast duck for the Fuji, but everything else on the menu is a go. I'll check back in a little while."

After a few minutes of discussion, Tanner and Natalie agreed on the special, with sundried tomatoes, green peppers, black olives and reindeer sausage. Natalie planned to ask for no olives on one half, but when Cindy returned, Tanner ordered. "Medium North Pole. Hold the olives, please."

"Can do. I'll get this to the kitchen."

Once she'd left Natalie asked, "You don't like olives? I saw you eat some."

"I can take them or leave them, but I thought you didn't like them. I can change the order if you want."

"No, you're right. I don't. I'm just surprised you remember."

"Are you?" Tanner raised an eyebrow. "Apparently you don't realize how unforgettable you are."

"Unforgettable good or unforgettable bad?" Natalie couldn't resist asking.

"Good," Tanner asserted. He leaned closer and whispered, "Definitely good."

CHAPTER FOURTEEN

EXCITED YIPS AND BARKS filled the air when Tanner and Natalie arrived at the kennel around noon. They'd come by earlier, right after finishing an amazing breakfast at the B&B—those cinnamon rolls alone were good enough to make Tanner want to move in permanently—but the teenager who was filling water bowls at the kennel said Barb had gone on an overnight trip and wouldn't be back until later in the day. So, they'd gone for coffee and discussed their plans, until Natalie had admitted she'd never visited the SeaLife Center in Seward.

"We took Evie and Maya last summer when they came to visit," Tanner told her, "and I can't, in good conscience, allow you to move out of Alaska without seeing Pilot, the Stellar Sea Lion." Natalie had agreed, and so they'd spent the last two hours watching fish, seals, ducks and other sea animals. The sea lion was in fine form, swimming up to the glass in the tank to greet them and turning flips to show off for Natalie. Natalie had especially loved watching the sea otters, and her laughter at their antics made Tanner glad he'd insisted.

Unfortunately, it looked as if the visit to the SeaLife Center meant they'd missed Dane once again, if indeed Dane was the overnight client. Back at the kennels, the only person in sight was a dark-haired woman busy harnessing a team of huskies. She looked up and waved. "Hi. I'm Barb. Welcome."

"Hello." Natalie walked closer, an expression of delight on her face as she surveyed the dogs. "I'm Natalie, and this is Tanner. Ursula from The Forget-Me-Not B&B suggested we stop by."

Barb smiled. "Ursula is a good friend. Are you interested in taking a mushing tour?"

A look of longing passed over Natalie's face, but she shook her head. "No, we just wanted to ask—"

"About your last tour," Tanner interrupted, figuring Barb would have the same privacy policy as Ursula, and not wanting to get her suspicions up. "We heard it was an overnight and we wondered how that worked. Do you camp in tents?"

"Actually, last night we stayed in a remote lodge, not far from here."

"Really? I'm surprised a remote lodge could

stay open all winter. Do people mostly come by snow machine?"

"No, it's been closed up for about six months, but my client had the key and wanted to spend several hours inspecting it, so we stayed overnight."

"Why was he inspecting it?" Natalie asked. Tanner wondered, as well. What about a remote lodge near Seward would be of interest to Dane?

Barb shrugged. "I assume he's looking to buy. Anyway, a real estate agent from town gave him the key. He seemed to like what he saw." Barb scratched the nearest husky's head. "You want to see it? We can't go inside, but you can look through the windows. It's only about a ninety-minute ride by dogsled, and I was about to take my younger team out for a run anyway."

"I suppose we should head back to the B&B now," Natalie whispered to Tanner. "Dane's obviously come and gone."

But Tanner had seen the look of yearning on her face when Barb had suggested a sled ride. Besides, he was curious. "Why don't we take that ride? We have no guarantee that Dane has returned to the B&B yet, and I'd like to see this lodge." He looked at his watch. "Although, that means we'll miss lunch."

"After that huge breakfast, I don't need lunch," Natalie said. She looked at the huskies, wiggling and barking, eager to be off. "If you think we should check out the lodge—"

"I really do," Tanner asserted. He was rewarded by a huge smile.

"We'll do it," Natalie told Barb.

"We have a malamute with us," Tanner said. "Can he come along?"

Barb looked toward Tanner's truck, where Vitus had moved himself to the driver's seat and was staring at them through the windshield. "He's gorgeous. Unfortunately, I don't have a harness to fit him, and I'm afraid if we let him run loose either we'd lose him on the trail or my dogs would get in a tangle trying to follow him where they shouldn't. He can stay here, though. I have an empty pen."

A short time later, Vitus was standing on a wooden platform in a chain-link enclosure, howling in protest at being left behind. Twelve huskies jumped up and down and yipped, eager to be on their way. "I'm afraid it's a tight fit for two people in the basket," Barb said. "I've been considering investing in one of those sleds with benches, but this is the biggest sled I own right now."

"We'll be fine." Tanner climbed into the sled first and made room for Natalie. She squeezed in just ahead of him and tucked the blanket Barb had provided around them. Tanner hadn't foreseen the opportunity to get closer to Natalie, but he wasn't about to squander it. He put his arms around her, and she settled back against his chest.

"Line out," Barb called to the dogs. They leaned into their harnesses, muscles quivering in anticipation. "Are you guys ready?"

"We're ready," Natalie said, tugging her hat lower on her head.

"Hike!" The moment Barb gave the command, the dogs leaped ahead, jerking the sled forward and quickly picking up speed. Vitus's howls faded as they rounded a curve and followed the trail into the forest.

It was a perfect day for the outing, with little wind, enough clouds to hold in the heat and occasional patches of sun that made the snow sparkle. The dogs soon settled into a steady trot, their plumy tails waving behind them. One of the wheel dogs was almost solid white, but with three distinct black spots on his back. His cohort on the other side was black and tan, with a streak of reddish fur along the underside of her tail like a flag. Both seemed delighted to run.

"This reminds me of that old joke," Tanner whispered to Natalie.

Natalie laughed. "You mean that if you're not the lead dog, the scenery never changes?"

"That's the one."

"It does, though." Natalie waved her hand toward an opening in the forest revealing a snow-covered mountain vista. "It's beautiful here."

"It really is," Tanner agreed, admiring the pink glow of her cheeks and her bright eyes. "Are you warm enough?"

"I'm great." She smiled and snuggled a little closer. Tanner would have liked to taste those smiling lips, but perhaps this wasn't the time nor place. Not that there would be many more times and places for the two of them. Once they found Dane, and she saw for herself what kind of man he was, Natalie would be gone, and he'd probably never see her again. Oh, maybe she'd come to Alaska to visit her friend sometimes, and maybe she'd give him a call when she did, but he doubted it. She was starting a new life, and Natalie didn't seem like the kind to look back.

A glimpse of a log building appeared through the trees. Tanner checked his watch. Somehow almost an hour and a half had passed in what seemed like only minutes. The trail dropped, and the lodge disappeared until they reached the bottom of the hill, curved around a grove of bare alders and broke out of the trees to a frozen lake. A long boat and float-plane dock lined the far side of the lake, with the lodge rising up behind it.

A semicircular window filled the second-story gable facing the lake, with multiple glass doors leading to expansive decks on both levels below. Two wings, probably guest rooms, jut-ted out to each side. As they drew closer, Tan-ner could see that the trim around the windows and doors could use new paint, but overall the property looked to be in good shape. Too good.

"Whoa." Barb brought the dogs to a stop in front of the lodge. Two sets of tracks, one matching those Barb was leaving now and an-other bigger set from bunny boots led to the door of the lodge and around the perimeter. Natalie and Tanner climbed out of the sled.

"It's lovely," Natalie commented.

"Yes." Tanner walked to the window and pressed his face against the glass. The inside looked to be just as nice as the outside, with an enormous central fireplace and exposed beams, although everything was covered with dust and cobwebs. He circled the building and discovered a large outbuilding, big enough to park a dozen cars, or more likely to store boats and ATVs, since there was no road. A log picnic pavilion nestled at the edge of a rise and overlooked the lake. Tanner frowned.

"What's wrong?" Natalie asked.

"I'm just wondering if we're on the wrong track. I mean, Dane does well with his art, and he inherited some money from our grandfather just like I did, but look at this place. I can't imagine any way Dane could afford it. Or any reason he'd want to."

"You think Barb's client was someone else?"

"I'm starting to."

"Hmm." Natalie pressed a knuckle to her jaw. "We assumed Ursula sent us here to help us find Dane, but maybe she steered us toward Barb to keep us out of the way rather than to help us."

Tanner thought about that. "It seems unlikely. Dane isn't hiding, he's just busy. Besides, Ursula and Mac seem completely straightforward."

"People aren't always what they seem." She licked her lips. "I think we should head back to Seward."

"All right. Let's see if Barb is ready to go."

"Do you think she's in on it?"

Tanner shook his head. "First of all, we don't know there is an *it*. And second, she offered to take us here but wasn't particularly insistent."

"True. Then we don't have to worry that

she's purposely delaying our return." Natalie turned and tromped back toward the sled.

Tanner hurried to catch up with her. "We'll find him."

"I hope so." Natalie didn't look at him. "SeaLife Center, mushing tour—we need to quit letting ourselves get distracted."

"I've rather enjoyed some of the distractions." Tanner tried to reach for her hand, but Natalie was having none of it.

"That's what makes them distractions. I don't have that much time. We need to focus."

"Right." It was the equivalent of a cold bucket of water in the face. "Focus."

Even though they were just as close in proximity on the way back to town, Natalie seemed a million miles away. Before the kennel came into sight, they could hear a welcoming chorus of howling, led by a familiar melodious baritone. When Natalie and Tanner climbed out of the sled within his sight, Vitus rested his enormous front paws against the fence and yowled louder.

"Coming," Tanner said. Dodging Vitus's tongue, he clipped the dog's leash to his collar. "He didn't howl the entire time we were gone, did he?" Tanner asked the teenage kennel worker who was helping Barb with her team.

"No. As soon as you were out of sight, he

took a nap and didn't wake up until he heard the team coming back."

Natalie rubbed the big dog's head and slipped him a bit of bacon from breakfast that she'd saved just for that purpose. "I'm sorry you couldn't go, Vitus."

A wiggle of his tail assured them they were forgiven. Tanner handed the leash and keys to Natalie. "Could you please put him in the car while I settle up?"

Tanner added a big tip to the amount Barb had quoted and promised to post a review on-line. "We really appreciate you taking us to the lodge. I know Natalie enjoyed it."

"I hope so." Barb unbuckled another dog and handed him over to her helper. "When you were getting into the sled after looking at the lodge, I thought she seemed kind of annoyed."

"It had nothing to do with you," Tanner assured her. "She's just focused on her next goal. Believe me, she loved the dogsled ride. Thank you."

Tanner's stomach growled as he made his way to the SUV where Natalie was waiting. "What do you say we go to town for an early dinner?"

She frowned. "We're here to find your cousin. We should return to the B&B to see if he's there."

"It's a thirty-minute drive to the B&B and then fifteen back to town if he's not. Let's check first." He pulled out his phone. Natalie didn't look convinced, but didn't argue.

After two rings, Ursula picked up. "Forget-Me-Not B&B."

"Hi, this is Tanner Rockford. We just got back from a mushing trip, and I was wondering if your other guest has returned."

"Hello, Tanner. No, I'm afraid I haven't seen him yet, but I do expect him this evening."

"You talked to him?"

"Not directly, but he sent a message through a friend."

"I see. We'll see you this evening then, Ursula." He put away the phone. "He's not there, but she expects him later."

"What if she's lying?"

After hearing Natalie's story about her own father stealing her identity, he could understand why she didn't trust easily, but nothing about Ursula struck him as dishonest. "Why would she do that? True, she wouldn't give his name because of her privacy policy, but other than that, she's been nothing but helpful to us."

"I don't trust helpful people. They usually want something."

"I'm sure she does." Tanner hid a laugh. "She wants us to have a good time and tell everyone we know about her B&B. Really, Natalie, there's no reason Dane would be trying to avoid me, and certainly no reason for Ursula to keep us apart. Besides, I'm starved. I want to eat first."

She raised her chin. "I still think we should check it out."

He sighed. "I'll tell you what. Let's stop in town for takeout on the way to the B&B. The deli there makes a good Reuben. Agreed?"

"Fine. But if we arrive and find out Dane's been there and left, I'm holding you responsible."

"Duly noted." Fifteen minutes later, Tanner parked on Fourth Avenue, across the street from a jewelry store next to the deli. He opened his door, careful not to bump the ancient Jeep Wagoneer parked beside him. It looked as though a good shake would reduce it to a pile of rust.

Natalie climbed out of the truck to accompany him, but Vitus, obviously anxious after one abandonment that day, started to whine. Natalie reached for his leash. "Just get me a turkey sandwich or something. I'll take the dog for a walk."

"All right. Thanks." Tanner crossed the street and got in line behind a woman with four kids, each of whom wanted something different and complicated. He studied the menu and made his selections, and then turned to look out the window while waiting his turn. Natalie was strolling along the sidewalk with Vitus.

Suddenly, Vitus stopped and raised his head, staring in Tanner's direction. A moment later, he was charging across the street, dragging Natalie behind him. Fortunately, there was a lull in traffic, because she wouldn't have been able to stop the dog for any amount of money.

Tanner ran out the door just in time to see Vitus rear up to throw his paws on a man's shoulders and lick his face. His tail thrashed madly. Vitus had found his owner. Dane threw his arms around the dog. "Hey, boy. Where did you come from?"

Tanner trotted over. "Hey, coz."

"Tanner?" Without pushing the dog away, Dane reached out to give Tanner a one-armed hug. Then he turned to Natalie, who was still trying to untangle herself from Vitus's leash. "What's going on?"

"We've been looking for you." Tanner almost blurted out the news from Brooke, but Natalie caught his eye and he remembered his promise. Instead he said, "Dane, this is Natalie. Natalie, my cousin, Dane Rockford."

"Hello." Dane managed to reach around the dog to shake Natalie's hand, and then turned back to Tanner for an explanation. "Why were you looking for me?"

"I, uh, was worried about you. I wanted to see what kept you from coming home for Christmas."

"I called to tell you I wouldn't be there." Dane looked puzzled. Tanner couldn't blame him. He'd never come chasing after Dane before. "I had some business and it took a little longer than I thought it would."

"Does this business have anything to do with a remote lodge about ninety minutes away by dogsled?" Natalie asked.

Dane blinked. "Yes, actually. I'm sorry, who are you again?"

"Natalie Weiss," Tanner repeated, suddenly realizing they needed a backstory. Better change the subject until he could get Natalie up to speed. "We met on the train from Fairbanks. Oh, by the way, I picked up your mail while I was there. It's in the car."

"You can give it to me later. It's usually nothing but ads."

"I'll get it." Ignoring his protest, Natalie hurried to cross the street to the car.

Dane unhooked the dog's paws from his shoulders and set him on four feet. Vitus leaned against his leg as though he didn't plan to let Dane get out of touching distance. "Thanks for taking care of Vitus for so long."

"No problem." Tanner stroked the dog's head. "We're buds. Right, Vitus?"

The dog gave a polite wag, but never took his adoring eyes off Dane. Dane scratched the dog's ears. "Was everything okay at the cabin? No earthquake damage?"

"No, we got lucky."

"And Gen's girls had a good Christmas?"

Tanner grinned. "They did. Want to grab a bite and catch up?"

"Sure."

Natalie trotted back, carrying the stack of envelopes and thrust them at Dane. "Here you are."

"Thanks." Dane started to tuck the entire stack under his arm until he noticed the bright yellow envelope on top. After catching sight of the return address, he handed Tanner everything else and ripped it open. A smile grew wider as he read. When he finished, he looked up from the letter and stared off into space.

"Well?" Tanner asked. "Who's the letter from?"

Dane glanced up as though he'd momentarily forgotten Tanner was there. "Brooke. A woman I met a couple of months ago. She's…" Dane couldn't seem to come up with the words, but his goofy grin said it all. "She says she wants to see me."

"Are you going?"

"Heck, yeah. I already have a train reservation. I just wish I didn't have to wait until Saturday to go up."

"What? How could you have a reservation?" Natalie asked. "You just got the letter."

Dane shrugged. "I told Brooke I'd be back as soon as I finished my business. I'm glad she wrote, though." Dane's gaze returned to the letter as though making sure the words hadn't changed. Again, they drew a grin.

Tanner suppressed a chuckle. He'd never seen Dane lovestruck before. "I could drive you to Fairbanks tomorrow."

"Could you? That would be great. One of the gallery owners in Anchorage loaned me her spare car—" he nodded toward the Wagoneer across the street "—but I wouldn't want to drive a borrowed car all the way to Fairbanks. I'll need to return it."

"Funny you would mention Brooke and Fairbanks," Natalie commented casually, as though she didn't know exactly what the letter said. "I have a friend who lives there named Brooke Jenkins."

Dane turned wide eyes toward her. "You're *that* Natalie? Brooke's college roommate?"

Natalie smiled. "That's me."

"And you and Tanner met on the train from Fairbanks? What are the odds?"

"They've got to be huge," Tanner admitted, sneaking a side look at Natalie.

"I guess. Are you going home tonight? My stuff is at a B&B here, but I could check out and meet you in Anchorage if you want."

"We're checked into The Forget-Me-Not, too. We might as well stay the night. Tomorrow, we'll follow you into Anchorage, you can return the car and we'll drive up to Fairbanks. Sound like a plan?"

"Great." Dane nodded in satisfaction and then raised his eyebrows. "Wait—you're staying at the same B&B? The Forget-Me-Not Inn?"

"Yeah. I told you we were looking for you. Come on. Let's grab that bite. We need to talk."

CHAPTER FIFTEEN

THEY SETTLED ON the diner at the end of the block. Vitus had to wait in the car once again, but Dane assured him he'd be back shortly and the malamute curled up in Tanner's back seat for a nap. While Dane was getting the dog settled, Tanner whispered to Natalie, "We need to let Dane think we're dating, or he'll wonder why you're here."

Natalie looked momentarily startled, but then she nodded. "You're right." When Dane shut the door, she reached for Tanner's hand. "Ready to go, babe?"

"Um, sure, honeybunch." Tanner managed to hold in a chuckle at the look she flashed him when Dane was looking the other way. The three of them walked to the diner and settled into a red vinyl booth in the corner.

Natalie scooted a little closer to Tanner and reached for one of the menus propped between the napkin holder and the sugar jar. "Oh, look, Tanner. They have Reuben sandwiches. I know you love a good Reuben."

Dane looked from one to the other. "You say you just met on the train from Fairbanks?"

"Yes, funny story. We had lunch together on the train and then later when the train stopped in Hurricane Gulch, I got confused and got off." Natalie was actually selling the ditzy girlfriend pretty well. "Tanner rescued me and let me stay with your family until the next train." She gazed at Tanner and even batted her eyelashes.

Tanner swallowed a laugh and put an arm around her shoulders. "Yep. She stayed with us over Christmas, earthquake and all."

"Wow. That's quite a story." Dane's response was so deadpan, Tanner couldn't tell if he was buying it or not.

"Order me the chicken sandwich with sweet potato fries, would you, babe? I'll be right back." Natalie slid out of the booth and made her way toward the restrooms.

Dane watched her go. "So, you and Brooke's college roommate are dating?"

"I guess so."

"Huh." Dane turned his menu over. "Brooke said Natalie was getting her PhD and moving to New Mexico at the end of the semester."

"She is."

"So why are you getting involved with someone who's about to leave the state?"

A very good question, and one Tanner had been avoiding asking himself. Not that he was really involved with Natalie. A couple of kisses did not equal a relationship. "We're not. She just had some time to kill before she flies out, so she came to Seward with me. Oh, I almost forgot. Mom sent this." Tanner pulled the package from his pocket and handed it over, glad for an excuse to change the subject.

Dane tore the wrapping paper. "It's Grandpa's knife." He ran his finger reverently over the bone handle. "I love it. Tell her thanks."

"Tell her yourself and call your dad while you're at it. They're both worried about you. You can use my phone."

Dane gave a sheepish smile. "Sorry. I didn't plan to disappear for so long. It took longer to find what I needed than I thought it would. I should have called."

The server stepped up. "Are you ready to order?" By the time they'd given their orders, Natalie had returned. Once the server left, Tanner turned to Dane. "So, what's the deal with this lodge?"

"I bought it."

Tanner blinked. "You bought a lodge. Just like that."

"Yeah, like an hour ago. That's why I didn't make it for Christmas. There were five siblings selling it and some were only in town for Christmas, including one from overseas, so we needed to get the closing done right away. I'd gone and inspected the outside several times, but there was some mix-up with the realtor being out of town and nobody was sure who had the only key, so I finally got in to see the inside yesterday. Fortunately, it's in good shape. The whole process was kind of a fiasco, but I got a fair price."

"Did you take out a mortgage, or are you buying over time, or—"

"Nope. Cash."

"Okay, I'm confused. Putting aside what you want with a remote lodge, where did you get the cash to pay for it? I know your art sells well, but not that well."

Dane grinned. "Do you remember that real estate developer I talked to at Granddad's funeral? The one you chased off?"

"Yeah."

"Well, I contacted him later. I did some research, looked at the plans for their new development in Eagle River and decided to invest. It's paid off quite well."

"Why didn't you tell me you'd invested in real estate?"

"None of your business." Dane shrugged.

"Besides, you would have tried to talk me out of it."

He was right. Tanner would have pointed out the risks and encouraged Dane to invest in something safe. Tanner had been willing to use his own share to start a business much riskier than real estate, but he'd been trying to protect Dane from losses. Obviously, Dane didn't need his protection. "Sorry. Guess I overstepped."

Dane grinned. "No harm done."

"So, are you going to live in this backcountry lodge?" Natalie asked.

"That's the plan."

"We saw it today," she said. "The innkeeper recommended dogsled rides, and the musher mentioned she'd just gotten back from an overnight at this lodge, so we hired her to take us there. It's very nice."

"Thanks. I believe it will be a good investment."

Did Dane mean he was going to flip the lodge? Or hold it for a few years assuming the price would rise? Tanner couldn't imagine he was going to run it as a hotel. Dealing with the public was about the last thing Dane would choose to do. But before he could ask more, their food arrived.

Tanner bit into his sandwich. He'd get the details from Dane later, when they were alone.

If Dane hadn't thought this plan through, there was no need to have the discussion in front of Natalie. On the other hand, Dane had apparently made a tidy sum in real estate despite his attempt to help, so why worry?

"Mmm, these are delicious. Try one, babe." Natalie held a sweet potato fry in front of his face. Tanner obediently opened his mouth and let her feed him the fry. She gave a little wink, and Tanner had to smile. The woman literally had him eating out of her hand.

NATALIE SMOOTHED THE rose-colored quilt on her bed and took a last look around her room to make sure she hadn't forgotten anything. The aroma of fresh bread, cinnamon and sausage wafted down the hallway. It was a lovely inn, but Natalie couldn't help feeling a little nostalgic for the bedroom in the cabin. She'd enjoyed the rainfall showerhead and ample hot water in her shower this morning, but it didn't compare to Tanner washing her hair over a galvanized tub.

She caught a glimpse of herself in the mirror over the dresser and noticed the smile on her face. She'd been smiling since she woke up this morning, thinking of the expression on Brooke's face when Dane showed up tonight. An evening with Dane had erased some of her doubts. Based on Tanner and Gen's comments, Natalie had almost expected Dane to be a social disaster, but she found his mild awkwardness more endearing than off-putting. He didn't waste time on small talk, but when he spoke, he said what he meant. And he was obviously taken with Brooke.

Natalie wasn't completely reassured—he had disappeared without a trace for almost two months—but she was feeling better about his potential relationship with Brooke and the baby. Not that Dane knew about the baby yet. They'd kept their promise to let Brooke be the one to tell him, although it had been a struggle to tell Dane as much of the story as they could without giving everything away.

She'd rather enjoyed overplaying Tanner's girlfriend, but she got the impression Dane wasn't quite buying their story and was just too polite to call them on it. Which was fine; he'd know the whole tale soon enough, once they got to Fairbanks.

Tanner tapped on the open door frame. "Hi. Breakfast is ready."

"So am I." She closed her bag and latched it. "I'll call Brooke after breakfast and let her know to expect us. What time do you think we'll arrive?"

Tanner shook his head, laughing. "Dane wants to surprise her."

"Really?" Natalie smiled. "*He* wants to surprise *her*?"

"That's what he says. Do you mind?"

"Actually, Brooke will love that." She checked the hall to make sure Dane wasn't within earshot. "He doesn't suspect?"

"Hard to tell, but he isn't asking questions." He grabbed her bag and grinned. "Come on. Ursula's cinnamon rolls are calling my name."

He laid a hand on her back to guide her ahead of him into the hallway. She liked the weight of it there, like a caress. If only—but no. In exactly three days, Natalie was leaving the state. She and Tanner had no future.

They reached the dining room, where Dane greeted them from one of the round tables. Tanner pulled out a chair for her. "No cappuccino, but there's excellent coffee. Double cream, light sugar?"

"Perfect."

Tanner fetched the coffee and sat beside her at the table just as Ursula emerged from the kitchen carrying a tray. She transferred two covered dishes and a plate of cinnamon rolls to their table. "Since you're my only guests, no need for you to have to fill your plates at the buffet." She removed the covers to reveal eggs in one dish and sausages in the other. "I scrambled the eggs with onions and peppers, the way Dane likes them, but if anyone wants them cooked differently, I can do that."

"It all looks delicious," Natalie told her. "Thank you."

Breakfast lived up to its billing. Ursula insisted on packing a few extra cinnamon rolls in a box for the road. She gave Dane a hug and wished him luck before they left. Natalie wasn't quite sure what the luck was for, but she didn't ask.

The nine-hour trip went by more quickly than Natalie would have expected, even with two stops in Anchorage for Dane to return the car and to give his nieces their Christmas presents. Each girl received a hand-carved animal. Maya's was a fox, carved from some reddish wood and polished until it gleamed. Evie unwrapped a puffin, with its hooked beak and big eyes. Both girls were overjoyed. They presented their uncle with a sparkly fish like the one they'd given Tanner, and Dane thanked them graciously.

Around six thirty, Tanner pulled into Brooke's driveway. His headlights flashed against her front window before he stopped the car. As they were climbing out, Brooke flipped on the light and stepped onto the front porch, pulling on her coat over her work uniform. "Hello?" she called.

Vitus's ears perked up and he jumped from the car, running past Dane to Brooke. "Vitus?" Natalie could tell the moment Dane reached the circle of light from the porch by the way Brooke's face lit up. "Dane!" She flew down the porch steps.

"Brooke!" He dropped something he was carrying and caught her in mid-step, swinging her in a circle before setting her on her feet. She threw her arms around his neck and pulled him into a kiss. The kiss went on for several seconds before Tanner's chuckle alerted Brooke that Dane wasn't alone.

She looked over his shoulder. "Natalie?"

"It's me. And this is Tanner, Dane's cousin."

"You found him!"

"Dane got your letter," Natalie said, hoping Brooke got the hint to soft-pedal Natalie's role in all of this. "But he was already planning to take the train up on Saturday. Tanner just gave him a ride so he could get here faster."

"You were already coming before you got the letter?" Brooke asked Dane.

"Sure. I told you I'd be back as soon as I finished my business. Let me show you." Dane picked up the folder he had dropped and pulled out some papers. "It's a remote lodge, not too far from Seward, built on a lake. It has twelve guest rooms, a floatplane dock, and a garage big enough to park boats and snow machines and still have room for a workshop."

"It's beautiful," Brooke said, obviously confused as to why Dane was showing her this. "Are you thinking of spending some time there?"

"No, I bought it." Dane told her. "For you."

"For me?"

"Well, for us. You told me it was your dream. Remember, we said you could manage the lodge and restaurant, and I could be the fishing guide?"

"And in the winter, you'd work on your art, and I'd work on marketing and planning? Of course, I remember." Brooke was almost quivering with excitement. "But I thought we were just building castles in the clouds. I never thought you were serious."

He looked crestfallen. "You don't like it?"

"Well, of course I do. I love it! Who wouldn't?" Brooke looked more closely at the pictures. "It's absolutely beautiful, and it has so much potential. But I don't understand what you mean about buying it for me."

"Sorry. I'm doing everything backward." Dane pulled a small box from his pocket and sank into the snow on one knee. When he opened the box, something flashed in the porchlight. "Brooke, I love you so much. Will you marry me?"

Natalie's jaw dropped. Dane was proposing marriage? He and Brooke barely knew each other. Beside her, Tanner stiffened. He must not have seen this coming either.

"Oh, Dane." Brooke touched the ring. "It's beautiful. I love you, too."

"So, will you marry me?"

"I…" Brooke hesitated. "I need to tell you something first." She looked over as though she'd just remembered Tanner and Natalie were there. "Everyone come inside where it's warm."

"Sorry, you're probably cold," Dane said. "I should have waited until—"

"It's fine," Brooke assured him. She took Dane's hand in her own and pulled him to his feet. "Come on in."

They filed into Brooke's living room. She led Dane to the love seat and sat beside him. Natalie perched on the edge of the couch. Vitus padded across the room and laid his head in Brooke's lap, staring up at her adoringly. She smiled and stroked his head.

There was a pause, while everyone waited for someone to speak first. Brooke caught

Natalie's eye and tipped her head toward the kitchen door.

"I'll just get Tanner a glass of water," Natalie said. When Tanner looked at her questioningly, she took his hand and tugged him toward the kitchen.

"I don't need water," Tanner said, once they arrived.

"I know. But they need privacy," Natalie whispered and positioned herself beside the kitchen door, just out of sight from the living room. "Now be quiet so I can hear."

Tanner muttered, "Privacy, huh?" But he came up behind her to eavesdrop, as well.

"You're a good boy, Vitus," Brooke was saying. "Are you good with kids?"

"He's great with kids," Dane said. "My nieces love him."

"That's good. I think it's important for children to be around animals."

"Why—oh! Are you saying?"

"Yes," Brooke told him. "I'm pregnant."

"A baby?" Natalie detected shock in Dane's voice, but she couldn't tell if he was upset. "You're having a baby? Oh my gosh. That's incredible!" There was a pause with some sounds, possibly a kiss. "We're having a baby."

"You're happy?"

"I'm…yes, so happy. Oh, Brooke, this is so

amazing. But you haven't answered my question. Will you marry me?"

"Are you sure about this? We talked about it, but we haven't known each other that long."

"I've never been surer of anything. You're having my baby. I feel like the luckiest man in the world. The only thing that would make it better is if you'll agree to be my wife. Will you?"

"I will."

Natalie silently counted to thirty before returning to the living room, making more noise than necessary in the process. Tanner followed.

"We're getting married!" Brooke jumped up and flashed her ring.

"Wow, that's… Congratulations!" Natalie said, hugging her friend and then taking her ring hand. "Let me see."

"Congratulations to you both." Tanner gave his cousin a one-armed hug and shoulder thump before turning to Brooke and hugging her.

"And more good news. I just found out we're having a baby," Dane told them.

"That is big news!" Tanner managed to sound surprised. "Congratulations again."

"Let's celebrate." Dane turned to Brooke. "How about that Greek restaurant?"

"I'd love that! Just let me change out of my work clothes."

Natalie followed Brooke to her bedroom. As soon as Natalie closed the door behind her, Brooke enfolded her in another hug. "Oh, Nat, thank you so much for finding him. And we're getting married. Can you believe it?"

"Uh, no. I didn't see that coming. At least not this soon." Natalie searched Brooke's face. "Are you sure? You could tell him you need more time."

"But I don't need more time. I love Dane, and he loves me."

"How can you be sure? You hardly know each other."

"I do know him. He's sweet, and funny, and kind and loyal."

"He disappeared for two months, Brooke."

"To find a lodge. He bought a lodge for us! I still can't believe that. We talked about how someday we'd do it together, but I had no idea—"

"That's just it, Brooke. You have no idea. How do you know it's not a scam?"

"I saw the papers."

"But what if the deal falls apart?"

"Then I'll keep my job and we'll live here. I'll have the baby and he'll sell his art, and we'll be fine." Brooke shed her uniform and reached for a pair of jeans.

"Don't you think buying you a lodge is a little over the top? Usually, when people offer something extravagant, it's because they want something from you."

Brooke buttoned her jeans. "You know, Nat, not every man is like your father."

"They're not all like yours either." Brooke's dad and mom had been happily married forever. After putting in twenty years with the Air Force, Brooke's dad and mom had gone to work for an international hunger relief charity. Last Natalie had heard, they were living somewhere in Africa. "Speaking of, have you told your parents about the baby?"

"Not yet. If I told my mom, she'd be on the next plane here, and this is a busy time for them. Besides, I wanted to wait until you found Dane so they can meet him when they do come." Brooke gazed down at the ring on her finger. "They'll love him. He's perfect."

"Nobody's perfect. You just haven't discovered his flaws."

"He's perfect for me. He loves me. He wants us to make a life together. And he wanted it even before I told him about the baby." Brooke was getting that stubborn look that Natalie knew from experience meant she wasn't budging. Time to change tactics.

"Dane is good-looking," Natalie admitted.

"I know." Brooke disappeared into her closet. "Tanner is, too. Don't you think?"

"Um, sure, I guess."

Brooke laughed. "Like you haven't noticed. I can see the sparks. You should go for it. We could be cousin-in-laws…or is it cousins-in-law? You know what I mean."

"Tanner's family was at the cabin," Natalie commented, deliberately redirecting the conversation. "They're eager to meet you."

"They are?" Brooke leaned out of the closet while she buttoned a shirt. "Do you think they'll like me?"

Natalie laughed. "Brooke, it's impossible not to like you. Now finish getting dressed so we can go out. I'm starved."

"Me, too." Brooke pulled a sweater over her head. "But then I'm always starved. That or nauseous, but that's getting better." She stepped out of the closet. "Dane was so surprised. I guess we should tell him the whole story about you looking for him. I don't want to go into marriage with any secrets."

"Exactly." Natalie laid a hand on Brooke's shoulder. "Take your time. Find out all his secrets, too. Don't rush into anything you'll regret."

Brooke rolled her eyes. "You're so suspicious. If you were Cinderella, you'd never make it to the ball because you'd be too busy trying to figure out the fairy godmother's angle."

Natalie laughed. "Don't you know you're my fairy godmother?"

"Me?"

"Sure. Who went with me to talk to the dean after my tuition check bounced because my father had forged all those checks? Who took me in as a roommate when I couldn't get an apartment because my credit rating was shot? Who let me stay with her whenever I needed to be in Fairbanks for my degree?"

"You've done just as much for me. And now you've found Dane."

"As it turns out, he was on his way here anyway. Tanner and I only sped up the process by a few days."

"Doesn't matter." Brooke sat on the bed to pull on a pair of socks with dancing reindeer on them. "You brought him home to me. For that, I'll always be grateful."

When Natalie and Brooke came out of the bedroom, Dane was waiting. "Tanner's warming up the car. Are you ready?"

Brooke slipped her hand into his. "I'm ready."

THEY COULD SMELL fresh bread and good food as soon as they got out of the car in the restaurant parking lot. "I hope they're not out of spanakopita," Dane said.

Brooke laughed. "I think we ate here three

nights in a row because Dane loves their spana-kopita so much."

"Almost as much as you love moussaka," Dane teased her.

The hostess jumped up to hug Brooke as soon as they came through the door. "Hi. Good to see you."

"You, too, Suz. Was your mom surprised when you gave her the scrapbook you made for Christmas?"

"She loved it. You were right."

"I knew she would."

The older man who owned the restaurant had spotted Brooke and had made his way from the kitchen. "Brooke, it's good to see you."

"You, too, Thanos."

"And you've brought your young man who likes my spanakopita so much."

She laughed. "Yes. And this is Tanner, Dane's cousin, and you remember my friend Natalie?"

"Yes, of course." They exchanged greetings. Thanos reached for her ring hand. "And what have we here?"

Brooke beamed at him. "As of tonight, Dane and I are engaged."

"But this is wonderful. You are a lucky man," he told Dane.

"The luckiest," Dane agreed.

Thanos seated them at the best table. "They don't need menus," he asserted, whisking them away from the hostess. "I know what to serve." He gave Dane a conspiratorial smile. "There will be spanakopita."

A few minutes later, the waiter brought a platter of assorted appetizers. "Mmm, dolmades." Brooke dipped a leaf-wrapped bundle into tzatziki sauce and took a bite. "So good. Taste."

She offered the rest of the dolmade to Dane, who opened his mouth and allowed her to feed him. They were almost too cute. She leaned over to kiss him before saying, "Dane, we have a confession. Natalie didn't just happen to meet Tanner on the train."

"No?"

"No. She'd been watching the mailbox store, looking for you, and when he collected your mail, she followed him."

"Why?"

"She thought he was you." Together, they told the story, although Natalie left out her suspicions about Dane being married. Dane laughed when Natalie admitted she'd followed Tanner off the train with no plan on how to get back to Anchorage, but by the time he'd heard the whole story, he was frowning.

"I'm sorry." Dane leaned closer to Brooke.

"I didn't realize you might need to reach me. I didn't mean to worry you."

"I knew you'd come back."

"But I should have checked in sooner. I wanted to find a place for us first to surprise you, but I shouldn't have been away for so long." He paused. "What's your schedule tomorrow?"

"Since I worked over Christmas, I have the next two days off."

"Great. We can pick up our marriage license, make an appointment with the judge, and then let's stop by and get me a cell phone so you can always reach me."

"Marriage license?" Natalie burst out. "Tomorrow?"

Brooke's eyes widened in delight. "Yes! We applied before Dane left town, and they told us there was a three-day waiting period. It should be ready by now."

"You applied for a marriage license? Why didn't you tell me?" Natalie demanded.

Brooke laughed. "Because I didn't want to see your head explode."

"They said the license is good for three months," Dane said. "I hope they can fit us in tomorrow afternoon."

"Hey, slow down," Tanner spoke up. "You

popped the question less than an hour ago. Give her a little while to get used to the idea."

"Yes, that isn't much time to plan a wedding," Natalie seconded him. "What with finding a dress, and flowers, and cake…" Natalie couldn't think of what else might be involved in wedding planning, but she was sure there were many more details. "Brooke might need several months or a year to get a wedding together." And to give her time to get to know her future husband before she committed.

"No." Brooke gazed into Dane's eyes, smiling. "I don't need a big wedding. I just want Dane."

"But don't you want your parents here?" Natalie persisted.

"They'll understand. My dad says he knew from the moment he saw my mom that she was the woman he was going to marry."

"That's how I felt," Dane told her.

Oh please. It was all very sweet to say things like that, but this wasn't some fairy tale. Brooke couldn't marry a guy she hardly knew just because she was pregnant. Even though he'd bought them a lodge to live in and run. Especially because he'd bought the lodge. After all, he'd gone and done it without asking for Brooke's input, even though she was the expert. Granted, he seemed to have chosen well. And Brooke did love to be surprised. But still…

Tanner seemed to agree. "What about your family?" he was asking Dane. "Your dad, and my mom and Gen and the girls. Your dad's on the slope this week. Don't you want to wait and plan something special with family?"

Dane and Brooke looked at each other in wordless conversation. Brooke took his hand and leaned closer, presenting a united force. "You're here. Natalie's as close to me as any family. Natalie, your flight isn't until the first, right? We'd love to have you as witnesses to our marriage. Can you stay here for a couple of days?"

"I really think—" Natalie began.

"I don't—" Tanner said at the same time.

They both stopped, waiting for the other, but it was Dane who spoke first. "We love each other, and we have a baby on the way. We're getting married. You can stay and celebrate with us, or you can go. But either way, it's happening."

Brooke nodded in agreement. "It's happening."

Tanner looked to Natalie with raised eyebrows. Slowly, she nodded. "Well, then. If it's happening, I want to be a part of it. I'll be here to support you."

Tanner nodded. "I will be, too. Brooke, I'm proud to welcome you to the Rockford family."

CHAPTER SIXTEEN

SIX HOURS TO make sure her best friend in the world wasn't making a terrible mistake. And at the same time, Natalie was determined to make sure this marriage, if it did take place, got off to the best start possible. Could she do both?

"What do you think of this one?" Brooke held up a pale pink dress with a lace bodice and chiffon skirt.

"It's pretty, but don't you want white?" Natalie asked.

Brooke shrugged. "The only white dress I've found in my size so far had a sequin Christmas tree on the front. It was in the clearance section."

This was all happening so fast. Early in the morning Dane and Brooke had gone off together and returned home with a new cell phone and a date at the courthouse for four thirty this afternoon.

Natalie examined the pink dress doubtfully. "We could try another bridal shop."

Brooke shook her head. "The last one said a minimum of three months even for rush orders."

"Well, why not wait a few months and have the wedding you really want, with the perfect dress, and your family here, and a big celebration? You love parties."

"And I plan to have lots of them, but that's not what's important to me right now. Becoming Dane's wife is."

"How do you know, for sure? You were only together for two weeks."

"Two weeks can be plenty of time if you really connect. Almost from the beginning, it felt as though we'd known each other for years."

How could Brooke put her trust in a man so quickly? People were basically selfish. If someone granted a favor, it was almost always because they hoped for an even bigger favor in return. At least that was Natalie's experience. On the other hand, she'd only known Tanner for ten days, and—she pushed that thought away. Right now, she needed to focus on Natalie's situation.

Natalie pulled a beige dress from the rack and immediately returned it. "But why the hurry? Do you really think the two of you living alone in a backcountry lodge in the middle of winter when you're pregnant is a good idea? You could wait until after breakup."

"Dane says the lodge is only thirty minutes from Seward by snow machine. And we won't be alone for long. Once I get the place stocked and ready, I'll hire staff and we'll begin taking in visitors. Just looking at the pictures has given me so many ideas, and I know I'll have more once I've seen the place in person. I can hardly believe Dane actually bought me a lodge."

Natalie could hardly believe it either. "Are you absolutely sure you're not falling in love with the idea of running your own place, rather than with him?"

Brooke laughed. "Natalie, I was ready to go live with him in that cabin with no plumbing if that's what he wanted. I just want to be with Dane."

"You should talk this over with your parents."

"I called them last night and told them everything. Dad asked if I truly loved Dane. Then they talked to Dane for a while, privately. When Dane called me back to the phone, they gave us their blessing."

"Just like that?"

"Mom said that I know what true love looks like. They trust my judgment."

"Wow, that's, um…sweet." Considering how many times Brooke had been ripped off and taken advantage of, Natalie couldn't imagine why they would.

Brooke grinned at her. "I know what you're thinking."

"You do?"

"You think I have terrible judgment when it comes to people. And I see why you'd think that. But I know what I'm doing. When I loaned fifty bucks to the new housekeeper at work yesterday, for instance, I knew there was a good chance she won't pay me back. It was a calculated risk."

"You loaned someone you just met fifty dollars?"

"She needed the money for groceries until her first payday on Friday. That's not the point. The point is that I was willing to lose the fifty dollars. But I'm not stupid. I wouldn't tie myself, much less my child, to a man unless I believed he truly loved me. Unless he was a man I trust completely."

Brooke hung the pink dress back on the rack and turned to Natalie. "You know I moved a lot growing up. I learned to make friends quickly, but I've been very selective about my closest friends. There are very few people in my life that I know I can always count on. Like you."

Natalie blinked back the tears collecting in her eyes. "Oh Brooke. Getting assigned to the same dorm room as you was the luckiest day of my life." She wrapped her arms around her best friend.

"For me, too." Brooke hugged her back. "Along with the night I got a flat tire on the way home from work and met Dane. These things happen for a reason, Nat."

Did they? Or was this just another example of Brooke's rose-colored world? Even if events were completely random, Brooke could be counted on to make the best of every situation. And often, her faith was justified.

Natalie stepped back and smiled at her friend. "Come on. Let's try another store. Somewhere in this town the perfect dress is waiting for you. We just have to find it."

DANE'S MAUL SANK into the wood, and the two split logs tumbled onto the ground. Tanner picked them up and stacked them with the rest in Brooke's woodshed. "Why are you doing all this? Brooke says she's selling the house."

"Just burning off some energy." Dane positioned another log on the chopping block. "Besides, I'm going to try to talk her out of that. She should keep the house for at least a year or so, just in case." Another single stroke of the maul yielded two more fireplace logs.

"In case of what?"

"In case she doesn't like running a back-country lodge after all. If she isn't happy, we can move up here together."

"You'd be willing to do that? To live in town?"

"For Brooke? I'd live in a high-rise apartment in downtown Seattle."

Tanner laughed. "That's some sacrifice."

Dane set up another log. "Brooke is worth it."

From what Tanner had seen of her and the way her face softened when she looked at Dane, he had to agree. But why the rush? "You sound awfully sure of that."

"I am."

Tanner waited for him to split the log before moving in to pick up the pieces. "You know, you're concerned she might not be happy in a backcountry lodge, but how about you? Are you going to be happy with strangers coming and going and traipsing all over your property?"

"There's a private apartment in the back with a separate entrance, lots of room in the garage and plenty of wild country. I'll prob-ably partition off my workshop area from the rest of the garage so I can work uninterrupted. Brooke knows how to hire the right people. I've always worked as a fishing guide during the summers, and we plan to offer that as an option to guests, but otherwise the lodge is Brooke's baby." Dane set up and split another log.

"Speaking of babies…"

"Yeah, I know." Dane rested the maul on the ground and grinned. "It's like winning the lottery, and then getting a bonus prize on top of everything."

"Well, that's one way of looking at it." Tanner stacked a few more logs. "In fact, that's a really good way of looking at it." Tanner grinned back at his cousin. "You'll bring Brooke and the baby to the cabin for Christmas next year, right?"

"Either that, or the whole family will come to the lodge. It's going to be a good life, Tanner. I know it."

"I know it, too." Tanner slapped his cousin on the shoulder. "Give me that maul. You're not the only one who needs to burn off excess energy, you know."

"I CAN BE on the next flight up," Debbie offered, when Tanner called her to fill her in on the news.

"I know, but that's not what Dane wants. Brooke's parents are overseas and can't be here, and they don't want to wait. He's promised to bring Brooke down to meet you all as soon as his dad is back from his rotation on the slope."

"This woman he's marrying, Brooke, you like her?"

"I do," Tanner said. "She's just like Natalie said, friendly and warm, and she's crazy about Dane. You just have to see them together to know that."

"I'm glad. Dane needs someone who can get him out of his shell once in a while."

"Well, she's done that. Wait until I tell you what he's been doing that kept him away for the last month." He gave her the whole story about the lodge and their plans for it, despite several interruptions and observations from his mother along the way.

Once he'd finished, she sighed. "It sounds lovely. I have to give Dane credit. When the perfect woman happened into his life, he didn't hesitate. That takes courage."

"That's true." Tanner had the uncomfortable feeling she wasn't talking only about Dane.

"Well, give them both a hug for me, and let me know if there's anything at all I can do to help. I'll call Gen and fill her in, and we'll look forward to meeting Brooke in two weeks when

Russ gets back. No more or I'm hunting them down. You'll tell Dane?"

"I'll pass that along. Love you, Mom."

"I love you, too, Tanner. Is Natalie there?"

"Yes, she's in the kitchen."

"Let me speak to her, please."

Tanner took the phone to Natalie, who was standing at the counter with her spiral notebook in front of her and her phone to her ear. "Yes, that sounds delicious. See you then." She hung up and turned to Tanner. "What's up?"

"My mom wants to talk with you."

Natalie accepted the phone. "Hi, Debbie." A smile spread over her face as she listened. "Can you really? That's so sweet. She'll love it. Yes, I will. Bye, Debbie." She hung up and handed the phone to him.

"So, what are you and Mom cooking up?"

"I can't tell you, but if she can make it happen, it's going to be a nice surprise for Brooke." Natalie chuckled. "Your mom is so great."

"I know," Tanner said. "She thinks the same of you."

"Does she?"

"Do you think she involves just anyone in her schemes?"

"I'm honored." Natalie checked off something in her spiral notebook. "It's going to be a glorious wedding."

Natalie zipped Brooke into her dress and handed her the bouquet of white roses with pine cones and juniper. She stepped back to take in the whole effect. Brooke's blond hair was swept up in a loose knot with a spray of baby's breath. Her cheeks were pink with excitement, and the light in her eyes fairly radiated happiness. Natalie smiled. "What a beautiful bride you are."

Brooke turned to look into the full-length mirror in her bedroom. "I can't believe we found the perfect dress in a consignment shop. I never would have thought to look there if you hadn't suggested it." The long-sleeved white lace skimmed her curves and flared out into a trumpet hem at knee level. Via a family friend with a private plane, Debbie's surprise had arrived: a sapphire pendant on a silver chain that had been her mother-in-law's forty-fifth anniversary present. It now hung at Brooke's throat above the sweetheart neckline of her dress. Her shoes were her something new, a pair of silver pumps Natalie had bought for the department Christmas party she'd never ended up attending.

"So, you're feeling good?" Natalie asked. "No nausea?"

"None. I haven't had a moment of morning

sickness since Dane arrived. It's like now everything is the way it's supposed to be."

A knock sounded at the door. "We should go soon." Tanner's voice. "The appointment is in half an hour."

"One minute." Natalie smoothed the skirt of the emerald green velvet she'd found at the same shop and gathered her own bouquet and bag. "I've got the ring, lipstick, a handkerchief and my camera. I think that's everything."

"I'm ready," Brooke said.

Natalie looked her over and nodded. "Yes, you are."

Natalie stepped into the living room first. Dane and Tanner were there, looking handsome and very much alike in their dark suits and fresh haircuts. Tanner held Natalie's coat for her. "You look amazing."

"Wait until you see Brooke." Natalie watched Dane's face and could tell by the light in his eyes the exact moment he spotted his bride.

He stepped forward to take her left hand and pressed it to his chest. "Brooke, you are the most beautiful woman I've ever seen."

Brooke touched the sapphire at her throat. "This was your grandmother's. Your aunt sent it so I could have something borrowed and something blue."

"Beautiful," he said again.

Brooke cradled his cheek. "I love you, Dane." She stood on her tiptoes to press a kiss to his lips and then smiled at him. "Let's go get married."

THE JUDGE AT the courthouse was charming, complimenting Dane on his lovely bride and chatting about their future plans while his clerk got the paperwork together. The clerk even took Natalie's camera and offered to take pictures during the ceremony. The traditional vows were short and simple. Dane and Brooke promised each other a lifetime together with no hesitation. The ceremony ended with some advice from the judge, and even though he probably repeated it to every couple he married, it was clearly heartfelt.

"My parents were married for sixty-one years. According to my mother, the secrets of a happy marriage are kindness, respect and affection. When I asked my father, he said, 'Whatever your mother says. She's always right.' Which may have been the true key to their successful marriage."

He paused for their laughter before continuing. "So, based on my mother's wisdom, my wife and I developed three habits that have served us well, and I'm passing them on to you. Every day of your lives together look for some little act of kindness you can perform. Look for a way to show your spouse you value them. And never end the day without a good-night kiss." He chuckled. "And that said, I now pronounce you husband and wife. Norman Dane Rockford, you may kiss your bride."

Dane gazed into Brooke's eyes as though he couldn't believe his luck before he gathered her up in his arms and kissed her. Natalie, Tanner and the clerk applauded. After posing for a few more photos and signing the marriage certificate, they were done.

Afterward, they all went out for dinner in a private room in the back of the Greek restaurant. Thanos outdid himself with appetizers and entrées, including spanakopita. At the end of the meal, a waiter brought in the flourless almond wedding cake Natalie had requested and all the employees gathered around to cheer when Dane and Brooke fed one another the first piece.

Once they'd finished dinner, Tanner loaded them in the car. After a few minutes, Dane took his eyes from his bride long enough to notice where they were. "This isn't the way home."

"Nope," Tanner said. "You're booked into a suite tonight." He pulled under the canopy of the top hotel in Fairbanks. Dane and Brooke seemed a little dazed as they all climbed out of the car.

"But you're leaving in the morning," Dane said.

"Yes, I have to get Natalie back to Anchorage. But don't worry. We've already moved Brooke's car to the parking lot here, so you don't have to worry about a ride. Order room service for whatever you need. The bill's taken care of."

"Here's your room key." Natalie slipped the key card into Brooke's hand. "Room 421. Your luggage and car keys are already in the room."

"Oh my goodness, this is exciting! Thank you, Tanner and Natalie." Brooke hugged them in turn. "For everything."

"You're welcome. You just go be happy, okay?" Natalie's gaze took in Brooke and Dane.

Brooke's rings sparkled as she took Dane's hand. "We will be."

CHAPTER SEVENTEEN

TANNER PULLED UP in the driveway of Brooke's house. He went around to open Natalie's door, but she was already climbing out, high heels and all, despite the ice and snow. He offered his arm. "You don't ever wait for help, do you?"

"Maybe not, but I'm learning to accept it when offered," Natalie said, grasping his elbow. "If I hadn't had your help arranging for the hotel, shuttling the car and taking Dane to buy a suit, I never would have gotten everything done in time."

Vitus greeted them at the door, tail wagging. Tanner ran a hand over his head, but the dog was looking past him, at the car. "It's okay, Vitus. Dane and Brooke are spending the night away, but they'll be back here tomorrow."

"They were pleased about the hotel."

"They were pleased about everything. Especially that wedding cake. Having dinner at the Greek restaurant was a great idea. In fact, all your ideas were great." He helped her off with her coat and hung it on the rack. "That dress—"

"I know. It's like it was custom-made for Brooke. Such a stroke of luck to have found it."

"Brooke was beautiful, for sure, but I was referring to your dress." Tanner cast an appreciative glance from her toes to her face. "You're gorgeous. You know that, right?"

"I—" Natalie felt her cheeks growing warm, which was ridiculous. She was a grown woman. Surely, she could take a simple compliment without making a big deal out of it. "Thank you." She stepped out of her shoes and wiggled her toes. "That feels good."

"I'll bet." He loosened his tie. "Let's both go change, and then I'll plug in the car so it will start tomorrow and build a fire in the fireplace. I don't suppose Brooke would happen to have a Scrabble game lying around?"

"Of course, she does. I gave it to her."

He raised his eyebrows. "Well, then, one more game for old times' sake?"

"You're on."

Natalie paused in front of the mirror in Brooke's room. She did look good in this dress. The green brought out the reddish highlights in her hair, and the fit flattered her figure. That's why she'd bought it in the first place. So why should Tanner's compliment leave her flustered?

She shrugged off the dress and pulled on the jeans she'd been wearing this morning before they got ready for the wedding. Reaching for her flannel shirt, she started to pull it on when she remembered a chenille sweater in Brooke's closet. Yes, there it was, almost the exact shade of green as the dress she'd just taken off. Brooke wouldn't mind if she borrowed it; they'd been sharing clothes since college.

Natalie pulled on the sweater, ran a brush through her hair and swiped on a dash of lip balm. She could hear Tanner whistling as he arranged the wood in the fireplace. He was just putting the match to the paper when she walked into the room. It gave her a moment to study in profile the face that had become so familiar. She took in the subtle bend in his eyebrows, the firm jaw, the way his mouth seemed always to be poised for a smile. He looked toward her, and that latent smile grew into a real one. "Hi, there."

"Hello."

"I found the game." He nodded toward the coffee table.

"Good." Natalie sat in a wing chair on one side of the coffee table and Tanner took the one across from her. They looked at each other for a moment, but neither of them made a move to open the box.

Tanner was the one to break the silence. "Do you really want to play?"

"Not especially, but—"

"Me either."

"Then why did you suggest it?"

"I don't know." Tanner looked down at the table and back up at her. "I guess I was trying to re-create the feeling of those late nights at the cabin with you."

So those evenings had been special for him, too. Natalie smiled. "You know what I'd really like to do?"

"What?"

"I'd like to make some hot cocoa, and then sit on the couch with the lights turned low and just watch the fire with you."

"You really do have the best ideas."

She laughed. "I know."

THE FIRE CRACKLED, as clusters of orange-tipped flames lapped at the top log, catching a foothold in the bark and spreading warmth through the room. Natalie's head rested on Tanner's shoulder. Her hair smelled of something clean and light, like the air after a rain. He rubbed his hand up and down her arm, feeling the softness of her sweater, and she snuggled even closer. He wouldn't complain if they stayed right there all night.

Because tomorrow everything would change. Tomorrow they were driving back to Anchorage, and the next morning she would be leaving Alaska. Permanently.

Natalie was the most appealing woman he'd met in…ever? Strong and independent, but the lengths she was willing to go to help her friend demonstrated how much she cared. She'd been great with Evie and Maya, too, patient, playful, caring. And if she was slow to trust, well who could blame her after what her father pulled? But it would take time to earn her trust, and time was one thing they didn't have.

But they had tonight.

She looked up at him, the sparks from the fire reflecting in her eyes. He touched her cheek and bent just close enough to brush his lips against hers. She closed her eyes, and her face went soft and vulnerable. Each of her eyelids received a kiss and then he tasted her lips once more.

She reached for him, cupping his face in her hands and tilting her head just a bit so that their lips fit together as though they were made for one another. Maybe they were.

Vitus let out a sudden snore and they both jumped. Natalie laughed. "I forgot we weren't alone."

Tanner winked. "Don't worry. He's very discreet. I've been trying to get Dane's secret recipe for moose jerky for years, but Vitus won't tell."

"Not even for bacon?"

"Not." He kissed her forehead. "Even." Her soft cheek. "For." The tip of her perfect nose. "Bacon." And once more he turned his full attention to her lips.

After a long, sweet kiss, Natalie snuggled her head against his shoulder. Together they watched the fire turn to coals.

Tanner stroked her arm through the sleeve of her sweater. "I suppose I should get up and throw another log on the fire."

Natalie let out a breath. "No, it's late, and we've got a long drive tomorrow. I'm going to bed." She gathered the pillow and blankets he'd used the night before and made up the couch for him. "There. Do you have everything you need?"

He'd always thought so, up until the last few days. Now, after spending time in Natalie's company, he wasn't so sure. But he smiled anyway. "I'm fine. Sleep well, Natalie. I'll see you in the morning."

THE MORNING DAWNED partly cloudy and not too cold, at least by Fairbanks's standards. No snow in the forecast, good for driving. Natalie and Tanner worked together to assemble a lasagna to leave in the refrigerator so that Dane and Brooke wouldn't need to cook when they got home. Then they packed their bags, walked the dog and gave him a fond goodbye. Vitus watched them out the front window as they backed from the drive, his plume of a tail wagging slowly.

Natalie waved to him. "Will he be all right by himself until they come home?"

"He'll be fine. He's used to Dane being busy working all day, although I'm sure he'll miss having Maya and Evie to play with."

"It won't be too many years before Dane and Brooke's baby will be big enough to play."

"I'm still getting used to the idea of Dane with a family." Tanner grinned. "Maya and Evie are going to be thrilled at the idea of a new baby cousin."

"You don't think they caught on when we were talking on the train?"

"No, they were both zonked. But if Gen hasn't already told them, I'm sure she will soon. You were right about Brooke, by the way. I like her a lot. And she's perfect for Dane, to counteract his hermit tendencies."

"I noticed you didn't insist on a paternity test before the wedding."

"No. There was no need. It's clear they're crazy about each other. Even if the baby wasn't Dane's, and I'm sure he or she is, they belong together."

"I've got to admit, when I realized Dane bought a lodge because of Brooke's dream to run one, I was suspicious."

Tanner laughed. "I'm sure you were."

"No really, think about it. Why would a man do something that extravagant to get a woman to marry him unless he had nothing else to offer?"

It seemed obvious to Tanner. "Because he loves her, and he wants her to be happy?"

"Yes, I came to the same conclusion." Natalie gave a wry smile. "Eventually."

Tanner nodded slowly. "I understand why you'd want to protect Brooke. I have the same instincts when it comes to Dane, which is why I originally wanted a paternity test, and why I ran off those real estate developers way back when. Fortunately for Dane and Brooke, he didn't listen to me about that."

Natalie chuckled. "Despite your advice, your cousin invested in real estate and your mom won't move out of her house."

"And despite yours, your friend wouldn't

give up her trust in Dane," Tanner shot back. "Considering you and I have so much wisdom to share, the people around us aren't exactly cooperative." He laughed. "Sometimes, it seems, we might possibly be wrong."

"Sometimes," Natalie agreed. "Although if I'd been around to advise Brooke when someone backed into her car in a parking lot, it would have saved her some money."

"Well, share a little of that wisdom with me regarding Gen's situation. She's considering a job as a receptionist, but she has a bachelor's degree in psychology, and I think if she keeps looking, she can find something better. Besides, in less than two years both girls will be in school, which will make everything easier. I don't think she should take the job."

"But she doesn't agree?"

"No. They only moved up a month ago, and Christmas isn't really the best time for job hunting, but she's already getting discouraged. I think she feels that a job in hand is worth two dozen in the ads."

"Was she working before?"

"No, she's been out of the workforce since Evie was born."

"Well, it seems to me Gen has things pretty together. She knows what she needs. It's really her choice, isn't it?"

"I guess so. It's just…" he hesitated.

"What?"

Tanner shrugged. "My dad was always the one everyone turned to when they needed help. When he was dying, he asked me for my promise that I'd always watch over my mom and the rest of the family."

"You would have done that anyway." Natalie wasn't sure how she knew this, but she was certain of it.

"You're right. I would have. But it eased his mind to have my promise."

"And because you gave your promise, what? You have to meddle in everyone's personal decisions?"

"Is that what I'm doing?"

"Maybe you should ask your sister. Or your mother."

"Touché." Gen had called him overprotective more than once, and maybe she was right. It was nice having Natalie to talk to, to give him perspective. It was nice having Natalie around, period. "We'll be coming up to Denali Park soon. Shall we stop for lunch at Denali village?"

"Sure. There's a place kind of up the hill a little way—"

He grinned. "The one with the incredible nachos?"

"You've had them?"

"Only every time I come this way. I love the ones with smoked salmon and black beans."

"My favorite, too."

He chuckled. "Wisdom, beauty and great taste in food. You're the total package, Natalie Weiss."

"Flatterer." Natalie looked away, but not before he caught the trace of a smile. "Do you write the advertising copy for your fly-tying merchandise?"

"No. We hire professionals for that. Opinions are strictly my own. I just call 'em as I see 'em."

"There's your turnoff," she pointed out, even though he'd already begun pulling into the left turn lane. He debated teasing her a little more, just to see how long it took before her cheeks turned that delectable shade of pink, but he decided not to push it.

They were later than usual for lunch, and only a few other tables were occupied in the restaurant, which was part of a hotel complex. The view through the glass wall on the west side overlooked the log resort buildings at the Denali entrance. Sadly, clouds obscured their view of the mountains, but the peaceful, snow-covered landscape still would have made dining there special, even without sharing the platter of nachos, which were every bit as good as Tanner remembered.

"Dessert?" the server asked as she cleared the table.

Natalie shook her head, and Tanner replied, "I guess we'd better get back on the road."

"You're not headed to Anchorage, are you?" the server asked.

"Yes. Why?"

"Radio says the highway's shut down. A tractor trailer overturned north of Talkeetna. Might be a while."

Tanner looked at Natalie. She shrugged. "As long as I make my flight in the morning, I'm good."

"In that case," Tanner said, "maybe we should see the dessert menu." While the server was getting the menus, Tanner pulled up the news on his phone. "Looks like nobody was hurt, but they're predicting two hours before the highway opens. We might as well get comfortable."

Tanner and Natalie chatted over chocolate raspberry torte and coffee. He told her some of the history of his company, and she shared a few stories about her experiences teaching. Natalie received a call from Brooke, verifying that Vitus was fine and thanking them again for all they'd done.

Eventually Tanner paid the check and they left the table so that the server could prepare it for the dinner crowd, but the update said the highway would remain closed for at least another half hour. They bundled up and stood outside on the deck, looking across at the park entrance.

Tanner rested one hand on Natalie's back and pointed with the other. "There's the train station." Was it only eleven days ago that they'd passed through on the train? "My dad and Uncle Russ used to take Gen, Dane and me camping in Denali every summer. We'd ride the bus out to one of the far stops and then backpack for two or three days. There's some beautiful country out there."

"My mom took me to Denali once," Natalie said, with surprise in her voice. "I'd forgotten all about it. I was probably nine or ten. She borrowed a pickup with a camper from someone and we stayed at the campground near the entrance for two nights. We took the bus all the way to the end of the line, and we saw a grizzly mom with three cubs. I was so excited."

"I wonder if we might have been on the same bus?" Tanner reached for her hand.

"Mathematically unlikely, but it's fun to think about." She intertwined her fingers in his. "You know, it's funny. I've resented my mother for so long because she always acted like I was nothing but a complication in her life, an annoyance. But now that I look back, that really started when I was a teenager. It was different before that."

"Different how?"

"She came to the play our class put on in elementary school. And she used to drive me to the library. We'd always go to the Governor's Picnic at the Park Strip—" Natalie chuckled "—but that may have been more about the free food than a family outing. Still, it was fun. For some reason, being around you and your family has brought back some happy memories I'd buried under my resentment."

"That's good, right?"

"Yes, very good." Suddenly, the clouds shifted and the peak at the top of Denali came into view. The low winter sun washed the snow-covered mountain in pink. Natalie gasped. "Wow, look at the alpenglow."

"Beautiful." Tanner squeezed her hand as they gazed at the mountaintop together. Less than a minute later, more clouds had blown in, and Denali had once more disappeared from view.

"I'll never forget," Natalie vowed, turning toward Tanner. "As long as I live, I'll always remember seeing Denali with you."

Tanner would always remember, as well. But looking at her face, seeing the excitement and wonder there, Tanner made up his mind. This couldn't be their last day together. Surely, life wouldn't have thrown them together only to tear them apart. He'd never considered a long-distance relationship before, but somehow, they were going to have to find a way to make this work. Because never seeing Natalie again after tomorrow was not an option.

BECAUSE OF THE DELAY, they made most of the drive to Anchorage in darkness. When they were almost through Wasilla, a string of popping noises sounded. "Fireworks," Tanner said.

Natalie peered out the window, looking for the source of the sound. In the far distance, a shower of sparkles from a bottle rocket sank toward the earth. "What with all the hunt for Dane and the wedding and everything, I'd almost forgotten about New Year's Eve celebrations."

"I know. It's been wild. But in a good way."

Another rocket sent out a shower of green and gold. Natalie watched the sprinkles die away as they left town. "I've always liked fireworks." In fact, her original plan had been to attend the firework show in downtown Anchorage, as a fitting goodbye to her old life in Alaska.

Forty-five minutes later, they drove into Anchorage. "What do you think?" Tanner said when their exit sign appeared. "Home or downtown to watch the fireworks?"

Natalie didn't hesitate. "Fireworks."

"I was hoping you'd say that. If it's the same schedule as last year, the performers and food start on the square about five and fireworks begin at eight."

"Yes." Natalie checked her phone. "But it's already seven forty-five. We'll never find parking close enough to get to the square in time."

"I have a backup plan." Tanner turned off before they arrived at the square, skirted the southern edge of downtown and drove west until they came to a smallish office building. He pulled into an underground garage, punched in a code and parked in a spot marked Reserved.

"What are we doing here?" Natalie asked.

"You'll see." He took her hand and led her to an elevator. Tanner punched the top button for the fourth floor. The elevator opened into a long hallway lined with doors. At the end of the hall, he pulled out his keys and unlocked a door marked Rockford Flies.

"This is your office?" Natalie followed him into a small reception area.

"Officially. I usually work from home, but my partner, Rob, does business here." He slipped off his coat and reached to help her with hers before hanging them on hooks near the door. Another key unlocked one of the doors behind the reception area.

Tanner flipped a light switch and ushered her inside, where a long conference table with several chairs took up most of the space. A coffee machine, tray and mugs sat on a console table nearby. Windows lined two walls, and just as he shut the door behind her, the first rocket of the night exploded into an enormous chrysanthemum over the harbor.

"Oh, wow." She took a step closer to the glass. "It's like the fireworks are right outside the room."

Tanner dimmed the lights to a soft glow. As the second rocket burst into a horsetail shape, he came up behind her and slipped his arms around her waist. She leaned back against his chest, comfortable in his arms.

In between fireworks, their faces reflected back at them in the glass. Tanner looked happy, pleased at her excitement. He did love taking care of people. It wasn't just his promise to his father. He was hardwired to look out for the people he loved. And wouldn't it be lovely to be one of them?

Was that possible? Could Tanner ever love her? When their eyes met in the reflection, his seemed to soften, the same way she'd seen Dane's eyes soften when he looked at Brooke. But Brooke was utterly lovable. Natalie was prickly, independent and skeptical. She didn't want or need to be taken care of. And yet, it felt so good to be leaning into Tanner's strength right now.

Another boom, and this time the blast separated into five whistling streaks, each of which then exploded into different-colored starbursts. Why was she having these thoughts about Tanner now? She was this close to getting everything she'd been working toward for fourteen years. Tonight would be their last together.

Suddenly, the fireworks were a little less bright, a little less joyous. But she stayed in Tanner's arms, watching, treasuring their last scrap of time together. When the last stars from the grand finale burned away, Natalie took a deep breath, turned and slipped her arms around his neck.

He gazed at her, examining her face feature by feature as though she was the most wondrous thing he'd ever seen. And then slowly, ever so slowly, he leaned in to touch his lips to hers. Soft, gentle, and then deeper and more urgent, the kiss grew. She pulled him nearer, pushing away everything except this moment. Her heart pounded, or maybe it was his; they were so close she couldn't tell. His scent, the clean, woodsy scent, filled her nose. Natalie closed her eyes and simply felt.

At some point, she couldn't say if it was a minute or an hour, Tanner ended the kiss and pressed his forehead to hers. "Natalie." He breathed in a long breath. "Are you absolutely sure you want to move to New Mexico?"

She didn't. Not right now. Right this minute, she wanted nothing more than to stay in Tanner's arms for the rest of her life.

And there it was. The cost.

Anything valuable came at a cost. Accepting her father's offer had cost Natalie her good credit. Falling for Tanner could cost her the career she'd spent fourteen years preparing for. She couldn't let that happen.

Instead, she touched his face and laughed as though he'd made a joke. "Don't tempt me." She stepped back, putting a safe distance between them. "Well, the fireworks show was fabulous, but I have an early flight in the morning. Can you direct me to the restroom before we go?"

"Of course." He opened the door to reception and pointed. "At the end of that hallway."

"Thanks." As soon as she'd closed the door behind her, Natalie leaned against it and sucked in a shaky breath. A kiss or two, and she'd come this close to throwing away everything she'd worked for. Time to get real. Tanner was attracted to her, but he didn't love her. He couldn't. Because if he did, he wouldn't be asking her to give up her dream.

She pulled out her phone and looked for airport hotels. Since it was New Year's Eve, the first two were full, but the third call yielded a reservation. She washed her hands, smoothed her hair and waited until the face in the mirror was composed before stepping out to face Tanner.

"Are you all right?" He looked concerned, and no wonder considering how long she'd been absent.

"I'm fine." She gave what she hoped was a reassuring smile.

"Well, then, let's go home."

"Actually, could you drop me at my hotel?"

"Hotel?"

"I have a reservation at Jewel Lake Gardens."

"Why? You know you're welcome to stay with me."

Natalie shook her head. "You're all the way across town. It's not convenient for you."

He frowned. "It's not that far."

"Still, this will save time in the morning. It's better this way."

He hesitated, but eventually nodded. "All right. I'll take you to your hotel." He reached for her coat and held it for her before he pulled on his own. They made the drive to the hotel in silence. When they arrived, he went around to get her bag. She took it from him. "Thank you, Tanner. It's been...amazing."

"Yes."

She reached up and brushed a kiss across his lips. "Don't come in. I have a reservation. I'm fine."

"What time is your flight in the morning? I'll pick you up."

"No need. They have a shuttle."

"I'll pick you up," he repeated. "What time should I be here?"

"I... Seven o'clock."

"All right. I'll be in the lobby tomorrow at seven."

"Thank you." One more quick kiss and she turned toward the door.

"I'll see you in the morning."

She flashed a smile over her shoulder. "Good night, Tanner. Happy New Year."

AT SIX THIRTY-FIVE the next morning, Tanner waited at the red light on International Airport Road, rehearsing what he was going to say. It was only a five-minute drive from the hotel to the airport, so he'd have to talk fast.

"Natalie, I know we haven't known each other for long…" Lame. "Natalie, the time we spent together…" That wasn't right either. Maybe just cut to the chase. "I know they say long-distance relationships are tough, but you and I have something special, and I don't want to lose that. What if—"

The car behind him honked, and he realized the light was green. Waving an apology, he moved forward. He was going to be early, but that didn't matter. He'd wait.

A shuttle bus pulled out of the parking lot as Tanner pulled in. He was lucky enough to snag a spot only a few spaces down from the front door. A man walked by with a yellow Lab who sniffed along the bare bushes at the front of the hotel. Still fifteen minutes to go. Tanner looked in the rearview mirror, smoothed his hair and went inside the lobby.

Several people lined up at the front desk, and others were coming and going, dragging luggage across the tile floor. Over in the corner, a woman with a white terrier in her lap sat facing outside. The dog's eyes were glued to the Labrador.

Tanner found an out-of-the-way spot where he could keep an eye on the elevator and the lobby. How could he convince Natalie of the possibilities? Should he say the "L" word? Or would the idea that he might be falling in love with her only send Natalie running? For some reason, that kiss last night had shaken her. Either she sensed the depths of his feelings and it scared her, or maybe it was her own feelings she found frightening. How could he reassure her?

He looked at his watch. Seven-oh-four. Knowing Natalie, he'd expected her precisely on time, but even the most punctual people had to deal with slow elevators and unexpected interruptions. He paced up and down the lobby, still considering his options. Ten minutes later, he was starting to worry. He pulled out his phone and then realized that somehow, since they'd been practically joined at the hip for the past twelve days, he'd never asked for Natalie's phone number. Stupid.

The line had died away at the front desk. Tanner crossed the lobby. "Hi. I'm picking up Natalie Weiss. Could you call her room please and let her know I'm here?"

"Tanner Rockford?"

"Yes."

"Here." The clerk handed him an envelope with his name on the front.

"What? But Natalie—"

"She checked out earlier and said to give you this. That's all I know." The clerk shifted his attention to a ringing phone.

Tanner carried the envelope to his car and stared at it for a moment, not quite sure if he wanted to open it or not. The car next to him started, sending up a cloud of condensation and fogging his view. He pulled open the flap and took out a sheet torn from a spiral notebook.

Dear Tanner,

Sorry to have missed you, but I was mistaken about the time of my flight and had to leave early.

No, that's not true, and I owe you the truth at the very least. Tanner, I purposely gave you the wrong time last night, because seeing you this morning would have made leaving even harder. The days I've spent with you have been the most special I've ever experienced, but it's time to move on. I'm turning the page to a new life starting today, and that life isn't in Alaska.

Thank you for all your help in finding

Dane and with the wedding. Give Vitus a hug, and all your family my warmest wishes. I hope for only good things for you for all your life.
Love, Natalie.

CHAPTER EIGHTEEN

"HERE YOU ARE. Come on. It's time to cut the cake, and they're waiting for you." Gen tapped her foot.

Tanner reluctantly slid the latest K. Krisman novel back onto a shelf in the cozy reading nook Brooke had created under the main staircase of the lodge, now officially named Rockford Backcountry Resort. She and Dane had done wonders in the past two months, refurbishing, refurnishing and generally transforming the place from a cobweb-covered haunted house to a luxury retreat. He followed Gen to the main lobby, where Brooke and Dane, flanked by Brooke's parents and Russ, posed for photos in front of a multitiered cake decorated with violets.

Maya and Evie, dressed in matching frilly dresses, crowded to the front to ogle the cake. Mom hovered nearby, ready to stop any small fingers that might be tempted to taste-test the frosting. This weekend served double duty as a delayed wedding reception and a trial run before the lodge officially opened next Wednesday.

Brooke picked up a silver serrated knife and beamed as Dane gently placed his big paw over her hand. Together they sliced into the cake, and then fed one another bites while everyone clapped.

Tanner couldn't help remembering that little almond wedding cake in the back room of the Greek restaurant. The smile on Natalie's face as she'd watched her friend feed cake to her new husband. How all the waiters had cheered.

He'd half expected Natalie to be there for the weekend, but apparently her new life didn't include weekend jaunts to Alaska, even for her best friend's wedding reception. Or maybe Brooke, knowing how busy she was, hadn't invited her. Tanner didn't know, and he wouldn't ask. In fact, he was doing everything in his power to avoid thinking about Natalie this weekend. So far, it wasn't working.

"Doesn't she look beautiful?" Gen sighed.

Tanner had to agree. Brooke wore a soft white sweaterdress and a radiant smile. Her blond hair glowed under the lights from one of four wrought-iron chandeliers. Dane whispered something in her ear and she laughed, her hand brushing across the front of her dress to touch the beginnings of a baby bump.

Mom stepped in to serve the cake, while two of the new staff carried trays laden with flutes of sparkling cider for the guests. Once everyone had been served and found a spot at one of the round tables scattered through the space, Brooke's father tapped his glass. Laying a hand on Dane's shoulder, he officially welcomed him to the family. He kissed his daughter's cheek and reached for her hand to join it with Dane's and then proposed a toast to a long and happy marriage.

Tanner drank to the toast, and to Uncle Russ's toast, as well. He even managed to make small talk with the people at his table while he finished his cake. But when the music and dancing started, he slipped upstairs to the balcony, to breathe the fresh air and look out into the night. As his eyes adjusted, he began to see the shapes of trees and bushes, dark against the tattered spring snow cover.

He spotted what might have been the glint of eyes in the shadows, and then a rustle of dead leaves and twigs as something dived into the brush. Moments later, a great horned owl rose silently from the woods and perched on the gable of Dane's workshop, his talons empty. Lucky for whatever creature escaped, unlucky for the owl. After a short rest, the owl took off to seek more game.

Which was worse, never finding what you sought, or finding it only to see it get away? Not that Tanner had been looking for love, but somehow, he'd found it. Yes, love. He'd tried to tell himself it was only an attraction fueled by the intensity of their situation, but if that were the case, his feelings for Natalie would have faded in the past two months. They hadn't. And his life, the same life that had felt fulfilling and full before Natalie pushed her way in, now seemed like half a life.

He'd found her online easily enough. There weren't that many colleges in South Central New Mexico, and they all listed their staff. Even a picture, her expression unsmiling but kind, in front of a bookcase of leather-bound volumes that was probably a roll-down backdrop the photographer used for all academic portraits. Her students rated her as tough but fair. Tanner would have to agree with that assessment.

Was she happy? He hoped so. After all, this was her dream, the one she'd worked toward for so many years, and against so many odds. Someone opened a door, and the music carried up to the balcony. Tanner supposed he should get back to the party. This was Dane and Brooke's night, after all. But his feet remained rooted to the spot.

"Can you believe what they've done to this place?" Gen stepped onto the balcony. "The bed in my room is like a cloud. I may sleep all day tomorrow."

"Mmm-hmm," Tanner replied, without looking up.

"And that dinner. I don't know what Dane and Brooke are paying Mrs. Jackson, but she's worth every penny. Did you taste that mushroom risotto?"

"Good."

"It's a shame the firemen's convention they have booked the first week plans to use the ledge for firefighting practice and burn it down."

"Uh-huh."

Gen burst out laughing. "I knew you weren't listening."

"Sorry." He shook his head to clear it. "You said something about a fire?"

"Why don't you just call her?"

"Who?"

"You know who. Natalie. The reason you've been such a bear for the last two months."

"I haven't been a bear." Had he? He'd tried not to let his mood affect Gen or the girls.

"Mostly a hibernating bear. Like tonight, slipping off while everyone else is enjoying the party. It's clear you miss her. Why don't you call?"

"Maybe because I don't have her phone number?"

"Smooth move." Gen rolled her eyes. "But I suspect you could get it from Brooke if you asked nicely."

"No, you don't get it. Natalie specifically didn't give me her phone number because she didn't want me to call her."

"You don't know that."

"I do. Her life is there now. Mine is here."

"Why?"

"Why is my life here? Well, there's my business for starters."

"Which you do mostly from home while Rob runs the office. Try again."

"I promised Dad I'd take care of Mom."

"I'm here now. So's Uncle Russ. Dane is only two hours from Anchorage. You're not the only one who can help, you know."

"What about you and the girls?"

"What about us? I'm working now, even if it is only three days a week." She'd decided against the full-time receptionist job, but was enjoying occasional shifts working as a barista. "I hate to break it to you, but you're not indispensable. Sometimes I think you get wrapped up in everybody else's life so that you don't have to take care of your own."

"That's not true." Was it?

"Okay, then make the call."

Tanner thought about it. "What would I say if I did call?"

"Who am I, Cyrano de Bergerac? Come on downstairs for now. I understand there may be a conga line forming soon, and your nieces want you in it."

"I'll be there in just a minute." After she left, Tanner took one last look out from the balcony, at the new moon rising over the trees. A new moon. A new start? Something to think about. But right now, it was time to join the party. Suddenly, he was in the mood to celebrate.

"THAT'S VERY SWEET of you to ask, but I don't think so." Natalie shifted the receiver to her other ear. She was trying her best not to hurt Brian's feelings, but a second date with the history professor was out of the question.

"Oh. I thought you enjoyed dinner the other night." Poor guy. He sounded so confused. And no wonder. Despite her lack of enthusiasm, she'd accepted the date, dressed up and been as charming as she knew how. Fake it till you make it, they said. Bad theory as it turned out.

"The dinner was very nice, thank you. And the flowers you sent are lovely." Natalie glanced at the red tulips on the windowsill. They really were. And there was nothing particularly wrong with Brian…except that he wasn't Tanner. "I'm sorry, Brian. You're a great guy, but I just don't believe we're well suited."

"I see." Drat, she had hurt his feelings. She could hear it in his voice.

"I am sorry." Natalie picked up the pen on her desk and clicked the point in and out.

"No. If that's how you feel, it's better to say so."

"Thank you for understanding. And thanks again for the beautiful flowers. Goodbye, Brian." She hung up the phone and let her forehead fall forward to rest on the desk. Darn that Tanner. Did he have to ruin her for every other guy in the world?

Natalie had been out with three perfectly pleasant, good-looking and intelligent men since she'd started working at the college and yet couldn't seem to scare up even a flicker of attraction for any of them. Dating was overrated anyway. She'd only tried it because she'd told Brooke it was part of her plan, but three duds in a row should probably tell her something.

Other than the dating scene, everything was going according to plan. The facilities were spacious and up-to-date. Her colleagues, while prone to the usual intradepartmental gossip, were generally friendly and helpful. She liked her students, and her classes were going well. By taking over Dr. Benarjee's lease, she'd lucked into a garden apartment within walking distance of the campus. The town itself was a vibrant mix of locals, college students and snowbirds, which encouraged a surprising variety of restaurants and cultural events. This was the life she'd always wanted.

So why were her thoughts constantly drifting back to Alaska? She kept up with Brooke, of course, phoning often and studying the pictures Brooke had posted on the lodge's new website. Natalie had hated missing Brooke and Dane's second wedding reception two weeks ago, but she'd been scheduled in the tutoring lab that weekend and being the new person, she hadn't wanted to ask anyone to trade. At least, that's what she told herself. Not that it had anything to do with the probability of seeing Tanner there.

Natalie allowed herself one sigh before turning her attention to the stack of ungraded papers from her freshman calculus class, but when she turned to retrieve them, there was the wooden crescent moon Tanner had made for her, hanging in the window. The rowan wood, a reminder of the mountain ash berries they'd gathered with Evie and Maya, and the green beads around the crescent moon, like the northern lights. Their first kiss.

Maybe if she didn't want to think about Alaska, she shouldn't surround herself with so many reminders, but she couldn't bear to take it down. She ran her finger over the smooth wood, thinking of their time together in the cabin.

Time to focus. She started grading and had almost made it to the bottom of the stack when there was a knock at her door. She glanced at the time on her phone. Her posted office hours had ended forty-five minutes ago, but since she was here, she might as well give the student whatever help they needed. "Come in."

The door opened, and Natalie blinked, wondering if her imagination had somehow superimposed Tanner's face on someone else. But no, it really was him, with one foot in the office and one out, as though he might retreat at any moment. "Tanner?"

"Hi, Natalie. I hope I'm not disturbing you."

She was most certainly disturbed, but it was so good to see his face. "Come in."

"Oh, good. I was afraid I was being stalker-ish." He stepped closer to the desk.

"What in the world are you doing here?" Natalie asked. And how did he even know where she was? Unless Brooke had let it slip, which, come to think of it, was quite likely.

He laughed. "Would you believe I was riding a train and got off at the wrong stop?"

"I would not." She grinned. "Who would believe such a story?"

"Nobody as cynical as you, for sure. How about 'I was in the neighborhood?'"

"Still not buying it."

"Well, it happens to be true, in a roundabout way. You see, I was talking to my mom, and she mentioned she'd almost fallen in the drive-way getting the mail the other day, and maybe she needed less ice in her life."

"So, what, you brought her here on vaca-tion?" A likely story.

"Actually, she's looking into buying a condo here. There's a senior-friendly development that might work for her."

Natalie scoffed. "You're here, in the same town where I happen to be living and work-ing, to buy your mom a condo."

"Possibly." He glanced at his wrist. "Say, it's past six. Will you have dinner with me?"

"What about your mom?"

"She's being wined and dined by the sales agents."

Natalie raised her eyebrows. "And you're okay leaving your mom alone with sales agents?"

Tanner's sheepish grin was her answer. "I was dismissed."

She laughed. "Okay, let's get something to eat and you can tell me more about your mom's sudden urge to move south. Do you like Turkish food?"

"I don't think I've ever tried it, but I'm open to new experiences."

Sure, he was. His whole life was based on family tradition. Nevertheless, she took him to a restaurant she'd discovered just a couple of blocks off campus. Getting a table was no problem on a Tuesday evening, and soon they were seated in a quiet booth and she was guiding him through the menu. "Doner kebab is almost like a seasoned rotisserie meatloaf, and kofte are spicy little meatballs."

"That sounds good." He closed his menu as the server showed up with tea. "So, baba ghanoush looks like the go-to appetizer, yes?" he asked Natalie.

"I love it."

"Good." They placed their orders. Once the server had gone, Tanner sipped from the small glass resting on a colorful plate. "You missed quite a party at the lodge."

"I know. I wish I could have been there. Brooke sent pictures."

"She's worked miracles. They've had guests every day since they opened, and they're booked solid starting Memorial Day. Have you seen their website?"

"I have. Wonderful pictures."

"Dane took those."

"Did he? I assumed they'd hired a professional. He's very talented."

"Yes."

Natalie waited for Tanner to go on, but he didn't. He shifted in his seat. The silence began to grow awkward. That had never happened before with Tanner, Natalie realized. "How are Gen and the girls?"

"They're doing well. Gen is working three days a week, and she has them in a preschool program they like. But the big news is that Gen has decided to go back to school for her master's starting next fall. She wants to be a school counselor."

"She'd be great at that. She's so good with kids."

"I think so, too. And, apparently, her ex's girlfriend kicked him out and he's been forced to find a paying job, so Gen will be getting some child support now. We've agreed that she and the girls will stay in my house until she finishes her degree."

Their appetizer arrived. Tanner dipped a pita wedge into the dish and tasted it. "This is really good. What did you say it was made of?"

"Eggplant." She smiled at his enthusiasm. Maybe he was open to new experiences.

"I like it." He finished off his pita wedge. "I think this may become one of my favorite restaurants if I stay."

Natalie's head snapped up. "What do you mean, if you stay?"

Tanner twitched his shoulders. "It's a nice town. Sunshine feels good. And the Pecos River, which is one of the premier trout rivers in the country, is only about four hours from here."

"Be serious."

"I am." He took a deep breath in and out. "Okay, here goes. Natalie, I can't stop thinking about you. I know, we spent less than two weeks together, and unless you happen to be Dane and Brooke, that's not enough to base a future on, but it is enough to know I want more."

"Tanner, what are you saying?"

"I'm saying that if you feel the same, I want to move here. I want to spend time together with you, doing ordinary things. Taking walks, watching TV, talking about the latest K. Krisman novel. I want to hear about your day and rub your shoulders when you're feeling tense. I want to tell you about mine."

"You can't move here!"

"Oh." His face fell. "I—I'm sorry. When we kissed in Anchorage that night, I thought you felt—" He started to push back his chair.

"I did. I do! But what about your company?"

"Oh, that." Relief flooded his face. "I mostly work remotely, anyway, trying out products, choosing collections for kits, writing books. I'd need to spend time in Anchorage now and then, and I do have a series to film there this summer, but I could use this as my base."

"And your family?"

"Well, as I said, Mom is considering the snowbird lifestyle. She still wants to summer in Alaska, but Russ and Gen are there for her. Gen's feeling a lot better now that she has a plan. Dane and Brooke are thriving. They don't need me there every day."

"But you need them." She'd seen how involved he was with his family.

"I need you." He reached for her hand. "I love you, Natalie. I'm not saying that to pressure—"

"I love you, too." The words seemed to fall from her mouth without conscious thought, but she knew they were true. "I love you, Tanner. But what if it's different without Christmas and earthquakes and missing persons and a wedding to plan? What if I don't turn out to be who you think I am?"

"That doesn't worry me. I know who you are." He stroked her cheek. "I love who you are. I just want to give you the time to get used to having someone around who loves you. See if you can push that independent spirit aside just far enough to let me into your life. I'm not asking for a commitment, not yet." His eyes locked onto hers. "You have the power. Anytime, you tell me to leave, I'm gone."

"You'd do that? You'd disrupt your whole life on the off chance we turn out to be compatible?"

"I believe the odds are in our favor."

Could that be true? A thought occurred to her. "Is Debbie really considering a condo, or was that just an excuse?"

"Oh, she really is. We had a talk last week. I told her I was considering moving here to be with you, and would she be okay with that? She was two steps ahead, as usual. She'd already been looking through the real estate ads online. She said she didn't want to be the reason we couldn't be together."

"Aw. That's the sweetest thing I ever heard."

Tanner smiled. "And besides, she tells me there's a serious needlework community here. I have no idea what a needlework community looks like, but she's stoked."

"Where would you live?"

"I don't know yet. Do you want to go house hunting with me this weekend?"

He really meant it. He loved her. And he got her. He understood that she needed time, that this whole idea of coupledom was foreign to her. And yet, he still wanted her. "Yes." She leaned across the table to kiss him, but there was still too much space between them. She dashed around and slid into his side of the booth where she could kiss him properly.

Twice.

"I would love to help you find a place here." She kissed him once more. "So we can be together."

CHAPTER NINETEEN

FROM HER SPOT on the balcony of Brooke and Dane's lodge, Natalie could get a bird's-eye view of the activities below. Gen and Brooke rearranged platters on a long table in the pavilion. Rather than moving with her usual nimble grace, Brooke almost waddled under the weight of her enormous belly. Hard to believe she still had over a month before her due date. Natalie would have suspected twins if she hadn't seen the ultrasound image of one perfect little girl. Evie and Maya were ecstatic about the idea of a new baby girl in the family.

At the dock, a group of men had loaded their baggage and were climbing into the floatplane that had delivered Brooke's mom and dad to the lodge a little while ago. The guys were the last of the registered guests to go, Brooke had told her. The next three days were family only.

Below on the lawn, Evie threw a ball for Vitus. He obligingly fetched it, but instead of bringing it back, he turned it into a game of tag, sprinting across the grass with Evie and Maya right behind him.

In two weeks, when the sockeye run was due in, Tanner would begin filming his series of fishing shows, starting right here at Rockford Backcountry Lodge. He and Dane would be fishing the creek that flowed into the lake in front of them. Tanner's partner, Rob, had come to scout the place earlier and agreed it was ideal for the show.

Dane emerged from the porch below and strode across the grass to the pavilion, where he gave his wife a kiss and seemed to be attempting to usher her to one of the Adirondack chairs that lined the edge of the lawn. She shook her head, but after Gen said something, she laughed and went with Dane, who held her hand to help her ease into a chair. He got her a glass of water and bent down to kiss her once again. Natalie smiled to herself. Brooke had been right about him all along.

"Are you ready to go down?" Tanner stepped onto the balcony and rested a hand on her back. "Mom and Russ will be coming in by water taxi anytime now."

"I'm ready." She turned, and he kissed her. That was one of the things that had taken some getting used to, this casual kissing. Tanner kissed her hello, he kissed her goodbye, and sometimes he would get that little twinkle in his eye in the middle of a conversation and she knew a kiss was coming. It had startled her at first, but she'd grown to love it. She returned the kiss, and together they descended the stairs to the lobby, where they found Brooke's parents just coming out of their room.

"Natalie! It's so good to see you." Brooke's mom opened her arms for a hug. "And you, too, Tanner."

"Major Jenkins, Captain Jenkins," Tanner greeted them.

"Now, we talked about that. It's Bob and Sue." Bob gave Tanner a hearty handshake and a slap on the shoulder.

"Are you excited about becoming grandparents?" Natalie asked as she turned from Sue to hug Bob.

"Sue just about bought out the store when we went shopping during our stopover in Atlanta," Bob told her with a grin. "We had to buy an extra suitcase just to haul it all up here."

"Hey, who's the one who ordered the custom crib two months ago?" Sue retorted. "Have you seen it yet, Natalie?"

"Yes, the nursery was the first thing Brooke showed me when we arrived this morning. The crib is beautiful."

"We'd better get outside," Bob said. "Have Debbie and Russ arrived yet?"

"I think I see the boat approaching now," Tanner answered as he held the door open.

Once they stepped outside, Evie and Maya came running to the porch to dispense greetings and hugs, even though they'd already done it when Tanner and Natalie arrived two hours ago. Vitus shoved his head under Natalie's hand. She rubbed his ears.

"Look." Tanner pointed. "There's your grandma and Uncle Russ coming on a boat."

"Let's go!" Maya and Evie took off across the grass, with Vitus right behind them.

"I'd better go see about their luggage." Tanner followed them.

Once everyone had gathered, they all moved to the pavilion for what Brooke called a picnic lunch, but Natalie would have termed a gourmet feast. Smoked salmon dip, steamed clams, grilled sausages, and a variety of salads and sides lined the table.

Lunch took longer than usual, with everyone catching up and telling stories. Laughter rang out often. Once they'd finished eating, Tanner suggested lawn games. The staff cleared the first round of dishes and carried them inside. Natalie went to help load a cart with the leftover food, but Dane stopped her. "I can handle this. Go sit with Brooke, would you? Otherwise, she'll be over here loading steam trays."

Knowing it was true, Natalie walked to the lawn and relaxed in the chair beside Brooke's. "You really know how to throw a party. That was some spread."

"Thank you." Brooke beamed. "I was so lucky to find Mrs. Jackson. Everything she cooks is amazing."

"Do you think she'll stay here in the backcountry?"

"She loves it. We all do." Brooke shifted her weight in the chair and rearranged her tunic over her belly.

Natalie smiled. "And how is our little sweetheart doing?"

"Growing and going. The doctor says she's right on schedule. Oh, here. Feel." Brooke pressed Natalie's hand against her belly.

Natalie felt a flutter, and then a solid kick. "Oh my goodness. That's amazing. A tiny soccer player growing inside you."

"Did I tell you one of the housekeepers is expecting, too? Our kids will be within six months of each other. Built-in playmates." Brooke leaned closer. "So, I've been dying to know. How is everything between you and Tanner?"

"It's good. Really good." Natalie laughed. "Sometimes I have to pinch myself. We both like living in New Mexico, but it's wonderful that we can come back to Alaska for the summer. We have so much fun just being together. In fact…" She hesitated.

"In fact, what?"

Natalie continued in a low voice. "Well, after our time here, we're going to the family cabin for a week or so before they start shooting the fishing series. Just the two of us."

"And?"

Natalie swallowed. "And I saw a ring box in his luggage. I'm ninety percent sure he's going to propose."

Brooke squealed and tried to jump up but couldn't make it out of her chair. Natalie laughed and perched on the edge of Brooke's chair so she could hug her friend.

Once Brooke had finished congratulating her, Natalie looked around to make sure no one was within listening distance. "I'm a little nervous, though."

"Why? You just said you get along great."

"Yeah, but I know Tanner wants kids."

"And you don't?"

"I do, but it scares me. What do I know about being a mother?"

"What does anyone know? You love your children and do your best. That's what my mom says."

"But what if it changes things? What if Tanner…" Natalie stopped, unable to find the words.

"What if Tanner leaves you, the way your dad left you and your mom? That's what you're afraid of, isn't it?"

Natalie nodded. Sometimes Brooke could read her mind better than she could. "Tanner is nothing like my father. I know that. He would never, ever, desert his family. But if he were unhappy—"

Brooke laughed.

"Hey, this is no laughing matter."

"It is, though. Look." Brooke pointed.

Natalie turned to see Tanner patiently instructing Maya and Evie on how to throw a beanbag. When Maya's fell short, he picked it up and brought it to her for another try, showing her again how to swing her arm to get momentum. When her beanbag went through the hole, he cheered and gave her a high five.

Brooke took Natalie's hand and squeezed it. "Nat, what you have there is a family man. Might as well get used to him, because Tanner loves you, and for men like him, love means forever."

Natalie blinked back the tears that rose in her eyes. "You're right." This was a man she could trust. A man she did trust, literally with her life. "You're absolutely right."

As though he felt her gaze, Tanner turned in their direction. He waved, handed the bean-bags off to Gen, and walked over. "Hi. What's up over here?"

"We were just talking," Brooke said.

"About what?"

Natalie stood and slipped her arms around his neck. "About how much I love you."

"Oh really?" Tanner rested his hands on her waist and kissed her forehead. "I like this conversation. Visiting Alaska and spending time with Brooke must put you in a good mood."

"For sure."

"I'm glad." He grinned. "Because I have something to ask you later on."

Natalie didn't hesitate. "The answer is yes."

Tanner quirked an eyebrow. "You haven't heard the question."

"Doesn't matter. I trust you." Natalie pulled him closer. Just before their lips touched, she whispered, "For you, my answer will always be yes."

* * * * *

For more great romances in
Beth Carpenter's Northern Lights series
from Harlequin Heartwarming,
visit www.Harlequin.com today!

Get 4 FREE REWARDS!

We'll send you 2 FREE Books plus 2 FREE Mystery Gifts.

Love Inspired books feature uplifting stories where faith helps guide you through life's challenges and discover the promise of a new beginning.

FREE Value Over $20

Get 4 FREE REWARDS!

We'll send you 2 FREE Books plus 2 FREE Mystery Gifts.

Love Inspired Suspense books showcase how courage and optimism unite in stories of faith and love in the face of danger.

FREE Value Over $20

THE WESTERN HEARTS COLLECTION!

19 FREE BOOKS in all!

COWBOYS. RANCHERS. RODEO REBELS.
Here are their charming love stories in one prized Collection:
51 emotional and heart-filled romances that capture the majesty and rugged beauty of the American West!

YES! Please send me **The Western Hearts Collection** in Larger Print. This collection begins with 3 FREE books and 2 FREE gifts in the first shipment. Along with my 3 free books, I'll also get the next 4 books from The Western Hearts Collection, in LARGER PRINT, which I may either return and owe nothing, or keep for the low price of $5.45 U.S./$6.23 CDN each plus $2.99 U.S./$7.49 CDN for shipping and handling per shipment*. If I decide to continue, about once a month for 8 months I will get 6 or 7 more books but will only need to pay for 4. That means 2 or 3 books in every shipment will be FREE! If I decide to keep the entire collection, I'll have paid for only 32 books because 19 books are FREE! I understand that accepting the 3 free books and gifts places me under no obligation to buy anything. I can always return a shipment and cancel at any time. My free books and gifts are mine to keep no matter what I decide.

☐ 270 HCN 5354   ☐ 470 HCN 5354

Name (please print)

Address   Apt. #

City   State/Province   Zip/Postal Code

Mail to the **Reader Service:**
IN U.S.A.: P.O. Box 1341, Buffalo, N.Y. 14240-8531
IN CANADA: P.O. Box 603, Fort Erie, Ontario L2A 5X3

Get 4 FREE REWARDS!

We'll send you 2 FREE Books plus 2 FREE Mystery Gifts.

Both the **Romance** and **Suspense** collections feature compelling novels written by many of today's bestselling authors.

YES! Please send me 2 FREE novels from the Essential Romance or Essential Suspense Collection and my 2 FREE gifts (gifts are worth about $10 retail). After receiving them, if I don't wish to receive any more books, I can return the shipping statement marked "cancel." If I don't cancel, I will receive 4 brand-new novels every month and be billed just $7.24 each in the U.S. or $7.49 each in Canada. That's a savings of up to 28% off the cover price. It's quite a bargain! Shipping and handling is just 50¢ per book in the U.S. and $1.25 per book in Canada.* I understand that accepting the 2 free books and gifts places me under no obligation to buy anything. I can always return a shipment and cancel at any time. The free books and gifts are mine to keep no matter what I decide.

Choose one: ☐ **Essential Romance**   ☐ **Essential Suspense**
                 (194/394 MDN GQ6M)   (191/391 MDN GQ6M)

Name (please print)

Address   Apt. #

City   State/Province   Zip/Postal Code

Email: Please check this box ☐ if you would like to receive newsletters and promotional emails from Harlequin Enterprises ULC and its affiliates. You can unsubscribe anytime.

Mail to the **Reader Service:**
IN U.S.A.: P.O. Box 1341, Buffalo, NY 14240-8531
IN CANADA: P.O. Box 603, Fort Erie, Ontario L2A 5X3

Want to try 2 free books from another series? Call 1-800-873-8635 or visit www.ReaderService.com.
